SHADOWBORNE

SHADOWBORNE

ROGER NORMAN

THE SUNDIAL PRESS

SHADOWBORNE
First published by The Sundial Press 2012

THE SUNDIAL PRESS
Sundial House, The Sheeplands, Sherborne, Dorset DT9 4BS
www.sundialpress.co.uk

Copyright
© Roger Norman 2012

Roger Norman has asserted his moral right to be identified as the author of this work in accordance with the Copyright, Designs and Patents Act, 1988

A CIP catalogue record for this book is available from the British Library

Front cover image: *Sherborne College* by Walter Tyndale

All rights reserved. This publication may not be reproduced,
stored in a retrieval system or transmitted in any form or
by any means, electronic, mechanical, photocopying, recording
or otherwise, without prior permission in writing from the publishers.

Copy editing and proofreading by Louise de Bruin

ISBN 978-1-908274-18-2

Printed in Great Britain by the MPG Books Group
Bodmin and King's Lynn.

For Alexi

The Britons (say historians) were naked civilized men, learned, studious, abstruse in thought and contemplation; naked, simple, plain in their acts and manners; wiser than after-ages. They were overwhelmed by brutal arms all but a small remnant; Strength, Beauty and Ugliness escaped the wreck, and remain for ever unsubdued, age after age.

William Blake

CONTENTS

I	Mr Grindlay's Top Shelf	1
II	The Immolation of Peggy Forgetmenot	14
III	The Apemen Have It	24
IV	Isadora	44
V	Science Five	56
VI	The Iniquitous Knacker	76
VII	The Aryan Dream	92
VIII	The Keep	113
IX	The Slape	142
X	Begone!	157
XI	Pitchfork	175
XII	Smell of a Rat	195
XIII	Skiaphagos	210
XIV	Moon in Gemini	233

Chapter One

MR GRINDLAY'S TOP SHELF

The lives of three wattles, the life of a hound
The lives of three hounds, the life of a steed
The lives of three steeds, the life of a man
The lives of three men, the life of an eagle,
The lives of three eagles, the life of a yew
The life of a yew, the length of an age –
Seven ages from Creation to Doom.
Traditional

SUNDAY EVENING in September and it was raining, a cold, pelting rain that made puddles under doorways, found the chinks in old stone, streamed wantonly down window-panes and danced wickedly on the leaded roofs. In the tall church-like library of Sherborne School, Mr Grindlay was putting his books in order. In his hands were the two weighty volumes of *The Descent of Man* by Charles Darwin. He was not sure where they belonged.

Philosophy? Obviously not. Next to Lyell's *Principles of Geology*, on the bottom shelf, among the crustaceans and fossils? No. The right place was the top shelf where only the tall and the inquisitive ventured. But the top shelf seemed further up than it once had, and Grindlay no longer liked to trust himself to his small three-stepped ladder.

Dr Hulme entered the dimly-lit room, shaking the rain from his hat and pulling off his dripping coat, flinging them over the back of a chair. 'Fine weather for ducks, Grindlay,' he said cheerily.

'I care nothing for ducks, Hulme. The weather in here is comfortable and the sound of the rain makes it more so. However, the water you have brought in with you is making a puddle on my floor. If you were to use the hooks provided for superfluous garments, you would notice that there is a piece of matting positioned underneath them to catch the spillage.'

'I'm only staying a minute, Grindlay. I have a proposition for you.'

'The minute you stay will be that of the greatest run-off from your coat, Hulme. Be good enough to hang it where it belongs.'

'My floor, did I hear, Grindlay?' Hulme thrust his hat and coat on a hook. 'I assumed that the library was a common resource for the use of the staff and the sixth form.'

'There is one key to the library, Hulme, which resides in my pocket. It is I who position the books, compile the catalogue and oversee the withdrawals. The floorboards are more familiar with my tread than with the collective tread of the rest of the staff put together. The floor is as much mine as that puddle is yours.'

'Only one key, Grindlay? Does the school custos not have one?'

'The key in question is not a common or garden latchkey, but an article of a certain age, of a design beyond the skill of the locksmiths of today. The custos once suggested he should have a replica, claiming to know a man who could manufacture it, but I dismissed the idea. The last thing I want is the custos muddying my floor or thumbing through my manuscripts.'

'The custos is not a man easily dismissed.'

'I did it simply, with a frown. You should acquire a proper frown, Hulme. You would find it useful. You are much given to smiles, which involve words to make their point, if the point is anything other than mere assent. To what proposition do you refer Hulme?'

The verbal sparring between the Head of Classics (and Librarian) and the Head of Modern Languages had a long history. Hulme was taller and louder. Grindlay, older and sharper, had more satisfaction from their exchanges, Hulme being easily provoked and easily vanquished.

Dr Hulme cleared his throat. 'I have been making the acquaintance of our new headmaster, Dr Runciman. I have had discussions with him. I have informed him on the customs and traditions of the school. I have offered him some advice. However, he is not a man to take advice. He wishes to initiate reforms, whatever that may mean. He must be prevented from such mistaken intentions, Grindlay. He must be stopped!'

'A new head likes a new broom, Hulme. It is in the nature of things.'

'I am not talking of a broom, Grindlay, but of a blunderbuss.'

'Then let him fire it once or twice and we shall see the extent of the damage.'

'Prevention is better than cure.'

'If you know the nature of the disease.'

'I know its nature and I know its name. It is Radicalism. It is Non-conformism. It is … Subversion!'

'Runciman is a young man new to Sherborne. He is the first headmaster in three hundred years – so I believe – who is not a cleric. He comes to us from Winchester, where there is a certain tendency to innovation. It is hardly a surprise that he has certain changes in mind. They may even be for the better.'

Hulme sighed. 'I sometimes wonder whether your heart is in quite the right place, Grindlay. I fear that your absorption in the Classics has undermined a certain manly integrity necessary to our modern world. Too much … too much Ovid and not enough Caesar.'

'When did you last read Caesar, Hulme?'

'You know perfectly well what I mean. A good school requires to be run by a general, not a poet.'

'Dr Runciman has poetic inclinations?'

'Like all reformers, he is a kind of romantic. An idealist. He is also married to a Russian, sprung from who-knows-where.'

'From Russia, one presumes.'

'But from forest or fen?'

'I have not closely observed the lady. She seems to conduct herself correctly.'

'Manners may be acquired as a gloss, Grindlay. I suspect her also of radicalism.'

There was a faint knock on the door of the library, the latch lifted and the heavy door swung inward to reveal a black glove, a black feather, the brim of an elaborate hat and the radical Russian lady herself.

Despite her correct conduct Isadora Runciman was an exotic creature in Sherborne town in 1877. She was tall, handsome and expensively dressed. She favoured black – black gowns, black hats, black cloaks – but these were enlivened by a purple sash or scarlet scarf or crimson ribbon, which made light of the black's severity and may even have been the source of Hulme's suspicions.

'Please forgive the intrusion, gentlemen,' Isadora said, closing the door behind her. 'I heard your voice from outside, Dr Hulme. There is a question it has been on my mind to ask you but the opportunity did not arise.'

Hulme rose from his chair. He was a well-built man with a large head, prominent in its parts – broad brow, strong chin, large ears – a head that might have looked very well as a portrait in oils. An artist choosing to emphasise a certain elegance of manner, while softening the traces of something brittle and supercilious in the expression, might have produced a canvas to fit impressively in the gallery of former Heads that hung in the Old Schoolroom.

'Do come in, madam,' said Hulme, with a slight bow. 'An unlooked-for pleasure.'

'But inopportune, perhaps, Dr Hulme?'

Her English was very good, but there were sounds that eluded her, and one of these lay at the heart of Dr Hulme's name. The name was pronounced Hume. Isadora had no problem with fume, or assume. She was distracted by the superfluous 'l'. What came out was something almost identical to 'whom'. 'Inopportune, perhaps, Dr Whom.'

'Not at all, dear lady.'

'I need not take up much of your valuable time. Good evening, Mr Grindlay.'

Grindlay rose a quarter-inch from his chair. 'It is unusual for the wife of the headmaster to visit the pedagogical domains of the school premises. Feathers may be ruffled, madam.'

'I am sure that I lack the means to ruffle your feathers, Mr Grindlay.'

Grindlay subsided, inclining his head. He was crusty, but under the crust lurked a certain humorousness, which in Hulme was absent. Isadora was right to suppose that she was incapable of ruffling him. He was immune to her beauty, her wit and her sex. His world was exclusively masculine. Some men had wives, some had daughters, some had sisters. Grindlay did not. Women were other people's problem. His work, which was also his life, required boys and books and stout doors that did not open unexpectedly. Having made his point to Mrs Runciman, he sat back to enjoy whatever exchanges might take place between the headmaster's wife and Dr Whom.

'What was it that you wished to question me on, madam?' Hume asked.

'You are head of Modern Languages I understand.'

'I am.'

'This means French and German, I take it.'

'That is so.'

'I wondered why there is no Russian.'

'It is a matter of history and geography, madam. Physical proximity and historical connection. Russia is a large nation, no doubt, but its orientation is different. To us, madam, Russia is a distant land, while Germany is not.'

'Russian might perhaps be added as an optional subject.'

'I doubt it, madam. Who would teach it? What text book would be used?'

'Teachers can be employed, text books can be bought, Dr Whom.'

'The existing curriculum would be disturbed. If Russian, why not Italian, or Spanish?'

'Why not? They might be more useful than Latin or Greek.'

Grindlay stirred. 'The Classics are not designed to be useful as domestic cutlery is useful. You do not use Latin in the way that you might use French, to greet a Frenchman for example, or to read the weather report when on vacation in Dieppe. The study of Latin grammar provides logical structures around which a proper mental activity may be built.'

'What is proper mental activity, Mr Grindlay?'

'I am surprised that you should need to ask, madam. The proper functions of the mind are to explore and to construct. *Explorare et construere.* And not to neglect or to destroy. *Negligere et destruere.* You will have noticed that most significant English words are children of Latin. To study Latin is to study the life and wisdom of the parent.'

'To study Russian is to study the heart and mind of a great culture.'

'It is a matter of curricular precedence, madam,' said Hulme.

'The existing curriculum is always to be preferred, then?'

'If there is to be a change, it must be at the expense of something. The question is: what is expendable, and who should decide it?'

'That is the business of the headmaster, I suppose, Mr Hulme.'

Hulme stole a look at Grindlay before replying.

'I shall be happy to consult the headmaster on the subject of additional optional languages.'

'I thank you. Good evening, gentlemen.'

'The woman did not hear my voice from outside,' Hulme said when she had gone. 'There are a dozen stone steps. She is a meddler, Grindlay. A novice headmaster with a meddlesome wife. A most unfortunate combination.'

'It might be argued that the study of the language of Pushkin would be more edifying than, for example, dressing up as soldiers and playing with guns in Coombe valley, Hulme.'

'Nonsense. Training the boys to handle a firearm is a patriotic obligation, not a recreation. When they come to raise a rifle in anger, as likely as not it'll be Russians they'll be facing across the palisades. What should we do, teach the boys to converse with the enemy or to drive 'em back to where they belong?'

'I prefer the Roman civil war, Grindlay answered. 'You should study it, Hulme. Yours is the part of Brutus, I fancy. Or is it Cassius, lean and hungry?'

'I have read the play. I once taught it to the third form.'

'Then you will remember what happened to Cassius.'

'I do not.'

'Suicide.' Grindlay laughed. The eyebrows went up, the jaw dropped and the eyes lit in a flash of pleasure.

'Your illustrations from the Classics are inapposite, Grindlay.'

'On the contrary. We have a new consul, young and ambitious. You disapprove of his appointment. You believe that you yourself would do a better job.'

'I am sure of it.'

'You have intimated that, if we act together, we can put a brake on the headmaster's urge to change the status quo. It is what Pompey and Crassus thought about Caesar. You came to recommend a triumvirate, Hulme. Perhaps next time it will be a conspiracy.'

'The school must be protected against the effect of hasty and ill-conceived changes. Good lord, the man wants to set up a prefect's council to handle matters of discipline! I shall oppose the scheme vigorously. The question is, do I have your support, Grindlay?'

'I am a Cato, not a Cassius.'

'I seem to remember that Cato also committed suicide.'

'I'm impressed that you should recall it. Yes, Marcus Porcius Cato took his own life, but not before a final reading of the *Phaedo*.'

'He spent his last hours reading Plato? Extraordinary thing to do.'

Hulme retrieved his hat and coat from their hook. 'The rain has let up, it seems. You will give serious consideration to my proposition I trust.'

'And you to mine, Hulme.'

'Did you propose something?'

'That we do not jump the gun.'

Dr Hulme grunted, and went out.

Grindlay returned to his work. It had occurred to him to ask Hulme to put Darwin on the top shelf, but he had no wish to draw his colleague's attention to the library's most precious items as well as what Grindlay preferred to keep out of the way. *Opus Aureum* by Thomas Aquinas, dated 1493, was there next to a very rare seventeenth-century bible in Cherokee. Also beyond the reach of the boys were certain treatises with provocative illustrations and one with marginal annotations in Latin which had shocked the librarian himself. Darwin did not really belong in this company, Grindlay thought as he painfully ascended the steps, but he could stay there until he weathered.

This matter of placing the books was important to Grindlay, as if it were the contents of his own mind that he was putting in order: upper regions for the rare and recondite, middle regions for the commonplace, lower regions for the unnecessary. He arrived at the top step of the ladder, picked up the first volume of *The Descent of Man*, which he had posted within the shelves at a convenient height, straightened up as far as he was able and checked, his eye caught by a slim, leather-bound manuscript.

Volume I of Darwin was pushed home and Grindlay went to grasp the manuscript. 'Bless me,' he murmured, 'I had forgotten this.'

The movement of his hand at the extremity of its reach upset the precarious balance of the old body and one foot slid from the step.

Grindlay teetered one-footed and one-handed and knew he was going over backwards.

The door of the library opened to admit a sixth former with a thatch of dark hair and a pile of books clutched to his side who reacted to the scene before him by dropping his books, springing promptly over the few yards that separated him from his Latin teacher and half-catching the old man as he fell. The boy went down too and bore the brunt of the collapse. Grindlay was extremely surprised but unhurt. It took him some time to roll off the boy's body and sit up.'

'Two-and-a-Half! You have saved me a bad bruising! Conceivably, from a broken back. Are you damaged?'

'Not a bit,' replied Two-and-a-Half getting up. 'Forgive me for saying so, sir, but you should avoid clambering on step-ladders.'

'It is hardly a ladder, Two-and-a-Half, and I was not clambering, but ascending carefully.'

'Not carefully enough, sir.'

'It's true that if you had not arrived so opportunely and reacted so swiftly, I would have been borne away on a stretcher. Age advances, the bones lose their bend, the neck grows stiff and the feet become clumsy. Why should the feet also age, I ask myself? Especially *my* feet, which have spent most of their life curled idly under desks. Damn you, foot,' he muttered, addressing the one that had lost its purchase on the top step. 'Behave yourself, sir, or you'll be the death of me!'

'Leave the books that have to be returned to the higher shelves, Mr Grindlay, and I'll put them away when I come.'

'I was not returning something, Two-and-a-Half. I was introducing a newcomer, the second part of which awaits its turn.' He gestured towards Volume II of Darwin.

The boy reached for the book, stepped nimbly up the steps and put it next to its companion volume.

'Why the top shelf for Charles Darwin, sir?' he asked.

'Read it and tell me!' He watched the boy's agile movements. 'You've grown tall. I shall have to abandon my old name for you.'

The boy laughed. 'Don't worry, sir, I've got used to it.'

The history of Two-and-a-Half dated to the boy's very first visit to Room VIII five years before, aged thirteen. He had stood up to answer a question and Grindlay had asked him how tall he was. 'Five foot two-and-a-half.' *'And a half,'* repeated the master. 'Let us not forget the half.' It was not forgotten, it stuck.

'Even absurd nicknames can acquire durability,' remarked Grindlay. 'My nickname among the boys is so old that I don't remember when I first heard it. You know it, of course.'

The boy nodded.

'Gnome obviously refers to my habit of creeping around with my shoulders bent and my chin on my neck. It is hardly flattering yet the origin of the word is rather different to what the boys imagine and I enjoy knowing what they do not.'

The boy waited for an explanation, but none came.

'I am going to have some supper to restore my equilibrium,' the old man continued. 'I shall return in a while. You may stay and browse, if you wish. If others come, do me the kindness to ensure that the normal regulations are observed.'

When the door closed, the boy looked up 'gnome' in the *Oxford English Dictionary*. 'One of a race of diminutive spirits fabled to inhabit the interior of the earth and to be the guardians of its treasures,' he read. The derivation was from the Greek, *gnomi*, meaning mind, and the root of the word know. The gnomes had originally been the knowing ones.

He put away the dictionary and retrieved the books he had dropped when he came in. He righted a chair overturned in Grindlay's fall and spotted a leather-bound manuscript under the reading table, dislodged by Darwin. He bent and picked it up. The leather was discoloured, its edges stiff and cracked. He opened it at random and saw it was hand-written, in Latin.

As he went to return it to the top shelf, loose papers protruding from between the pages caught his eye and he pulled them out. They were in English, and he knew the handwriting. The script was neater and more carefully formed than that of the brief comments at the foot of his essays, but it was unmistakably Grindlay's. 'The Book of Shadowborne', ran the title, dated 1648, and underneath: 'translated from the Latin by Gilbert Grindlay, 1837.' There was no author given.

He settled at the table with Grindlay's translation and had read only a few lines before he was drawn away, in that inimitable act of magic, into another dimension, lit by a light like candles along a dark passage, summoning the adventurer.

Chapter Two

THE IMMOLATION OF PEGGY FORGETMENOT

> *Sherborne then emerges into the light of history... as the capital of the Newer Wessex, the land west of the great forest of Selwood... like Winchester and Glastonbury, it is a rival of Westminster itself.*
> W.B. Wildman

'THE BOOK of Shadowborne' took the boy to a former Sherborne, its woodlands denser and more numerous, its tracks narrower and more perilous, closer to the demonic and the divine. There were passages of early history – or was it legend? Sherborne had once stood on the western edge of the great forest Selwood, which was peopled at some unspecified age by the diminutive Forest Folk before they were driven west and north, towards Wales. And here was an unexpected revelation: there had once been a great earthen mound on the site where the Old Castle was later built. It had been there when Aldhelm came as first bishop and was still there three centuries later when Roger of Caen wore the mitre. This energetic Norman, famous for the speed at which he conducted the holy services and more concerned with fortification than faith, had the mound flattened and the ground levelled for the building of his great palace, consigning to oblivion whatever was interred beneath the old pagan barrow.

The mound had long been known as the Shadow Mound, and it was from this, the manuscript related, that the town's name derived. Shadow in Greek was *Skia* and *Burnye* was mound in the old Kernevek tongue – thus Skiaburne, or Shadowborne. It was Bishop Aldhelm himself who had given the town its curious name, the boy read.

> Aldhelm's later life is full of contradictions. He was an old man given the task of a young man. He wrote in Latin but preferred Greek. He loved Malmesbury and ministered in Sherborne. He had the hands and the soul of a musician yet he employed them in prayer. He made studies of the stars but what we know of his thought was earthbound. He was a man of the church but his best-known book was a collection of riddles. What is a riddle? It is a verbal puzzle made of the marriage of opposites. Why should a prominent churchman compile a collection of riddles? Because his own life is a riddle. Because he keeps his real self concealed.

Was there no such thing as an innocent pastime in Saxon times, the boy asked himself. He read on. By the time of the Domesday Book, the town was called Scireburne, which people took to mean clear spring, a brighter and more auspicious derivation certainly, but as the writer pointed out, the river Yeo runs on a bed of clay among marshy meadows and there is nothing clear about it. As for the town's other water source, which the monks knew as the *Fons Limpidus*, it was an underground spring that in old English would have been Sherspryng or Sherfont. Besides, for the long centuries before Aldhelm the most prominent and impressive feature of the locality had been the Shadow Mound.

> From its beginnings and throughout its history, the mood of Sherborne town has been one of division. It is under the sign of Gemini the stargazers would say, although we would express it differently. Above the town, the rivers run north, below the town they run south. To the east was forest and wooded vales, to the west begins the country of moorland and meadow called Somerset. Sherborne itself is made of the abbey and the castle, and thus of peace and war. Even the Church itself was divided, between the monastery of the abbot and the cathedral of the bishop. It is the place where the north-south highway from Bristol to Dorchester meets the east-west highway, from London to Exeter. The Yeo itself is two: one flowing from Oborne and Poyntington and the other from the Caundle marshes. The crux of all these opposites is to be found at the place where the sorcerers of the Smiths confronted the magicians of the Forest Folk and the shadow pit was dug. In Sherborne to this day are to be found many people at war with themselves, which I have found to be a very common ailment in these parts, more common than can be explained by mere chance. It is the image of the shadow that captures the real and unchanging mood of the place.

Who wrote this, the boy thought. Who was the 'I' and who were the 'we'? He was leafing through the brittle pages searching for an answer when his eye was caught by an intriguing name, Peggy Forgetmenot. The passage that followed was so unlike what he had read before as to seem written by a different hand.

> They came for Peggy Forgetmenot at dead of night. All evening the cats had prowled restlessly and when the men arrived some of them fled and one of them leapt onto her pillow howling. She got up, reaching for her shawl, but she was still barefoot in her room when they battered down the kitchen door, with one man at the window in case she should jump out and flee across the fields. When they grabbed hold of her and tied her arms, she did not resist and when they shouted insults in her face, she made no response. They called her witch, demon-lover, fiend, servant of Satan. It was a chill night but she would need no coat where she was going, they said, and some of them laughed.
>
> They were five and one of them, a tall, dark, smirking man, took the lead. He would not have made a leader at any time when sanity and order prevailed. He was thrown up by the chaos of the times, like scum on a wild sea, and the men with him were no better. One was sunk in gloom, another in incomprehension. One carried a short-handled axe, another a pair of shears.
>
> The men are known in the story as Smirk, Sulk, Blunt, Poleaxe and Potter. The last of these was his real name, it seems.
>
> The smirking man was unarmed but for a large crucifix at his neck, which he brandished from time to time, a gesture in which there was fear underneath the defiance.

Thank the Lord, I bore no children, Peggy thought. Otherwise I could not endure it.

They tied her arms behind her back, then clumsily ransacked the place, smashing crockery and emptying the contents of drawers. There was little enough in the way of possessions in the two small rooms of the cottage and soon all of it lay scattered on the floor, where the men crushed whatever was breakable under their boots. She wondered at the rage in them against her teapot and teacups and she thought its source must be very far from her cottage, her belongings, her self. It comforted her to think that they were so far from her, in a different world almost, her persecutors and murderers.

Smirk did not join in the work of destruction, searching with cold eyes among the bits and bobs of her existence, picking up this or that before casting it away. He caught sight of the little shelf high up above the door and she saw a faint puzzlement cross his face as he took down the bible that lived there. He looked at her, and their eyes met. For a moment, the distance between them was gone, but he cast the bible away as if it were of no more significance than a tin mug or a cotton reel, and the smirk came back. It was the mask he wore to hide himself against humanity, so familiar to him that the features of his face had hardened around it and hinged on it. His smirk was the parody of humours he no longer knew.

The bible lay on the floor amongst the litter of her things. None of them trod on it, but none of them picked it up either, even though what they did that night was done in its name. Smirk reached up once more to the small shelf. His hand explored the darkened recess and closed around a miniature wooden box, which he put directly into his pocket, with a thief's intuition.

'We'll take the chickens before we fire the place,' he said. Out went Potter and Poleaxe. She heard the commotion in the hen coop and the bird shrieks cut short by muffled thuds.

They pushed her outside into the chill dark and bundled her into their cart. They tied her feet and bound them to her wrists behind her back. The horse shifted and snorted in its traces. One of the men led them a little way along the track. She lay in the shape of a bow, helpless in the back of the cart, listening to the shouts of the men. Soon she saw the glow of the fire and heard the crackle of the flames. They came to the cart and threw two sacks alongside her. Three of the men climbed up and sat with their backs to the driving box, shifting her with their feet to make room. She could feel the warmth of the dead birds in the sacks against her body and felt a sadness for their lives, for the cock-crowing dawns, the restless scratching and gleaning, the nests of glossy eggs, the mutters in the coop at dusk. Throughout her adult life, the hens had sustained her, and on her final journey, they warmed her with the last heat of their bodies. Now in the dark, the tears came to her eyes, because there would never be another cock-crowing dawn or muttering dusk or any of the small joys between.

I am not ready for the end, she thought.

She cried silently, bundled up in the black cart, until a sudden jolt of the wheels tipped her over and she looked up. The stars were bright in a clear moonless sky and there was the Hunter and the Badger and the Beehive. Her eye stopped at the tiny circlet of the

Daisy Chain. How often have I looked on those sparkling blooms, she wondered, and to her surprise it was not so many times that she had gazed on them, and felt their unique presence in the heavens. Even for a stargazer like herself, even for a woman who had not been much distracted by the mundane, the starry basket of precious secrets was still a rare thing. Never rarer than on that night, when she would take the picture of it with her wherever she was going.

She thought of what was in the box the man had taken from the shelf with the bible, and wondered what would become of it, but objects such as those had a way of directing their own fate, she knew.

The cart was climbing. The sound of the horse's breath came in gasps. 'We are too many for the horse up this slope,' she said aloud.

'Be silent, woman,' growled Blunt.

But she was right and they knew it, and before long they called a halt and two men got down, walking behind the cart as it laboured up the hill. She knew every curve of the lane, every tree almost, whose branches made black patterns in the sky above their heads.

When they reached the top of the hill, the two climbed back into the cart. One of them hacked at her in passing and the other pressed his knee into her groin as he clambered over her. The cart trundled slowly down along the long slope through the park and she thought they were taking her to the town where there might after all be some process of law and a chance, however slight, of reprieve. But their way led them instead to the shadowy ruins of the Old Castle, under the arched gateway and over the turf until they reached the keep.

Against one of the walls of the keep the wood for the pyre had been stacked and an iron stake had been hammered into the ground close by. The men were nervous and kept silent. They were in a hurry to get it done and in their haste, they hurt her, binding her too tightly to the stake.

'I can't breathe.' The words were forced from between her lips.

'There's no need for you to breathe,' sneered Smirk.

Really she could not get a proper breath, and when they lit the pile of twigs they had heaped at her feet, the smoke overcame her at once. Her head went forward on her breast and maybe she was never aware of the scorching of her legs, her thighs, her torso.

They built the fire up around her. The wood was old and dry, and soon they had to toss the sticks and stumps from a distance because the heat was too great.

The fuel burned fast and there was not enough of it to finish the job. In the dark, they dragged branches from the nearby copse, but still they could not heap it high enough to cover her blackened head. It was not with words that Peggy Forgetmenot cursed them but with the sight of her burnt, hairless skull looking at them from hollow eye sockets above the flames.

Men and women rising from their night's sleep in Sherborne town beyond the river looked up to see a pall of dark smoke over the castle keep. By the time it had dwindled to a slender thread of grey, most of them knew what had been done and to whom.

The five men returned at dusk with picks and shovels. 'We should say a few words over her bones,' Sulk suggested.

Smirk shrugged. 'Say something if you want to.'

But no one stepped forward, for what was on their minds could not be said aloud.

'Then let this be her send-off.' Smirk took a pair of dice from his pocket. For a moment he gazed at them as they lay on the palm of his hand. There was one white one and one red, the latter curiously marked. He threw them into the embers. 'Take these, slut, and be damned to you,' he said.

They covered the embers with soil dug from outside the keep. The smirking man made them continue until a thick layer of earth covered every trace of the fire, every charred log and flake of ash. They wondered at his thoroughness in concealing such a very public burning, but none of them suspected his real motive, which was to make it difficult for anyone to retrieve the objects he had cast into the woman's grave. Anyone? It was he himself who might be tempted.

The Law slept. No one was accused. There was no trial. There had been a fire at the castle in which someone was said to have died. Perhaps she had been struck by lightning. Among her neighbours – many of whom had been made well by the brews from Peggy's teapot against palsy and dropsy and plague and the ointments from her skilful fingers against tetter and rash and rot – the struck-by-lightning story took hold, soon burying what all of them knew was the truth as thoroughly as her ashes were buried in the keep. People who wander abroad on dark nights get struck by lightning, and Peggy was known for a wanderer by dark.

At dawn on the day after the burning, two hooded women, one elderly and one in middle age, arrived at the roofless cottage and searched among the remnants of Peggy Forgetmenot's life on earth. They saw the severed chicken heads which the cats had been at during the night. They saw where the cart had stood and the droppings of the carthorse. They picked through the fragments of crockery lying among the cinders on the floor of the house. They found the spine of her bible still attached to a blackened stub of text. They gathered all the pieces they could find of her teapot and these were the only objects they took away with them. Afterwards they walked up to the castle and came to the place of the fire. They saw the heap of fresh earth in the keep and the place from which it had been dug. They saw the flecks of ash and soot scattered over the precinct. They made a cross of two sticks bound with woodbine and set it on top of the mound. They gathered daisies from the meadow and made a daisy chain of a hundred tiny white and yellow blooms which they wound around the arms of the cross. The older woman spoke these words over the grave.

'Peggy walked this earth and is buried beneath it. She lived with the flowers and died with them. She grew under the trees and will always be among them. She learned under the stars and lies under them. Her story is our story and we will remember. May God have mercy on her soul. Amen.

'Amen,' the other repeated.

Chapter Three

THE APEMEN HAVE IT

The question of God's existence is beyond the scope of man's intellect
                                              Charles Darwin

TWO-AND-A-HALF was Louis Yeoman, son of a farmer in the Quantocks, where the Yeomans were a numerous tribe. Most were farmers but there was also a tailor in Taunton and a pork butcher in Bridgewater well-known for a violent way with the cleaver and some unusual cuts of meat. Louis' father was a narrow-minded and self-important widower with little time for his only son, who was cut from a different cloth.

The Michaelmas term of 1877 marked the beginning of Louis' last year at Sherborne School and the first term of Lionel Runciman's tenure as headmaster. Among Runciman's schemes to get his headship off to a lively start was a meeting of the Debating Society, with outside speakers. The motion for the debate was chosen by Runciman himself: 'This House Rejects the Theory that

Man is Descended from the Apes', which in 1877 was as lively a motion as you could get.

Asked by Runciman to recommend an artist for the poster, the art master suggested Louis, whose hobby consisted of pencil sketches drawn in the manner of Cruikshank, in which figures with outlandish bodies and pale faces spoke in balloons above their heads, against a background of angular carriages and bad-tempered horses or improbable furniture in disorderly homes.

So it was that news of the debate reached the boys by means of a poster in the cloisters featuring a large ape with a long beard sitting on a throne among clouds and swinging a sceptre. In danger of being struck by this object was a mitred bishop hopping on one leg and attempting to ward it off with a bible. The God of Chimps ran the title, in bold Gothic letters above the bearded ape. Below was the wording of the motion to be debated and at the bottom the names of the speakers. Proposing the motion was the Very Reverend Lord Bishop of Wells, seconded by the Reverend Jack Frazer, and opposing it were Mr Austin Kelynack and A.N. Other.

'Provocative,' commented the chaplain when he saw the poster. 'Impertinent,' said the Reverend Hulme. The senior staff agreed that the admirable HH, Runciman's predecessor, would never have allowed a debate of this kind, let alone the posting of a blasphemous advertisement. A protest was mooted in the Common Room, but the Bishop of Wells accepted the invitation to propose the motion, which put an end to that. Besides, as Hulme pointed out, the authority of the Bishop would certainly carry the day against an inexperienced history teacher, Kelynack whom Runciman had appointed that term and whoever he found to second him. Nobody knew the Reverend Jack Frazer, but as a churchman he was presumably a safe pair of hands.

For the debate, the reading tables were set back along three sides of the library and benches and chairs were brought in. The fifth form squatted on the tables, the sixth sat on the benches and staff and guests had the chairs. Runciman sat in the middle of the front row, flanked by his wife on one side and the Archdeacon on the other. Beyond them were Hulme, the chaplain and other reverend gentlemen. Seen from behind, Isadora Runciman's raven-black hair fell in perfect coils over the shoulders of a silk dress the colour of amethyst with sequins that glittered in the lamplight. As the four speakers battled with weighty thoughts on the origins of humankind that evening, their audience was much preoccupied by Mrs Runciman's hair and the bewitching sequins.

On the fourth side of the room, in a high-backed oak chair sat Biffen, head of English and president of the Debating Society. The proceedings began with his short speech describing the motion before the House as 'the most significant philosophical issue of our times'. He introduced the Bishop of Wells, a heavy man with a large hairless head and big hands that looked capable of tasks more muscular than the tending of Christ's flock.

'This House rejects the theory that man is descended from the ape,' the Bishop began loudly. 'I emphasise the word theory. It is a supposition, unproven and unprovable, based on observations in certain remote islands of the Pacific ocean made by a beetle collector. Large lizards and outsized crabs dwell amid an accretion of bird droppings and seaweed. In the fresh waters are found certain forms of animated slime that, it is said, do not occur elsewhere and could not have come by sea because of their dislike of salt water. According to the beetle collector, they developed there independently and it must be assumed that life forms developed independently elsewhere, through a process termed evolution.

'I shall happily apply to Mr Charles Darwin for advice if my beetroots are beset by slugs. Perhaps he will recommend a salt water moat through which the slugs cannot swim. But I shall not be applying to a collector of insects and toads for his opinion…' the Bishop thumped the table with his large fist, 'on the seven days of the Lord's creation, on man's eternal soul or his relations with his Maker!'

The Bishop was a man to whom belief in God gave conviction rather than humility. He was fond of the pulpit and enjoyed the power of his voice, preferring a heathenish bellow to a godly murmur. 'Blessed are the meek,' he had roared that morning in chapel, 'for they shall inherit the earth.' The Bishop knew what meekness was, he knew its virtues but he did not consider it necessary for himself.

His opening salvo at the debate was all the speech he had prepared. He was used to extemporising in the pulpit, and he had no qualms about doing so in a school debate. Informed that his opponents were a newly-arrived master and a sixth former, he had envisaged a pair of novices. After firing his first shots, his words drifted idly here and there, and the initial impact dissipated. The boys enjoyed the quip about the slugs but hardly listened to the rest, which seemed to their ears an amalgam of what they heard every day in chapel – that the existence of God was an unalterable fact entailing a list of unappealing duties.

The Bishop might have done better if he'd given any thought to the issue, but he anticipated a comfortable victory, assuming that most of his listeners thought as he did and that Darwin and his ilk were no more than a lunatic fringe thrown up by the universities. He knew nothing of his opponent and nothing of his own seconder who had been selected by the Dean of Wells and with whom he had not troubled to confer.

The fact was that in Austin Kelynack he was up against a intellect sharp and subtle and a speaker whose brisk and understated manner conveyed an authority of a very different kind to his own.

'I thank the Lord Bishop for stating so baldly the position of the medieval Church,' Kelynack began when his turn came. The word 'baldly' was greeted by the boys with titters, although it was 'medieval' that was the sap of the sentence.

'He has Augustine and Aquinas on his side, not to mention a tremendous tribe of deacons and deans, canons and candle-bearers. But we may doubt whether Augustine would have grasped the ideas of Newton or whether Aquinas would have made sense of Thomas Edison. As for the deacons and the deans, the prelates and the prebendaries, like ourselves they are mystified as to how Brunel erected his bridges or Stephenson powered his locomotives. They can hardly be blamed for failing to comprehend the implications of Lyell's geological researches or Hooker's work on tropical flora.

'However, we should be grateful to our own Lord Bishop, who has favoured us with a commendably succinct account of the theory of evolution, which by the way is far from being the exclusive property of Darwin but belongs to as many eminent naturalists and scientists as there are bishops in the House of Lords.

'Would it be fair, then, in our current debate, to range the spiritual lords of the realm in a contest against the lords – if I may put it this way – of the engine, the laboratory and the microscope?

'It would not be fair. On one side we have the pioneers of empirical research, the masters of inductive method, the ingenious innovators and inventors, and on the other we have only faith, immutable and impenetrable. On the one side, we have logical argument and objective reasoning. On the other, we have...'

'On the other side we have Christ our Lord,' thundered the Bishop.

Biffen intervened. 'With respect, Your Worship, I must ask you to keep your further remarks for the summing-up.'

'On the other, we have the cracked bells of superstition,' Kelynack finished.

Kelynack made an arresting figure. He was the tallest person in the room, a distinction emphasised by the peculiarly upright way in which he carried himself. There was not an ounce of fat on his body, and something in his bearing hinted that there never would be. He might have been thought handsome were it not for a certain elusiveness in his eye. There was a look about Austin Kelynack which unsettled people and made them wary.

The thrust of his speech that evening, after disposing of the ranks of bishops, was that the power of science to unravel myths and dismantle superstitions was something for which the young scholars in the room should be deeply grateful.

'The scales fall from our eyes,' he said, 'and what we see is not a divine vision but the objective truth. We are no longer enslaved by the past. We are free to achieve what we want to achieve, to become what we want to become, to prove ourselves the fittest to survive in the contest between man and man, nation and nation, race and race. We belong to an age of free thought and unlimited progress, and if the price we have to pay is the sneers of those who call us ape-men, it is a small one. Better an apeman than a slave!'

The final line of Kelynack's speech, an echo of Huxley's famous remark to Bishop Wilberforce some years before, was not destined to be its most memorable. For several weeks afterwards, as he made his upright way across the courts, cries of 'Lord of the Engine!' pursued him.

The Reverend Frazer took the floor to second the motion. He was an old man, somewhat disordered in appearance. The Bishop had looked at him askance when taking his seat. He appeared to have arrived in his gardening clothes, shapeless trousers of thick corduroy and an ancient green cardigan with a hole at one elbow. His hair was long and had long been left to its own devices. Some of the boys were tempted to laugh at this tattered old priest, but were restrained by an air of intensity that in it had more of the prophet than the gardener.

'In the beginning was the Word,' he began. His sharp eye travelled around the room. 'These are the opening words of the most intriguing part of the most read book in the world and deserve our close attention. When we see w-o-r-d our minds turn to something said or heard or written. However, in the beginning must refer to a time before anything else was, so there was no tongue to speak or ear to hear or hand to write. Whatever is meant by 'the Word' was without shape or form or substance in time and space. In Greek, 'the Word' is *Logos*, which might also be translated principle or cause, the presence of which cannot by its nature be detected by the five senses.

'No argument, therefore, based on measurement or observation – or as Mr Kelynack put it, empirical method – insisting that this *Logos* is a delusion, can be legitimate. Something that is beyond time and space and the senses can only be approached by intuition, or inspiration. The ancient philosophers of the great religions were agreed that the immaterial preceded the material and that this precedence cannot be affected by any events in the mundane sphere. It follows that all manifestations in the realm of time and space are dependent on a realm that is timeless and measureless, and of course invisible.'

He spoke without notes and addressed his remarks to the roof. Now he paused, glancing at his audience. Then he looked round at them more closely, apparently realising that most of them had not followed what he was saying. 'But it's very simple,' he continued frowning. 'What is not came before what is, and the whole secret of everything that is can be found in what is not!'

He tried again. 'Very well. Let us return to the motion before the House. What I am suggesting to you is that it is not the body of man that is important, and not even the mind, which is mostly beyond his control, but the capacity for imagination to reach where the senses cannot reach. The Logos, the first cause or principle, is accessible to the imagination of man, and it is this that separates him from the ape, or the horse, or the tiger.

'Since what the seer sees cannot be put into ordinary speech, which is itself a function of the sensible world, it must be conveyed in metaphors or myths. We tend to use the word myth as if it were a story for children, and eventually that is what it becomes. But the fact is that myths are rooted in the attempts of the wise to signal the direction of the truth.

'Let us consider the book of Genesis. It is true, but not in its details, which is only narrative dress. The snake, the fruit, the seduction of the woman: this is story. But inside the story is the idea that once upon a time, people lived in harmony with each other and with the world, and in that world there was no good and no evil but only being. That is the Garden of Eden. Once upon a time, I say. Aye, there's the rub, because someone will ask: when exactly?

'Then one of the diggers and delvers will find a pair of skeletons and announce the discovery of the human remains of Adam and Eve. There will be skull measurements and all manner of calculation and it will be determined that the tribe of the Adam-Evites were a people with a low brow who lived in a fertile spot with lots of fruit, until hit by a tidal wave, which when it first appeared on the horizon resembled a serpent...' He stopped and had another look around. Everyone appeared to be listening, but the looks on the faces were of incomprehension.

It was Jack Frazer's fate on earth to see with a prophet's eye and speak with a voice of fire and be treated as an eccentric old bird who made no sense.

'Where was I? Eden. The snake. Yes. Paradise is a metaphor for the knowledge of the spiritual truth, which is known to all souls before their imprisonment in a body, the forked carrot, with its pretensions... We forget who we really are and only by immense efforts can we recall... But do we make these immense efforts? No, we do not, because why should we? *Why should we?*'

These last words were shouted. James Biffen shifted in his chair and cleared his throat and nodded at the clock.

'Yes, yes, we are ruled by the clock. For thousands of years, or hundreds of thousands if the diggers and delvers are right, we carried on our business of hunting and cooking and making children with no more than an occasional glance at the position of the sun in the sky or the stars at night. The sky was enough of a clock all by itself, but now we need one in every room or even to carry one about with us. The slavery of man to time is increasing and perhaps soon the carrying of a clock will be compulsory. The old Hindus warned us of... of a growing and mistaken servitude to the sorts and dimensions of matter... and here comes Mister Charlie Darwin and his new version of Genesis, with the essential component *completely absent*.' He laughed a wild laugh.

'Darwin's version won't endure, of course, being a story of only one sentence. Once upon a time we were monkeys, our backs grew stiffer and our arms shorter and our brows expanded until we were capable of inventing all the things needed by people with stiff backs and large heads. No snake, no apple, even the question of clothing curiously omitted, which you will remember was a key element in the old tale. Everything of real significance omitted – good and evil, knowledge and nakedness, conscience and temptation – matters that every day puzzle and exercise us – to be replaced by this empty notion of progress. What is involved in so-called progress but more iron and more speed and more clocks and more fearsome instruments of destruction?'

'I must ask you, Reverend,' Biffen interrrupted, 'to bring your remarks to a conclusion.'

'I shall do so when I get there, Master Stickler. First, I have a word of encouragement for these boys, which one or two of them may heed. One alone would be enough to repay my journey here tonight.

'I referred to the immense efforts needed to recall who we really are. They lead to a path *more dangerous than the highest mountain*, and one which all but the boldest would rather avoid. Without clues, it seems, we are lost before we begin. But the clues are all around us.' He spoke these words with the emphasis appropriate to a tremendous mystery. 'They are in the writings of our poets, in the moods of the graveyards, at dawn or dusk in ancient places and in the whispers of the unrelenting wind. On lonely hilltops and in deep forests, the solitary wanderer can gather them like flowers. For the stay-at-homes, they can be heard in the old legends, told and retold by the fireside at night.

'Consider the goblins, the gnomes and the fairies... Have you ever wondered why these legendary folk have so many names? Why do the Scots tell of them, and the Welsh and the Irish and the Cornish and the Bretons and the Norsemen and the Chinamen and as far as I know every people on earth? Is the whole world mad that it makes stories of what is not there?

'The gods have become small. How else explain why they are so rarely seen in this age of the steam locomotive and the cotton mills? Soon they will be as small as midges and no one will see them at all. The old myths become fictions for the innocent. But think for a moment of the characteristics of the fairy, a delicate beauty, wings like gossamer...'

'Enough!' boomed the Bishop. 'Mr Frazer you have said enough! You are confused, sir, and you do us no service. Withdraw, my good sir. Be finished.'

'I am finished, Your Grace. Finished long since as a minister of the Church, and soon finished with the prison of the body. But if we are defeated in this vote, my Lord Bishop, you will have cause to thank me, since the blame may be put on my confusion rather than your own.'

Biffen intervened swiftly and the indignant response that leapt to the Bishop's lips stayed unspoken. 'I call on Mr Louis Yeoman,' Biffen went on hurriedly, 'as seconder to Mr Kelynack.'

If there was anybody there that evening who made Jack Frazer's journey worthwhile, it was Louis, who was to speak against him. Louis was not impressed by the logic of the old man's argument, which was erratic, nor by the hidden meaning of myth, which was obscure, but by his disdain for faster trains and more clocks and his appealing list of what might be learned by the solitary. There was something elevated and principled in the Reverend Jack Frazer and Louis wanted to go up to him and reassure him that one person at least had seen where the fairy's gossamer wings, so infuriating the Bishop, were leading. It didn't matter to Louis at that moment who was right, the Godly or the Godless – perhaps it didn't ever matter – what mattered was his sudden affinity with an old man in gardening trousers whom nobody understood.

It was more or less by chance that Louis came to be speaking for the Godless that night. Kelynack had seen his poster and come looking for him.

'The poster's good, Yeoman. And I know you can speak, because you recently proved it in sixth-form history. Be my seconder at the debate.'

'But I'm not even sure which side I stand on,' Louis responded.

Kelynack answered that agnosticism meant precisely that – a degree of doubt, a willingness to seek answers where orthodoxy was afraid to look. 'This is not the Last Judgement,' he said. 'It's a contest, made with words. We'll cause the priests to jump a bit and give the boys something other than rugby football to applaud. Here, read this and then give me your answer.'

He handed over a slim book called *Man's Place in Nature*.

'It was Huxley who coined the word agnostic,' Kelynack continued, indicating the author's name. 'He's not a firebrand. Just a freethinker.'

Louis liked the book from page one, which contained the first version of the later-famous queue of skeletons, with the gibbon on all fours becoming upright via stages of stooping ape, and *homo sapiens* at the head of the queue. Louis saw that Huxley's version of man's beginnings was less of a fairy-tale than Genesis. It matched the times they lived in, the age of the *Great Scientific Clubs* peopled by men with abundant beards, butterfly nets strapped to their carriages and rock hammers in their pockets. Earnest, methodical men with microscopes and a mission: the replacement of the Laws of God by the Laws of Nature. Louis wasn't sure how much difference it made, really, but a breath of fresh air blew through the stuffy churches. An ape stood in for Abraham, an elephant played the part of Elijah, the Devil was a dinosaur.

God wasn't denied, He was just omitted. Maybe there is, behind everything, some unintelligible higher power, or maybe not. There was the problem of the first cause, for example. How had the whole works been set in motion? A gas? Where did the gas come from? An explosion? What was it that blew up?

Louis did not share these large questions with Kelynack when they met in the library one evening to discuss their strategy for the debate. There was little common ground between them. The history master was an iconoclast, a rationalist, an atheist; Louis was simply exploring the various possibilities, still influenced by the old classical idea of a divine order, conveyed by Grindlay and, through him, by Plato and Socrates. Kelynack's idea of debate was to throw everything at your foe and see what happened. There was plenty to throw, he pointed out.

'God is a mental fog serving to obscure the truth,' he added. 'The fog clears in the light of rationality.'

That was all very well, Louis thought, but a mental fog was where most people lived, himself included. He worked away at a kind of speech, but he was no orator, no politician. He had more questions than answers. How could the wing be a product of natural selection? What was the good of the start of a wing unless it contained an awareness of what it would become?

Then there was the problem of the poets. Blake, Coleridge, John Donne. Their poetry seemed moved by faith and... and what? A kind of love. Their world, as far as Louis could understand it, was made of love. Where was love in the ideas of Darwin and Huxley? The engine of the Darwinian world was survival, and Huxley argued that man was the product of the same all-pervasive instinct. If it were true, Donne was ridiculous and William Blake insane. This made him think of John Clare, who had ended up in an asylum for lunatics. Is that what happened to men who explored the world of the spirit? Perhaps because they were chasing an illusion.

In the end, he had a speech. It was there in front of him when Biffen called on him to speak. Some bits of it might be alright, he thought. But as he got to his feet, he doubted that any of it was. His sudden compassion for the Reverend Frazer had stolen his wind.

He stood wordless, with the room watching him. He looked at his notes, but the words swarmed. There was a section, surely, on page two that he could use. Or was it page three? He shuffled the pages, aware of the dense expectant silence around him.

'Um,' he began. As the sound came out he knew it to be a catastrophic start. It was a sound close to Aum, it occurred to him, which was supposed to be the answer to everything if repeated often enough. 'Aum,' he continued.

Two coughs and a low muttering broke the silence.

'Aum is the magical word of the ancient Hindus. I was... I was trying it out, but it appears not to work.'

Jack Frazer caught the joke, and laughed. Louis glanced in his direction. The old clergyman was with him, but it was the wrong omen.

'I suppose the Reverend Frazer was going to say that the fairies are the last remaining traces of the angels.'

Each sentence he spoke could go in any number of directions, or none. Out of the corner of his eye, he saw Kelynack glaring at him.

'God is a kind of mental fog,' he stumbled on. He had liked the expression, and appreciated it. 'An excuse for muddled thinking.'

But what about The Word, in the beginning?

'The problem is that our muddled thinking is not sufficient to judge... to judge whether the principle came first. If it did, then Darwin must be wrong, unless apes can comprehend a principle. Obviously they can not. Nobody has suggested they can.

'But perhaps all of creation, I mean all animals, have an eternal soul. What they don't have is words, beyond a neigh or a grunt. Because they can't express it – can't conceive of it – doesn't mean that they don't have it. Maybe, even, they *are* it. They are God's children without knowing it.'

Even to his muddled mind it was clear that if his speech was going anywhere, it was in the wrong direction.

He felt that his audience was attentive, but only because they were watching for him to stumble, or fall flat. Damn them then! A contest made of words, Kelynack had said. He stiffened his back, like a man, and saw a way out.

'The motion of the debate does not define descent,' he went on. 'But Darwin and Huxley are concerned with the physical world, the realm of matter. Bones, teeth, fingernails. The physical resemblance between men and apes can't be missed. It's there is your nostrils, your knees and your navels.'

A ripple of laughter, friendlier.

'The body of man is a legacy of the apes, the scientists are saying. Why not? What does it matter? Physically man is descended from the ape, and that is why you will vote for us tonight. But…' Here he felt an elbow nudge him sharply in the ribs.

'No buts,' Kelynack hissed.

'But the awareness of an immortal soul, and with it the urge, or need, to reach for an understanding of… The Word, belongs to man alone.'

He sat down, clutching his futile sheaf of papers. A faint murmur of appreciation hummed briefly among the listeners. Some of the boys had sensed in his words the evidence of a real issue, not easily resolved. It was a sense missing from their classes with the self-righteous chaplain, the pompous Dr Hulme or the formidable HH.

Biffen opened the debate to the floor and Hulme was first to his feet.

'We are not here to argue the existence of man's soul, which is incontrovertible, nor that of animals, which is irrelevant. We are concerned with the scurrilous suggestion of man's simian origins, a theory which constitutes an attack on the dignity of man and the greatness of God. If man stands in the line of apes and monkeys, why should he not slobber like an ape and thieve like a monkey?

Why should he dress fittingly, respect the past, study languages or, for that matter, engineering? Why not grab what he can, steal from his neighbour, settle disputes by blows and burn down the churches and the libraries?

'I can assure you that is what it will come to, if this pestilence is not stamped out. God created man in his own image. Our nature is not determined by our navels or our knees, but our mind. It is the mind that directs, controls and decides. It is the mind that studies, invents and constructs. It is the mind that has produced a language of a million words.

'Man is characterised by three things: his upright posture, his hairlessness and his language. Where is the ape in these? This so-called evolution of Darwin and Huxley is looked at upside-down. If there is some remote connection between a man and an ape, it must be that the ape is a degenerate human. The human is the model: straight-backed, decently clothed, communicative. Perhaps at some point a starved remnant of humanity was forced to survive by taking to the trees and living on berries, and that is why our fingers and toes bear some resemblance to those of monkeys in a monkey house. I propose this as an alternative version, one which leaves the dignity of man and the greatness of God undefiled.'

The boys were familiar with Hulme's hectoring style, his predictions of social collapse, his emphasis on correct posture and neat dress. Here it was again, the same fare in a different pot. Besides, it was plain to the boys that Hulme was on his feet so promptly in order to impress the Bishop. His motive was revealed in two brief glances in the Bishop's direction, one as he rose to speak and the other as he resumed his seat. Boys in class may doodle and yawn, but they do not miss the signs that matter. Perhaps this was the real trace of the monkey in them, the legacy of the jungle, where the slightest movement among the leaves announces the advance of the snake or a faint shadow passing over the forest floor the coming of the eagle.

There were other contributions from the floor, but they were few. The boys had their eyes on the cakes and wine provided as refreshment.

The Bishop rose to make his summing-up. He valued his connection with the school. He was accustomed to think of it as a pasture not too far from home, with the boys as his flock. But it was Kelynack's speech to which the audience had responded, and that fool Frazer had only muddied the waters. The tide was against him. He should say something reassuring, avuncular, witty. Something to coax the sheep back to the fold. But there was too much indignation in him.

'I am the way, the truth and the light, Christ said,' he boomed. 'Christ is my shepherd, I shall not want, wrote the psalmist.' The word 'shepherd' was as close as he got to an avuncular tone, and he lost it at once. 'But you want more, it seems. You cannot be guided by Christ the Shepherd. It is Mammon you want. If you choose the broad road that leads to destruction, it is not the staff of Christ the Shepherd you will find, but the rod of God's just anger. I tell you it will be a terrible thing to meet your Maker unprepared.'

This was not the way. But he plunged on, gesturing in Kelynack's direction. 'Better an ape than a slave. Better a slave of God, I say, than a King of Apes! God! God! God! The Lord God of Hosts whose service is perfect freedom.'

The Bishop sat down. The Archdeacon led a round of applause, but it lacked enthusiasm. Kelynack rose on behalf of the opposition. He waited until the boys were hushed, then waited a moment more. 'Reason! Reason! Reason!' he repeated in a resounding voice. That was all.

The vote was taken and the Apemen had it, with a comfortable majority. The Bishop treated himself to a couple of brisk glasses of wine to restore his temper and found that they engendered more heat than good humour.

Chapter Four

ISADORA

She has heard a whisper say
A curse is on her if she stay

                              Alfred Tennyson

THE APE debate had caused Isadora to argue with her husband. She had seen the poster in the cloisters and told him she would like to attend.

'No, my dear, you may not be present at the debate.'

'On what grounds am I to be excluded?'

'On the grounds of your sex, Isadora. We shall be a roomful of men and boys. There will be no wives or daughters present.'

'It is in the rules, I suppose.'

'It is not a question of rules but of convention. This is a school for boys with a staff of men. Women are present at some social occasions. Otherwise they are absent.'

'If women were excluded from evening meetings at the Classical Society, you would not have met me.'

'The Classical Society is not the King's School.'

'And you are not the man I married. I married a young reformer and I find myself wed to a middle-aged conservative.'

'I am the headmaster of a school with traditions. If I do not maintain those traditions, I shall be failing in my duty to the Governors who employ me.'

'The chairman of the Board of Governors did not strike me as a traditionalist. Will he be present?'

'He will be invited.'

'Then invite his wife as well, and we shall be two.'

'I am sure that Lady Kenelm will not attend.'

'Invite Mrs Hulme.'

'Hulme will not want his wife there.'

'That makes two of you then. It is not about convention, Lionel. You do not want me to be conspicuous. You prefer to hide me away.'

'You are mistaken.'

'Perhaps you do not want me to be looked at. It is strange, because you hardly bother to look at me yourself.'

'I am sorry if you think so. It's true that I am preoccupied. The position is a taxing one.'

'Why did you marry me, Lionel?'

'For your charm, your vivacity... your beauty.'

'What is that you found beautiful in me?'

'Really, my dear, I'm surprised that...'

'Was it my eyes, my lips, my ankles, my bosom?'

'This is not seemly.'

'Was it seemly for a man to stare at a woman as you stared at me that first evening at the Classical Society? Yes, you stared. Do you think a woman doesn't notice when she is being admired? She has practised being looked at since she was a child. First you noticed my eyes. It was during your speech. You were talking of Thomas Arnold, but you were thinking of my eyes.'

How could he deny it?

'Afterwards, when you thought that no one was looking, you examined me. You examined the shape of my body.'

'I did not!'

'You did, certainly.'

'You were looking the other way.'

'When?' she flashed. 'When was I looking the other way?'

'You were talking to the headmaster of Fettes.'

'Yes, but when was I doing so?'

'When...'

'Lionel, there is nothing wrong in looking at a woman's bosom. When a woman dresses in a gown cut *so*,' – she gestured with her hand – 'she wishes to be looked at. It is expected that the glances be discreet, that they should not linger. In your case, they did.'

'Did what?'

'Lingered.'

'They did not!'

'Ah, so you admit that you were looking at my bosom?'

'Perhaps, for a moment. You are a handsome woman.'

'I was talking to Fettes... who, by the way, was looking at my bosom as I was talking to you.'

'The scoundrel!'

'But you were the scoundrel who pursued me most energetically. You married me, Lionel, because you wanted to have me.'

'Please let us bring this conversation to an end.'

'Now you have *had* me, and you no longer stare at me because where is the excitement in staring at what belongs to you?'

'I refuse to listen to talk in this vein.'

'Then allow me to attend the debate. Otherwise I shall assume that you do not want other men looking at me.'

'This is ridiculous.'

'I shall not speak. I shall listen, modestly.'

Runciman had yielded. He sent invitations to Lady Kenelm and Mrs Hulme, but as he had supposed, they were politely declined.

When Isadora took her seat at the Ape debate, she wished for a moment that there had been another woman amongst them, or an army general in full uniform, or a circus clown or anybody at all with some colour and style, but there was none but herself.

She enjoyed all four of the speeches, the Bishop's aggressive sermonising – so different to the grave Orthodox priesthood to which she was accustomed, the congenial eccentricity of the prophet in gardener's clothes and the brave honesty of the boy.

But it was Kelynack who interested her. Here is a different sort of man, she thought. She liked his clothes, combining a touch of the monastic – the severe cut of the black jacket – with a hint of the careless, his master's gown pushed back off the shoulders, the cravat flung loosely together. She liked that he made no attempt, with smiles or jokes or rhetorical tricks, to flatter or cajole. She liked that he wore no whiskers or sideburns or other concealments. Take me for what I am, he seemed to say, and if it doesn't please you, you can go to the devil.

After the debate, Isadora was at her husband's side for the wine and cakes. Since her husband chose to remain with the Bishop and the Archdeacon, she also remained. She caught the eye of Thomas Cuff, the head boy, signalled him to join her and was able by half-turning to talk to him without seeming to abandon her husband.

'Thomas,' she said quietly, 'I wish to be introduced to Mr Kelynack. You must send someone else for him, because if you go yourself, I shall lose my few feet of space.'

Cuff beckoned a prefect and sent him with the message for Kelynack.

When he came, he greeted her in Russian. The unexpected sound of her native tongue was delightful to her. For an instant, the old library of Sherborne School was lit in another light. It was St. Petersburg, with generals and ambassadors and trays of champagne, and the glitter and the game.

'You speak my language well.'

He bowed slightly. 'The language of Turgenev and Tolstoy deserves care,' he said.

'You have read Leo Nikolayevich Tolstoy?'

'With pleasure.'

'In Russian?'

'Yes, madam.'

'I should not have thought that his ideas would suit you.'

'How alert of you to perceive it. It is the breadth of his canvas that appeals.'

'You are a historian. But you are also a student of science, it seems.'

He held his head at a rigid perpendicular, looking down at her with his peculiar eyes, like pebbles seen through the waters of a stream.

'I know nothing of laboratories or microscopes, madam. It is the spirit of enquiry that I applaud.'

'We all applaud that, Mr Kelynack.'

'Do we? I fear we do not. There is an abbey to the south of us, a chapel to the west and a church to the north. If you went east, it is a certainty that you would also bump into one before long. These edifices and what they represent do not encourage people to think for themselves.'

'You are a Radical.'

'Cultures have roots. Nations have roots. If I wish to understand great matters, I must grasp their roots.'

He made a sudden swift gesture with his hand, as if clutching an object that lay between them. Involuntarily, she drew back.

'I startled you, Mrs Runciman.'

'You are theatrical, sir.'

He laughed. It was like the bark of a fox.

'I earn my living by instructing boys. Some of them are sleepy and dull. An element of the dramatic is required.'

It was not the suddenness of his gesture that had surprised her, but the hint of brutality in the way his hand had grasped the imaginary root, as if he were squeezing the life out of it. She wondered if there might be an aspect of these diffident Englishmen that she had not appreciated—something unpredictable and passionate.

During her nocturnal stroll a few days later, she saw a light coming from one of the classrooms, the door of which was ajar. Glancing in as she passed along the dark corridor, she saw Kelynack seated at the desk. She paused at the doorway, waiting to be observed. His eyes sprang towards her. Although the door was open, the swiftness of his glance and the sharp lift of the eyebrows were those of a man caught unawares in a world kept private. Isadora was intrigued. He had beautiful hands, she saw, with long slender fingers and there was an elegance in the way he held them.

'I was thinking of you, madam.'

'Of me?' She stepped into the room.

'Is that so surprising? But the train of my thoughts was professional. Dr Hulme mentioned in the staffroom your desire that Russian be taught in the school. He did not care for the idea. The expense of hiring an additional teacher, he said, was prohibitive. I have a spare hour or two on my timetable. With your permission, I might offer my services for optional Russian with the sixth.'

'I'm sure you do not require my permission, Mr Kelynack.'

'Only you, madam, are in a position to examine my credentials. Knowledge of the Russian language among the staff is restricted to a mispronunciation of Moscow and Sevastopol.'

'You wish me to set you a test?'

'I leave it up to you.'

'I shall give some thought to it.' She gestured at the articles on his desk. 'What are these objects?'

'Historical fribbles. Small clues buried under the turf for later generations to puzzle over. A spindle, a stirrup. Everyday medieval appurtenances. With the exception of *this*.' He picked up a large dark-coloured bead. 'It was this that I was examining as you passed. It is amber. I had started to rub it clean, as you see.'

A fishtail gasburner was lit at head height in the corner of the room, but the light was stingy and four candle stubs were also alight on the desk. Isadora bent over to see what Kelynack showed her and their heads came close to each other as if in some tableau of conspiracy. Where the jewel had been rubbed clean of the crusted grime, a red lustre emerged.

'A find of amber is always suggestive,' Kelynack said.

'Why is that?'

'It derives from a single source, the Baltic, and yet it is found in far-flung places. It was a traveller. But for what reason? It is not a diamond, prized for its brilliance, nor jade or ivory which can be carved into delicate shapes. It has not the glitter of a ruby or an emerald. It is not in fact a mineral at all, but pine resin become stone. Yet the evidence of the tombs indicates that it travelled further than any of them. Why would a man be given amber for his final journey?'

'As a charm or token, perhaps.'

'A token of what?'

'That may be beyond your understanding.'

'Why so?'

'I doubt that your study of history includes the mysteries of death.'

'There is little mystery in the last beat of a worn-out heart or the decomposition of bones in damp soil. I think of the amber as an emblem of the dead, signifying status or power. There may have been some superstition attached to it.'

'Superstition! A favourite word of the rationalist.'

'To denote an irrational and mistaken belief.'

'Reason, reason! you cried at the debate, Mr Kelynack. But reason may not help you with the puzzle of the amber. And now I must bid you good night.'

'Good night, madam. I hope to hear from you on the subject of the Russian lessons.'

'You should apply to my husband, I think.'

'Perhaps the husband may be circumvented.'

'Good night, Mr Kelynack.'

She left him holding the amber bead in his pianist's fingers, continuing her way out of the darkened postern gate of the school premises to the Abbey Close. Entering the abbey by the south door she wandered awhile in the church, where the moonlight caused the stained glass to glow strangely in the dark, as if the scenes depicted were animated by some spectral life. Isadora took a seat to contemplate this haunting illumination and found herself thinking of the amber's lustre, and of Austin Kelynack. The husband may be circumvented, he had said. He trod a precarious line in saying so. But he was someone little affected by rank, she thought. For the first time since arriving in Sherborne, she had encountered a man who treated her less like the headmaster's wife and more like...a woman.

'I must insist that you do not wander about the premises after dark,' Runciman said as they sat at supper the following evening.

'Perhaps you prefer that I take my walk before dawn.'

'Of course not.'

'During the day, the courts and the cloisters are busy and you have made it clear that you do not wish me to consort with the boys. Am I to be imprisoned then?'

'There are walks in other directions. You may go with your maid to Cheap Street or, if you wish, to the grounds of the castle.'

'We shall do so, if we please. But I am not thinking of walks with Françoise. I am thinking of the pleasure of being *toute seule*. Are you familiar with this need, Lionel?'

'It is a luxury that I have no time for.'

'And because you permit yourself to be put upon by those around you, I must suffer the same punishment?'

'Why not? You are my wife.'

'Your wife is not to be allowed her small luxuries?'

'I worry for you. Alone in the dark.'

'Thank you. But I am a creature of the dark. I enjoy the rising of the past in the dark of the present. I enjoy the ghosts of the monks in the shadows cast by moonlight.'

'Last night you were away for an hour.'

'You timed me?'

'I happened to look at the clock.'

'Then I shall time you in the bathroom, where you are very slow, and in the bedroom, where you are too quick. Besides, I left at nine-thirty and returned at the same hour.'

'You left at nine and returned at ten. Please discontinue your walks.'

'I shall not.'

The more he attempted to confine her, the more she shook herself free. So far from discontinuing her walks, she extended them, and often they included a visit to Room IV. She had a favourite costume for her nocturnal stroll, a full-length black frock that Russian peasant women wore in the region of the upper Volga, made of finer stuff but still a peasant frock, with long sleeves and buttons down the front. It was in this gown that Isadora felt most at ease with herself, as if she might really have been happy to remain all her life in the forests of Lukh. So Isadora before her walk exchanged the clothes of the headmaster's wife for a peasant gown, but in her growing feeling of constriction she modified her habit by wearing the black frock with nothing underneath it.

It entertained her to pass under the windows of the staffroom with but a single layer of material between her body and the outside air. It amused her to bid good night to the Vicar with her limbs naked under the folds of the gown. It was a pleasant thrill to converse with Kelynack in his classroom knowing that if a button of her bodice were undone, her bare flesh would be revealed to him.

In making this change of costume, there was naturally a moment when she stood with nothing on in the attic room that she had chosen for her private room. She took to prolonging the pleasure of this moment, first to a few minutes and then to ten or twenty, until there came a time when she would undress immediately on entering her room after supper, light the gas fire and remain naked while reading in her chair or contemplating the pendulum clock that had stopped at half-past nine. The window of the attic room stood back from the eaves of the roof and a passer-by below would have been unaware of the engaging scene above him even if he had happened to look up. There was, it is true, the east window of the school chapel on the other side of the headmaster's Green, the top of which was at a similar level, but the only figure at that window was facing in the opposite direction and, besides, had been crucified more than eighteen centuries before.

Chapter Five

SCIENCE FIVE

Poetry's unnat'ral; no man ever talked poetry 'cept a beadle on boxin' day... never you let yourself down to talk poetry, my boy. Begin again, Sammy.'

Charles Dickens

A FEW weeks after the debate, Louis made his way to Science Five to smoke his Sunday evening pipe. It was a curious room, with a high ceiling and banked forms. Formerly, this was Room V, used for the teaching of Classics to the juniors. When science was included in the curriculum, it became the Science Room, and the 'Five' remained because everyone was used to it. But the scientists, with their preference for modern idioms, dropped the Roman numeral, so Science Five it was. Later, HH converted the old silk-mill buildings to proper science labs and Science Five was utilised for whatever couldn't be fitted elsewhere. It was disliked by the boys because it was draughty, drab and excessively cold in winter and also because it was used for detention, on Saturday afternoons. The wit of the boys was scrawled inside the desks, visible only to whoever sat there. 'God is Dead and the Priests will Follow.' 'William Facey was here imprisoned', and the ubiquitous verse about Horace *et* Livy *et* the pit in the privy.

Conspicuous on the desks were names that rang of a previous age. The letters spelling out these names had slowly filled with ink and grime, with doses of polish to give them gloss, making them stand out blackly from the forms. Who was JOSEPH BLOBOLL, and what struggles had he endured in the parsing of Pliny and the complexities of Xenophon? Louis remembered Grindlay telling them that Sherborne boys used to have to sleep two to a bed. Had Bloboll shared a bed with THOMAS WINIFFE and been kept awake by Winiffe's bony knees?

It was in the top row of elevated desks in Science Five that Louis Yeoman smoked his pipe in the quiet of a Sunday evening. Smoking was forbidden and some previous leniency for the older boys had been revoked by the energetic HH, who had put a strict ban on the smoking of tobacco in the school precincts, even by masters. Louis' weekly pipe was a statement of a kind. The pipe itself, of best briar, had been a present from his grandfather, whom he had loved, and confiscated by his father, whom he never could. The retrieval of the pipe from his father's desk had been an act of daring on the boy's part, and the smoking of it in the school detention room had the appeal of the doubly forbidden.

He smoked with zest, gazing out of the big window at his side. The rays of the setting sun fell pleasantly over the rooftops of the chapel, the schoolhouse studies and the library, reaching a small attic window at the top of the headmaster's house and revealing to Louis' eyes the remarkable sight of Isadora Runciman perfectly naked. The vision was far off, but the final shafts of sunlight served as a spotlight which afterwards seemed to him more than mere accident. For an instant, the contours of the woman's body were lit up, as if for his benefit. There was the Russian lady, standing at a narrow window without clothes on, lit by the last of the day's celestial light.

The vision did not last long, but it was long enough. From that hour, Isadora became the mistress of Louis Yeoman's daydreams, the queen of his fantasy. The daydreams were oddly chaste but intense. The vision of a naked Isadora did not go away, nor did he wish it to.

As a sixth former, he was entitled to stand on the headmaster's Green before classes, and one sunny morning Isadora was there with her husband and Dr Hulme. Book in hand, Louis steered to a point immediately behind where Isadora stood, edging close enough to hear the rustle of her dress as she moved. Was that the scent of her perfume he caught, or did she always smell like... like a rose at night?

The next Sunday, at pipe-smoking time, there was a terrible anxiety inside him at the thought that he would watch for her and she would not be there. But of course she would not! The headmaster's wife was surely not in the habit of standing undressed at an attic window. It had been an inexplicable happening, never to be repeated. Nevertheless he went, shifting his pipe from this pocket to that, discovering that he had forgotten the matches and hurrying back for them, nervous of missing the setting sun. For her to be there with the sun gone down and nothing but a dim, indistinct tableau... Perhaps it was for the last of the sun that she stood there, in some magic ritual known to Russian women, harvesting with their bodies the sun's final flame.

As Louis went to climb the stairs to Science Five, he heard a voice coming from the room below. There was an urgency in the sound, as of someone in distress.

He stepped quietly to the doorway of the classroom and looked in. By the desk were two figures clasping each other, kissing. A floorboard creaked under his foot. Mr Kelynack and the headmaster's wife turned their faces to the door and sprang apart. There was a instant of stillness before Yeoman moved, not back to the stairs but on towards the doorway that led towards the abbey. He hurried through the wicket gate to the Close. Kelynack came up with him outside the abbey and caught his arm.

Beyond a slight breathlessness, Kelynack's manner was unruffled. 'You saw something back there, Yeoman. Or thought you did. It was a moment of theatre, of no significance. If you should repeat what you thought you saw, it would be damaging to the people concerned and to the school. It must not be spoken of, and I need to have your word on that.'

Louis looked at the man's taut, belligerent face. It was belligerence he saw, and not anxiety. But it made no difference to his reply, which was beyond doubt.

'You have my word, Mr Kelynack.'

'Thank you.' The master patted him on the shoulder. 'Join me in Bow House for tea and cake tomorrow.'

'I'm afraid that isn't possible.'

'The day after, then.'

'I have given you my word. I suppose it is all you need from me.'

Kelynack shrugged and walked back the way he had come. Louis went in the opposite direction, crossing Half Moon Street and down Digby Road, past the railway station to the bridge over the Yeo. There he lit his pipe and smoked it to the last leaf. He inhaled the smoke so deeply that he felt unsteady on his feet and for some time leaned against the parapet.

That was that then. What kind of woman was she, anyway? Undressed at the window. Embracing masters in their classrooms. But he had loved her for a week. For a week if she had said jump from this ship, he would have jumped. Run into those flames, he would have run.

He refilled his pipe and smoked again. It was getting dark and he should have been back inside the gates. A chill breeze blew down the brook between the darkening trees, invigorating him. What he had witnessed in Kelynack's room had saved him the humiliation of an unrequitable love. To depend like a puppet on another person, a stranger. And why? Because of the black hair falling about her white shoulders.

A locomotive with half-a-dozen carriages drew into the station, steam hissing, brakes squealing. Doors slammed and whistles blew as the train pulled out again. He barely registered its passage.

He set off up through the town. The school gates would be

locked and maybe the postern door as well. He became aware of raised voices, as of a procession ahead of him. Cheap Street was empty, but the sound grew louder, from the direction of the school. There were shouts, followed by the clanging of a bell. The dismal sound was unmistakable. It was the Panne, the fire bell. He hurried now, and when he turned the corner by the Conduit, he saw a red glow at the further end of the abbey, and sparks rising into the sky. He ran the length of the church and when he cleared its great bulk he could see the flames leaping from the roof of Science Five.

Smoke billowed from the postern door. He ran round to the main gate, where Rugg, the custos, was planted solidly in the way.

'Slow down, boy, slow down,' he said. 'Give us a hand with the gates. Headmaster don't want a crowd of onlookers in the courts. The engine'll be on the way, but it'll go round the back.'

They swung the big gates shut and fastened the bar.

'You've been out late, Yeoman.'

The boy nodded. 'I must go and help.'

'Get on with it then. There's a line of buckets through the cloisters.'

In the small courtyard between the chapel and the classroom block, the heat was intense. Three ladders stood up against the burning building, each with someone aloft silhouetted against the flames.

At the foot of the ladders was Corporal Timmins, directing the buckets. Timmins turned and saw him.

'Here's Yeoman,' he shouted. 'They thought you were inside. Go and tell the Head.' He gestured towards the cloisters and went on with his work.

'I'm Yeoman, sir,' Louis said to Runciman when he found him.

'Yeoman? Where the deuce were you? We've been hunting high and low for you. See me later.'

Louis saw his room-mate Morris in the bucket line and moved in next to him.

'Yeoman, for God's sake!'

'I'm alright.'

The full buckets were coming up the line and returning empty.

'I thought you were trapped in Science Five. Nobody had seen you.'

'I was down by the river.'

'How was I to guess? I know where you go on Sunday evenings.'

'Not this Sunday.'

'I've got you into trouble.'

'I was out of bounds, that's all.'

The fire engine arrived, the horses stamping and slipping on the cobbles. There were more ladders, axes and a big hose. The force of the hose allowed the firefighters to get in by the back gate and reach the stairs, which were still intact. The new ladders were set up on the other side of the building. Still it was three hours before the blaze was out and the naked roof timbers stood smoking against the sky. The ground was littered with sodden cinders. Soot and ash covered the hair and faces of the people.

A tea urn was set up in the cloisters and trestle-tables were laid with bread and jam. The blackened faces looked weird, with streaks of sweat and strangely white eyes, as if everyone had emerged rather different from a brush with death. Nobody had died, but something more had perished than rafters and floorboards, a work of man that had seemed permanent.

Runciman said a few words of thanks. But even after the bread was gone and the last drop of tea drunk, people lingered on, as if something more should happen. Most of the masters were there, among them Kelynack, almost unrecognisable with the soot thick in his hair and below it the clownish streaks of black and white.

'Kelynack was up one of the ladders,' Morris said at Yeoman's shoulder.

'Did he say he'd seen me?'

'Nobody had seen you. They were shouting your name but nobody had seen you.'

Yeoman saw Kelynack looking at him. The two white eyes in the piebald face. An instant of complicity.

'I'll have a word with you now, Yeoman,' Runciman ordered, coming up.

He strode across the courts with the boy at his heels.

'We can talk here,' Runciman said at the porch of his house. He opened the door and called for a lamp. Beyond the lamp when it came, Yeoman glimpsed the inquisitive face of a girl. The lamp was set on the low wall of the porch and the girl was gone.

'You were the object of some concern, Yeoman.'

'I'm sorry.'

'People risked their lives for you. Did you know that?'

'No.'

'Corporal Timmins smashed a window and climbed in. He was

driven out by the smoke. The custos tells me that you entered the school premises an hour after lock-up. Where were you?'

'Down by the river.'

'By the river, in the dark? You are aware of the rules, I suppose?'

'I was out of bounds.'

'Perhaps you think that the upper sixth is exempt from such rules?'

'No.'

'Explain yourself then.'

'I went for a smoke.'

'You went for a smoke. You broke two rules then.'

'I'm afraid I did.'

'Why did your study-mate think you were in Science Five?'

'I...I was in the habit of smoking a pipe there on Sunday evenings.'

'You're getting yourself in very deep, Yeoman. I trust you're aware of that.'

'Yes sir.'

'If you were in the habit of using Science Five for your pipe-smoking, why did you go to the river instead?'

'It was a warm night. I wanted to be out.'

'Empty your pockets.'

'Sir?'

'Turn your pockets out. Here on the wall.'

From one pocket came a few coins and a stub of pencil. From another came the pipe, tobacco and matches. From a third an unfinished poem:

In the red flame of the setting sun
Her naked body called me
A stranger seen suddenly, piercingly, near
In a too-strong spell that enthralled me.
What is it that summons? How does the summoned know?
By the beat of his heart and the pulse of his blood
In the red sun's duskward glow.

The last line was crossed out, written again, altered, abandoned.

'You were on your way to Science Five, with matches in your pocket. Later there is a fire in the room. What would you make of that if you were in my position, Yeoman?'

'I saw Mr Kelynack outside the abbey on my way to the river.'

'Be careful, Yeoman. Don't compound felony with perjury.'

'I saw Mr Kelynack outside the abbey.'

'Mr Kelynack was at the fire from the beginning. He was up on one of those ladders for an hour or more. If he had seen you in the Close, would he not have spoken up?'

'Maybe he didn't see me.'

'Maybe you didn't see him either. Maybe you didn't go to the river. Maybe you had your smoke in Science Five as usual. '

'Excuse me, sir, but why should I start a fire in Science Five?'

'That remains to be seen. Why should you break bounds at night and smoke a pipe despite strict rules to the contrary?'

'They are different crimes, sir. The boys would speak up for me, and some of the staff.'

'It is true that I am not acquainted with you, Yeoman. I shall speak to the staff, naturally.'

'Mr Biffen. Mr Grindlay.'

'To all of the staff. There is a puzzle here which must be solved. A fire breaks out in a classroom where nobody had any business on a Sunday evening. You were in the habit of smoking in that very classroom at that very time. I must warn you, Yeoman, that tomorrow I shall call in the police and that they will ask you some searching questions. I recommend the absolute truth as your best defence, whether innocent or guilty.' He nodded towards the pipe and matches where they lay on the wall. 'I shall keep these. You may take the poem.'

'Yes sir.'

'On second thoughts, I shall keep the poem as well for the time being.' He scanned it again. 'Who is the subject of this verse?'

'A woman.'

'Obviously. But which woman?'

'Any woman, sir. An ideal woman.'

'You may go, Yeoman.'

It was just the start of things. There would be further lies on the morrow. Yes, he had passed by the stairs to Science Five. No, there was no one in the room below. Yes, he had seen Mr Kelynack outside the abbey. No, they had not spoken. He had intended smoking his pipe in Science Five, but had changed his mind because it was a warm night. Had it been a warm night though?

He imagined a policeman's questions: Why in talking to the headmaster did you suggest that Kelynack had seen you, and then altered your story when it was obvious that he had not? Why do you write love poems?

By the time of the first lesson the next day, it seemed that there was no first former, no cook or cleaner who didn't know that Yeoman was suspected of starting the fire in Science Five. For a person who kept himself to himself on the margins of things, the covert glances and the whispered quarantine were an anguish.

In the classroom Hulme and the other boys avoided catching his eye. The not-looking was more pointed than the looking. Hulme made a show of setting forth on *La Langue Française, dixième chapitre*, but it was not long before he was launched on a history of fires in Sherborne. The fire in the schoolhouse studies in 1867. A fire in a farmer's barn when the whole school had gone to help and the farmer had cursed them for getting in the way 'as if it was some kind of show'. The forming of the Fire Brigade, the ringing of the Panne, 'the ugliest sound in the town'.

After half-an-hour, Yeoman gathered his books and left, saying he didn't feel well.

'He may well feel sick,' he heard Hulme tell the class as he left the room.

He retired to his study, awaiting a summons from the police. It came an hour later, borne by the custos.

'You saw me at the gate, Custos. Did I look like someone who'd just set a classroom on fire?'

'I said what I 'ad to say to the constable. Come on, boy. They're waiting for you in the library.'

There was a policeman, seated, and standing by the window at a little distance, Runciman. The constable was a thin, smiling person, with strands of lank hair combed carefully across his brow.

'My name is Bright. Bright by name and bright by nature!' He smiled. 'I expect we can clear up all this in no time.'

'I hope so.'

'Now. We have here the matches and the pipe. We have a statement from the headmaster that you went to…' he consulted his notebook, 'Science Five for a smoke, which you did regularly on a Sunday evening. That's not my province. A smoke's a smoke. Except on this occasion, where there was a smoke there was a fire.' Another little smile. Had he rehearsed this *bon mot*? 'But you did not have your smoke in Science Five. Am I right?'

'Yes.'

'You proceeded instead to the Abbey Close where you saw Mr Kelynack. But Mr Kelynack did not see you.'

'I thought he had seen me. Apparently he hadn't.'

'Ah. Apparently. After seeing, but not being seen by, Mr Kelynack, you then proceeded to the river and smoked your pipe.'

'Yes.'

'Where exactly?'

'On the bridge by the railway station.'

'Busy place, the station at around eight o'clock. Seven-fifty from London. People saw you there, I expect.'

'There was no train.'

'No Exeter train last night?' Bright said sharply.

'I didn't mean there was no train. I mean it didn't arrive while I was there. It must have been earlier than 7.50. Yes, it was earlier because the abbey clock struck the half-hour while I was talking to … when I saw Mr Kelynack in the Close.'

The officer's pencil noted the fact and the little smile returned.

'Let us go carefully. You talked to Mr Kelynack.'

'No.'

'While I was talking, you said.'

'To myself.'

'So. You were talking to yourself while you were seeing, but not being seen by, Mr Kelynack.'

Yeoman didn't answer. What could be said to such a question?

'Yes?' admonished the constable, his smile thin and tight on his lips.

'I saw Mr Kelynack and, since he looked my way, I assumed that he saw me. The clock chimed.'

'According to Mr Kelynack, he was eating buttered scones in his room.'

'At half past seven?'

'We will discuss the hour shortly. First I want to know if anyone passed you while you were on the bridge.'

'No. I don't think so.'

'He doesn't think so.' The pencil moved across the face of the notebook. 'And no train came in while you were there?'

'There was a train. I don't know what time it was. It came in while I was there, but I didn't really register the fact.'

'Oh, I like that! I do like that. A steam locomotive pulling half-a-dozen carriages thunders past you, but you did not *register the fact*.'

'I mean that I took no notice. But I remember it clearly enough now.'

'You took no notice but you recall it clearly.'

'I paid it no attention. My attention was elsewhere.'

'Dear me, Yeoman. Talking to yourself. Pipe-dreaming. Attention elsewhere. Had something happened to upset you?'

'Perhaps I am rather ... peculiar. Sometimes I'm unaware of my surroundings.'

'But you know where you are now, Yeoman, don't you. You're in trouble. What I think is that it was not the half-hour that sounded in the Close, but the hour. It was eight o'clock. By the time you arrived at the station, the 7.50 had been and gone. There was no train while you were on the bridge. You were upset. Yes indeed you were upset because you had started a fire in the school. You were running away from your fire. You stopped on the bridge to think about it and you thought you'd better get back. So you ran back to the school as fast as your legs would carry you, you arrived at the main gate, breathless and dishevelled, according to the custos.'

'Why didn't I use the gate into the master's garden where nobody would have seen me?'

'Because you're a thinker, Yeoman. A clever dick. upper sixth, isn't it? The fire's going and you started it. You don't take the garden gate because it looks like stealth, doesn't it. You go to the main entrance, help the custos with the gates, pretending that you hadn't a care in the world.'

'What is dishevelled supposed to mean?'

'You tell me, boy. You tell me.'

'I had run all the way round the buildings. My hair might have been out of place. But torn clothes, black on my hands – nothing like that.'

'Don't you go telling me my job, sonny. You stick to Latin verbs. If the custos says dishevelled and you say not, the difference of opinion will be noted and clarified. Now, let us return to the matter of the hour. The fire was discovered by the school gardener. According to the custos, you arrived at the main gate at 8.30 near enough. You said that you heard 7.30 strike outside the abbey. One hour is a very long time for the smoking of a pipe, Yeoman.'

'I smoked two pipes.'

'Two pipes! Well, I never. Would that be one after the other or was there an interval in between?'

'There was an interval.'

'Would it have been during that interval that the Exeter express steamed in?'

'I can't say.'

'Let us try to account for these sixty minutes. Five minutes to walk down and five back, would you say?'

'About that.'

'Two pipes loaded and smoked. Twenty minutes? Leaving half an hour for meditating on the bridge, during which you saw no one and failed to register the arrival of the 7.50.'

'I suppose so.'

'Do you suppose that you often spend half an hour lost to the world, Yeoman?'

'Not very often.'

'Perhaps this was the very first occasion that you spent half an hour thinking in the dark on your tod?'

'Sometimes when I have something on my mind, I like to spend time on my own.'

'Agreed, Yeoman. Agreed. Same for anyone. But the whole matter and crucial issue is *what was on your mind?*'

Louis kept silent

'I wonder if this has anything to do with it.' Runciman stepped forward and dropped the confiscated poem on the table in front of Yeoman. He glanced at it and looked away.

'No,' he said.

Bright picked it up. 'If I may, Headmaster...?'

Runciman nodded. 'It was in his pocket last night.'

'Well, well,' Bright said. 'I think we should hear this. In the red flame of the sunset, her nakedness enthralls me. Naked body? Piercingly? This is not to my taste. This is not very nice. No. A line is crossed here, Headmaster, don't you think?'

'Crossed out?'

'I mean a line of decency has been crossed. Wouldn't you think?'

'I see nothing indecent in the poem.'

'I'm surprised, sir. An eighteen-year-old boy writing of a woman's naked body?'

'Let us call it poetic licence, shall we?' Runciman said, holding out his hand for the paper.

'With your permission, Headmaster, I believe this paper constitutes evidence and should be duly recorded and filed.'

Yeoman grabbed the poem from the policeman's hand and tore

it into pieces. 'It's private. It is private to me and has nothing to do with anything. Please allow me to go. I have told you where I was and what I did. Please let me go.'

Bright was forestalled by Runciman.

'I'm sure the constable will agree to resume his questioning later.'

'Destroying the evidence!' Bright muttered.

'I shall recall the gist if necessary,' Runciman said. He gathered together the shreds of paper and returned them to the boy. 'You may go, Yeoman.'

Bright's notes of his morning's work were a few cramped lines of thin, childish script: Kelynack, hot buns in Bowhouse at eight. Custos: Breathless and dishevelled. Eight-thirty. Yeoman peculiar (his own word).

'The 7.50 was on time and Yeoman was not there to see it,' he later told the custos. 'That's the key to the case.'

This surmise was communicated by the custos to Hulme, by Hulme to the staffroom and from there, picking up speed, to the classrooms and corridors and kitchens. Mobs of diminutive boys from the lower school to whom Louis Yeoman was an aloof and inexplicable figure gathered in the road from where the ruined roof could best be observed, listening excitably to fresh-faced mobsters. That evening, the custos held forth volubly to his usual cronies at *The Antelope*, and winged rumour did the rest.

'This is not vandalism but sabotage,' Hulme told Grindlay the next morning. 'What else can you expect? A headmaster who commands no respect. New masters who cannot control their classes, including a papist from France. A rugby team which loses to Marlborough College by fifteen points...'

'Déchery is not a papist, Hulme.'

'He acts like one. And his French is incomprehensible. Gutter French.'

'So you say. But the qualities of your assistant French master are hardly the issue.'

'The issue is that a member of the upper sixth deliberately and maliciously set fire to the detention room.'

'I believe that the identity of the arsonist is still *sub judice*.'

'What doubt can there be? He was in or around Science Five with matches in his pocket. He was unable to account for his movements for an hour. A pipe-smoker, a poetaster.'

'You admire his skill as a boxer, I recall.'

'He did not deserve to be given the verdict in the final last year.'

'That does not make him a criminal, Hulme.'

'I have spoken to Constable Bright. The boy had indecent verses in his pocket, in his own hand.'

'Indecent?'

'A woman's naked body.'

'Ah. A subject also enjoyed by Catullus.'

'Grindlay, we are talking of a schoolboy of eighteen.'

'Catullus was about the same age at the time of those poems, I believe.'

'The goings-on of a pagan era are hardly pertinent, Grindlay. Constable Bright is convinced of the boy's guilt. According to him it is Runciman who is prevaricating.'

This much was true. Runciman's instinct was to believe Louis' story, despite the matter of the 7.50 train. But prompt action was expected and delay would be seen as indecisiveness. He summoned Yeoman and stood waiting for him at the bay window of his study, which commanded a view of the courts. Boys and masters strolled or stood in small knots, diminished, inconsequential.

'Yeoman,' he said when the boy came in, 'you are to be rusticated from this school for breaking bounds and the illicit smoking of tobacco. Your rustication will last for the rest of this term and for the term that follows. You will be permitted to return in time for the Oxbridge exams, but your upper-sixth privileges will be forfeited. On the matter of the fire, I have persuaded the police not to prosecute. Have you anything to say?'

'May I have my pipe back?'

'Is that all?'

'I suppose it is still mine.'

Runciman opened a drawer of his desk and took out the pipe and passed it to him.

'I shall send a letter to your father today. There will be no mention of the fire. You will pack your things and leave the school on Sunday.'

Chapter Six

THE INIQUITOUS KNACKER

> *... how meet beauty? Merely meet it; own,*
> *Home at heart, heaven's sweet gift;*
> *then leave, let that alone.*
>
> Gerard Manley Hopkins

THE FOLLOWING day, a wind blew from the northwest, strong enough for shoppers in Cheap Street to hang on to their hats. It blew on and off for a fortnight, whisking off roof tiles and chimney pots and driving the autumn leaves into deep piles in odd corners. Like all strong winds blowing in placid places, it disturbed and unsettled.

Louis kept to his study, skipping lessons and meals. Morris brought provisions from Tuffins and there was a box of Stubbard apples from home in the corner of their room. Louis sent his study-mate to the art room for a large sheet of drawing paper and set to work on a sketch in charcoal. A tall thin figure labelled 'The Iniquitous Knacker' stood with piebald face at the top of a ladder against a blazing building. In the cloud of smoke rising above his head were the words 'The Secret Must Be Kept'. Runciman was serving tea in the cloisters, wearing a cook's hat and designated 'The Chef'. Horns sprouted from either side of the hat. All that was visible of 'The Smirking Constable' next to him was a broad smile and the glint of a blade. Beyond him was a squat and bloated custos, labelled 'Lying Toad'. In the queue of boys passing buckets stood a boy with unruly hair and muddied clothes looking the wrong way and entitled 'The Dunce'. His gaze was directed to the top left-hand corner of the drawing where at a small window was the faint outline of a naked woman. 'Dark Queen of Hearts' ran the legend above the window. The tongue of flame flaring skyward at the centre of the sketch bore the words: 'Spontaneous Combustion of Science Five Caused by the Guilty Passion of the Iniquitous Knacker and His False Queen'.

Louis looked round his study, his home for three years. We get used to things so we assume we like them, he thought. We mistake familiarity for affection. What is this place? A hole for keeping boys in. Not even one per hole so that each may call it his own. Morris is a decent sort, but do I want to watch him pick his nose as he wrestles with Livy? Do I want his socks on the floor? Am I sad to leave this shared cell? No. Am I sorry to say good-bye to all this: the library, the art room, the books, boxing lessons with Timmins, tea and cake with the Biffens? Maybe I am.

I'm punished for looking at a woman's body. I saw her without her clothes on and I fell in love with her. How long was it for, one minute? Not that long. Less than a minute of looking but it caught me, held me, strung me like a puppet. If I hadn't seen her and loved her, would I have kept Kelynack's secret? I would have spoken up and damn them. Damn Kelynack for his cheating. Damn Runciman for not looking after his wife. Damn her? Even now I can't say that. Even now if I knew she was at the window again, I'd climb up into the gutted detention room to catch one more glimpse of her.

The thought took hold. Why not? It was still light.

He seemed to hear his own heartbeat as he went through the cloisters. A group of boys eyed him curiously from the noticeboard. In the burned building there were no gaslamps lit. Kelynack's room vacant and abandoned. The staircase intact, the upper stairs blackened. He picked his way through the charred classroom on builders' planks. A ladder stood under the glassless window. From the top of the ladder he could see beyond the chapel over the courts to the attic room, but the window was shut. He waited until it grew dark, listening to the gusting of the wind as it howled among the roofs. The attic window stayed shut and there was no movement from inside.

The next day, he packed his trunk and Morris helped him carry it to the main gate where they said good-bye, rather stiffly, like army officers at the end of a campaign.

'See you next spring, Louis.'

'Maybe not, Morris.'

Crossing the courts on the way back to his study, he saw the figure of a girl rise from the bench outside the headmaster's lodge and come towards him.

'I have waited very long.'

It was the girl who had brought the lamp for Runciman.

'I am sorry for your trouble,' he said.

She took a folded note from her pocket and slipped it into his hand. He was slow to react and the wind whisked it from his hand and blew it across the courts. The girl fled after it, followed by Louis. They trapped it finally in the corner of the courts where it was threatening to scale the walls.

She looked around to see if they had been observed. 'Nobody should see this.'

He watched her lips as she spoke, how boldly and friskily they made the words.

'Don't worry, I'll be careful.'

'You are handsome, Louis Yeoman.' She looked at him directly. 'I hope you will be lucky.' Then she went.

He read the note in his study: Dear Louis, What you have done is brave and generous and I shall not forget. Isadora Magdalensky.

He read it several times But it was not the headmaster's wife who was on his mind, it was her maid's frisky lips and the touch of her fingers on his hand. He was shocked at his fickleness.

The girl climbed the narrow stairs to the attic to tell her mistress the note was delivered.

'In an hour he must leave for his train, Françoise. There may be a reply. Wait for him. Make sure that he sees you.'

'I am hungry. I had no lunch.'

'Find something in the kitchen.'

They always spoke Russian when together. It was a pleasure to them both, their native tongue, which even if overheard would not be understood.

'If he is alone, I could go with him to the station.'

'It would be remarked.'

Françoise shrugged. 'Who is there to notice it? Dr Runciman is away.'

'In this town everything is remarked. Especially if it has to do with me.'

'No doubt it has been noticed that you meet with Kelynack.'

Isadora eyed her sharply. 'I take care that it is not.'

'Not so much that I don't know.'

'You don't count.'

'I count for much. I am your eyes and your ears.'

'So I need conceal nothing from you.'

'What I know may be known by others.'

The girl descended to the kitchen and foraged for food, sitting alone at the big deal table where the servants ate and munching her way through two apples and a thick slice of cheddar cheese. Afterwards she went out and waited on the bench as before.

When Louis appeared a little later, he carried a bottle-green travelling bag. He came over to her.

'She wants to know if there is a reply,' Françoise said.

'Tell her thank you.'

'I can come with you to the station if you like.'

'There's a trap going, with my trunk.'

'Send the trap and we will walk.'

So they went together to the station.

'Shall I carry your bag,' she asked.

'Of course not. Why should you?'

'Because it will give me pleasure,' she answered, taking it.

They went down Cheap Street together, driven by the wind. At the station, they sat on a bench and waited for the train.

'Why did you come?' he asked.

She shrugged. 'Why not?'

'Did you come because you think me handsome?'

She laughed. 'That was a tease. Many of the boys are handsome.'

'Like who?'

'Thomas Cuff, the head boy. He is handsome.'

'Would you carry his bag for him?'

'No. I would let him carry it himself.'

The trap arrived with his trunk. They watched it unloaded and put with the other luggage on the platform.

They sat next to each other in silence. He stole glances at her out of the corner of his eye.

'You may look at me if you want.'

But then he couldn't.

'Do you find me pretty?'.

'Yes.'

'Do you know my name?'

'No.'

'It is Françoise.'

'Françoise.'

'How nicely you say it!'

His train steamed in and clanked slowly to a halt.

'*Vous êtes délicieuse,*' he murmured, thinking she might not hear.

She heard, laughing with pleasure. She picked up his bag and passed it to him as he stood inside the carriage. 'Find me when you get back,' were her last words to him.

She went back up through the town, thinking of other things. A fine dog on South Street, the like of which she had never seen. Late roses in a garden, crimson and yellow, tossing hither and thither in the relentless wind.

'Enough of you, wind,' she cried. 'Stop it. Go somewhere else. You are blowing things apart and breaking things up.'

She turned up the sheltered alley by the Conduit. A tiny ginger kitten came mewing out of the staff garden and she picked it up, addressing it in Russian. 'He will fall in love with me, I suppose,' she told it. 'But we couldn't let him go off on his own could we?'

Françoise was not one to worry about the future. Yet she had a feeling that this affair between Isadora and Kelynack would turn out ill.

It was passion, and they were its slaves. At first they were discreet but soon they were not. The old mill became their trysting place, as it had been for others. The great wooden wheel was immobile, its paddles desiccated, its gears and axles gone to rust among rank weeds. He prised open a door and cleared a path between the fallen timbers and pulverised sacks. He brought blankets and made a den in the driest corner of the mill room. There they huddled together, with the world shut out and banished. Her evening excursions lasted one hour, then two. November came and she wore her coat of black astrakhan with fox-fur collar over her peasant gown. Once, it was midnight before she returned. Her husband was waiting for her and accused her outright.

'You are meeting someone and I wish to know whom.'

She denied nothing. How could she? Her coat was covered in hay seed and strands of straw. Her hair was roughly, hastily tied, her cheeks were wet, her eyes on fire.

'You are concerned only with whom,' she said contemptuously. 'Set your dogs on me then, and let them sniff him out.'

She was wild and imperious and he was frightened of her. He could have caught hold of her and bullied her, but there were blades in her eyes. He let her go upstairs and there was no talk between them the next day, or the next.

Dogs there were a-plenty but he felt that it was himself they would turn on, their nominal master. He sensed that the rumour of Isadora's affair was abroad. He strode the courts without meeting an eye. Hulme was supercilious. A knot of reverends on the Abbey Close fell silent at his approach and melted away.

Finally he summoned Constable Bright.

'This is a matter of extreme delicacy,' he told him. 'You will act for me personally and there will be a consideration for you if you bring me the information I need. No one must know what passes between us and I must have your word on it. If anyone asks the reason for your visit here, you will say that there is fresh evidence about the fire.'

'Her Majesty's officers are not permitted employment on matters other than her own, Headmaster,' Bright said, smiling.

'You will act as a private citizen, without uniform and without contract.'

'May I know the nature of the consideration?'

'For an evening's work, two guineas would seem an ample remuneration.'

'Five,' said Bright.

Runciman could not bargain with this man. 'Do I have your word that the matter will remain between us?'

'My lips are sealed.'

Runciman told him what he wanted, haltingly, suppressing his shame.

Bright already knew what 'the delicate matter' was. He knew the identity of the culprit. He must confirm it with his own eyes, that was all.

He waited that same evening on a bench on the Close, from where he could watch the gate on the side of the burned classroom as well as the entrance to the masters' garden. In case she should use the main gate, the custos had been instructed to send his boy at a run.

'The business of the fire,' he had told the custos with a wink.

'I know what sort of fire you do mean.'

In the event, it was the boy who alerted him and Bright caught up with his quarry going down the alley towards Acreman Street. He followed her in the dark, furtive, smirking. The wind was quiet that night, preparing for its next blast.

On the path to the mill, he trod warily, keeping his distance. When he reached the mill, she was gone and he quietly circled the ruin, listening. From the doorway he heard murmured voices. He waited for a few minutes – Enough for them to *get going*, he thought. Then he lit his lantern and strode inside. When the light found them in the corner, he shone it on their faces, then scurried off.

They had been on their feet, fully clothed. But the story that leaked out was salacious.

Next morning early he sought out the headmaster and told of the stalk down Acreman Street, the pursuit along the footpath. Runciman stood at the window, his back turned, unable to cut short the wretchedness. When in Bright's account the light fell at last on the man's face, still the name was withheld.

'Regrettably, Headmaster, it was a member of your staff.'

Runciman was motionless, staring out over the courts.

'One of your own appointments, I believe.'

Runciman waited.

'A gentleman of whom I know little.'

Runciman spun round. 'You don't know the man's name?'

'I do, Headmaster. I mean that...'

'His name, for God's sake.'

'Mr Kelynack.'

Runciman felt more relief than surprise. Not a tramp or gypsy. Not a landowner or squire's son. A man in his own employ who could be dismissed and disgraced. Even before Bright left the room, five pounds richer, Runciman pictured his revenge. As he climbed the stairs to the attic, Kelynack was hung, drawn and thrown out to rot.

He went in without knocking. Her eyes flashed as if she would eject him, then she saw that something was changed in him. Even in the way he stood at the door something was changed. He was gone from her and was a stranger again.

A world died for her and she glimpsed what it might have held: the comfortable years in the headmaster's house, the easy prizes and prestige.

'I have the name of the man,' he shouted. 'You will pack your bag and leave at once. I do not wish to see you again, here or elsewhere.'

An immensity of coldness.

'I shall require money for my journey.'

'You have made your bed. Lie on it,' he said, turning to go.

'The headmaster's wife should leave respectably and without drama. It would be better for both of us. If you are intelligent, you will behave as if nothing has happened. Your wife is going on a visit to London, that is all.'

'Who are you to talk of respect or intelligence?'

'I am who I am. I am an unfaithful wife, but I am not a murderer or a madwoman. If you want to cast me from your door, you may do so. It is what your enemies would prefer. Think of Hulme, Lionel.'

'Of whom?'

'Dr Hulme. You have not been clever with him. Be clever now. Admit to nothing. It was another woman at the mill.'

'Bright knows that it was you.'

'A man like Bright has his price and his price is not beyond your means.'

'I will not listen to you,' were his last words before going out and slamming the door behind him. But he had heard, and later that day, the trap took Isadora and Françoise to the railway station, for an extended visit, it was said, to Mrs Runciman's relatives in Russia.

Runciman sat at his desk thinking that his position as headmaster might survive the scandal as long as it were not openly referred to. That would mean silencing Bright and ignoring Kelynack until there was some other pretext to get rid of him. He raised his eyes to the window and saw the man himself approaching across the courts, apparently heading for his own door. He called his butler and instructed that Kelynack should not be admitted.

'The headmaster is not to be disturbed,' the butler told Kelynack at the front door.

'I'll risk that,' he answered, elbowing his way in. He opened the door to the head's study without knocking.

'Damn you, Kelynack,' Runciman said. 'Haven't you done enough without barging in here?'

'I bring my resignation, Runciman, which I imagine will please you.'

'I do not accept it. You will be dismissed in due course.'

'There can be no dismissal if there has already been a resignation. Here it is in writing. Dated and signed. The butler will witness it.' He went to the door. 'Come, my man. Jenkins, Jodhpur, whatever your wretched name is.'

'Joplin, do no enter this room or talk to this person,' Runciman called out.

Joplin remained discreetly out of sight.

'That won't do, Runciman. I'll be back with a lawyer.'

Instead he found the custos, who was closer and cheaper. Being solidly of the Hulme faction, the custos was more than willing to be bought for one shilling and be witness to this interesting scene.

They found the front door locked, but the custos had a key to the back one. Access was gained, despite Joplin's protests.

'Shut up, man. He's done for,' thundered the custos making for Runciman's study.

'The custos has read this letter and is witness to its delivery,' Kelynack said when they went in.

'I've a good mind to take a stick to you, sir,' Runciman threatened, rising from his desk.

The custos puffed up, in anticipation.

'You're not man enough,' Kelynack jibed. 'Not man enough to look after your wife and not man enough to raise your hand against me.'

'You'll regret this, Kelynack. I shall see to it that all positions in the public schools are closed to you.'

'You call this a position? Five bob's worth of baby-sitting at a third-rate school? Besides, your opinions won't be worth much at the headmasters' conference next year, or for years to come. Have you heard the ditty they're singing in the studies? Here's the first line: Runciman was once-a-man. Would you like to hear the rest?'

Runciman was not a violent type. In a life of scholarship, he had never had occasion to hit anyone. But to be mocked by the man who had made a cuckold of him and who was now to escape dismissal, that small revenge to which he looked forward, was too much.

'I won't stand for this Kelynack.'

His predecessor, the vigorous HH, was not a believer in corporal punishment, preferring to intimidate with a good bellow. But previous headmasters had been keen birchers, the common wisdom since medieval times being that if the headmaster did not make free use of the cane, matters would soon get out of hand. The cane cupboard was a prominent feature of the head's study and in it was a collection of canes, switches and rods handed down from more rumbustious times. Runciman had examined them with astonishment on his first occupation of the room and prayed that he would never have to use even the most innocuous of these seasoned instruments. But his prayer had not been answered. The time had come.

He marched to the cupboard and seized what came to hand. It was a slender cane of birch last used to chastise boys found drinking in the Plume of Feathers.

Kelynack's response to the headmaster advancing on him with a stick was to laugh, as at a charade, but when Runciman raised the stick with the unmistakable intention of bringing it down smartly on his person, Kelynack hopped aside. Not so the custos. As the man with the keys and the uniform and a stout cask-like figure, he did not hop. As Kelynack moved out, the custos moved custodially in and was mightily surprised – perhaps as surprised as he had ever been in his twenty year tenure of the dim cubby-hole by the main gate – to receive a stinging blow across the cheek.

It was a good cane, slender and strong with a proper whip to it. It was wielded by a man giving vent to the frustration that had built inside him. The blow was aimed at Kelynack, but included in its scope were Bright, Hulme, even perhaps Isadora herself. Perhaps not. Runciman was not a man to hit a woman. But he felt deeply wronged and cruelly deceived and this single act of violence was the only occasion when these feelings found expression. The blow was vicious, and the custos was cut to the quick. A red line sprang to his cheek. He put his hand to his face and examined the droplets of blood between his fingers. He looked up at the headmaster amazed then he turned on his heel and marched from the room.

'Good shot!' Kelynack said. He too went out, laughing.

The functions of school custos were not illustrious: patrolling, securing, bearing messages, ringing the bell for lessons. But his position had retained something of that of a medieval gatekeeper and access to the premises was in his hands. If a tradesman were chasing a contract or a cook wanted a job or a town bigwig had a complaint or request, the custos's little office was the first port of call.

Everyone in the town knew Walter Rugg and there was hardly a shopkeeper with whom he had no dealings. He had swelled and settled, like a cork stopper in a wine barrel. He occupied a small chair at a small desk in a dim room. He didn't ask for larger amenities or for an increased wage. He made his own amenities and increased his wage by his own devices, notably an unofficial commission on minor contracts, which he termed a charge. 'There'll be a charge,' he said, and there was. The size of the charge was rarely as modest as the surroundings in which the arrangement was made.

HH was a good Chief in the custos's view: an authoritative figure with an ambitious building programme that perfectly suited Rugg's ends. The subsequent appointment of an inexperienced, cautious person suited him less. What would be best of all was the elevation of Hulme, who had the necessary air of distinction without real substance. Hulme could be handled in a way that HH could not. Rugg treated him deferentially, but had little respect for him.

He had the welt on his cheek bandaged, and dressed himself in the uniform reserved for the first and last days of term and the weekend of Commemoration. He had his boy polish his boots and shine his buttons. Then he set off for the castle to see Lord Kenelm, chairman of the Board of Governors.

His injury, he told him, had been received at the hands of Dr Runciman, who had assaulted him with a cane when he had intervened to protect a member of staff.

'Might it not have been an accident, Custos?'

'Accident, my lord? No more accident than when I take off my belt and apply it to the boy's back. Dr Runciman is not liked by the staff and I suppose he don't care much for them. I am neutral on that point, nat'rally. But in this particular case, I was obligated to step in. Prompt action is required, my lord, if you'll forgive me saying so.'

'I take your point, Custos. Be good enough to ask Dr Runciman to wait on me this afternoon. Five o'clock would be convenient.'

Austin Kelynack and Lionel Runciman left Sherborne on the same day. The nor'wester died that evening, having unstitched the worlds of several people, as Françoise had foreseen.

Chapter Seven

THE ARYAN DREAM

We claim, and we shall wrest from theology, the entire domain of cosmological theory.

X-Club, 1868

AUSTIN KELYNACK had family, meaning there was land and money in it. His father, a London barrister, disapproved of him, and the feeling was mutual. Not so his grandfather, who preferred the grandson. This old man, Julius Kelynack, born before the close of the eighteenth century, during the first madness of George III, was the owner of the Gifford estate in southwest Wiltshire. It was family land he never himself farmed, living off the rents from the estate and engaging in a series of pursuits taken up with passion. His collection of shells occupied a tier of lacquered trays with miniature partitions, each containing a specimen. The identification and labelling of these molluscs was of more concern to Julius Kelynack than the state of the crops or the repeal of the Corn Laws. From shells he graduated to rocks, from rocks to fossils and from fossils to the stars. The stars themselves were uncollectable in this dimension, but their names and co-ordinates were energetically plotted and listed. One of the largest reflecting telescopes outside Greenwich was installed in a glass-domed observatory, and here Julius made notes on the movements of planets and peered into the deep reaches of the universe where, he did not doubt, there were great secrets to be revealed. The last passion eclipsed all others. The trays of shells and crates of rocks were consigned to basements where they were later deluged by the flood that swamped the valleys of Wiltshire and Hampshire during the biblical rains of the winter of 1881.

In his passion for collections and classifications, Julius was a man of his time. The era later known as mid-Victorian released a tremendous energy into the examination and ordering of the natural world. Never were so many butterflies impaled, so many beetles bothered, so many stones split and polished. Never before had mosses been the subject of conference, or the eggs of newts the object of such meticulous dissection.

When they told Julius on his deathbed of the loss of his molluscs and the submersion of his rocks, he muttered something interpreted by the nurse as 'dust to dust' which had them all nodding in appreciation of the old man's philosophy. Actually what he mumbled was 'drat the rocks', but such was the state of his vocal chords that the nurse can be forgiven her mistake. Besides, it amounted to much the same thing.

'Drat the rocks,' Julius said, because he had always been searching for the philosopher's stone, the key to the mysteries. Whether he found it is unknown, but there were moments in his star-gazing when some vast design seemed on the point of being revealed. In his last years, he abandoned the expensive telescope and preferred to lie on his back gazing with his own eyes through the glass dome into the heavens. He couldn't hear and could hardly speak, but his eyesight was unimpaired.

He wondered about the patterns discerned by the astrologers, and their endurance over millennia. It seemed to him that after all there might be more for man in what he could nightly see with his own eye – in something that, however mysteriously, related to the conditions on earth – than in the calculations of mass, velocity and distance to which the efforts of the astronomers tended. He sensed that understanding was a feeling, like hope or sorrow and doubted that the brain had much to do with it. It was the heart that understands, and drat the rocks.

Austin Kelynack when very young had toddled along with his grandpa as he poked about under boulders and examined flints. One of the earliest of his memories was of a journey in Julius's trap to the coast at Lyme Regis where they had spent the day pottering under the cliffs to the music of the sea. His grandfather unearthed a massive fossil of a lovely leaf-like form, so large that he needed a wheelbarrow to get it up to the trap. Night caught them on the way back but Grandfather Kelynack didn't slow the pace even when the rain came on, and the boy huddled at his grandfather's side in joy at the pelting rain and the black hedges flying by and the rhythm of the horses' hooves.

'Julius and Austin, champion team!' cried Julius as they dismounted. It was around that time that the boy started calling his grandfather by his first name, an impropriety that irritated the solemn father. Julius himself cared little for propriety, and his grandson grew up likewise.

It was the grandfather who felt real pride when Austin Kelynack was accepted to study at Trinity College, Cambridge. The father viewed scholarship as a distraction from real, money-getting, work, but Julius admired the boy for achieving something he himself had missed, a formal education. He read Austin's essays, talked to him of his reading, commended the choice of history as the subject of graduation, a rare choice in the 1860s, when education meant the Classics or theology and history was still very much regarded as a hobby for clergymen and rich scribblers.

Austin Kelynack's approach to history was not unlike his grandfather's approach to astronomy – something was to be hunted down and captured. It was the exercise of the intellect in pursuit of the secret of the human condition. In Austin's case, this was not a metaphysical secret, it was the key to the genealogy of race and power. He was impatient of nit-picking details, minor wars, lesser figures. He was drawn to grand movements and large cycles. His concern was with the great tides of history and he was aware that these tides were not set in motion by individuals but were caused by currents and storms which seemed an expression of the struggle for life itself, as if there were large histor in. He opened the door to the h, for which the smaller stuff must stand aside.

Kelynack's tutor at Cambridge, J.R. Seeley, a man also attracted by large themes, drew his pupil's attention to the trade in exotic articles such as cowrie shells and jade and Baltic amber from very early times.

'They were moving these things from one continent to another in Homeric times, Kelynack. They left a trail that can be followed.'

Staying on in Cambridge after graduation, financed by Julius, Kelynack studied Russian and Arabic and the thesis of Ibn Khaldun that the essential dynamic of history was the invigoration of decadent urban civilisations by nomadic conquerors.

A steady fall in agricultural rents obliged Julius to tighten his belt and Austin's allowance was one of the casualties. He took a position as history master at Sherborne School, viewing it as a temporary expedient. His salary was £200 a year. 'I'm cheap at five bob an hour,' he told his sixth formers. He never prepared a lesson and it took him ten minutes to set an exam. He marked essays by reading the first and last sentences, with brief glances at what was in between.

'If you want me actually to read your essay, it has to *arrest* me,' he said. 'Essay means attempt. You are learning by making attempts. That is the value of the exercise. My reading it or not is irrelevant. Pay attention to the first sentence and you may persuade me to read the second. I do not require the regurgitation of my own ideas. There can be no *syllabus* for history. There is no grammar, no way to measure progress. It is an ocean and most boys will do no more than paddle at the edge. One or two of you, however, may take the plunge. I will read the essays of those.'

If he was bored by the class, he read a book, which he kept handy. The boys were also free to read, or daydream, provided that they made no noise. Kelynack never had trouble keeping order.

'Anyone talking out of turn will be decapitated,' he warned them. In his classroom he kept a medieval broadsword, with which he severed imaginary heads. His pupils found Kelynack scary, and when he wanted to be, he was. His face was right for it, and those lean, long fingers. Once he raised the sword and brought it down savagely on the desk of a pupil in the front row, missing him by a whisker. The boy burst into tears.

'Don't blub,' Kelynack said, laughing. 'It might have sliced off a pound of your flesh.'

He was writing the book he hoped would earn him a Cambridge fellowship. It was a broad canvas, the nomad tribes and their empires, from the gates of China to the gates of Rome. Celts and Mongols, Huns and Vandals. Corners of the globe wild and magnificent. Histories that touched the great Middle Kingdom of Chung'kuo, the Islamic Caliphate, the desert Arabs and the domes of Byzantium. But without the books and maps he needed, his book might take five years to complete, and damned if he was going to spend five years sharing a staffroom with Hulme and Thorneycombe. He grew bored and idle. He gave up his studies of language. Spent vacant hours in front of blank pages. Tore up what he wrote. Altered the title of his book a dozen times. Redrafted the lay-out of chapters. Tinkered with the form of things as if the content might by some alchemy spring into existence ready-made. Instead, it dwindled, paled and staled.

Then came Isadora Runciman. The effect on him was immediate and dramatic. He was in love for the first and only time in his life. The mention of her name or a glimpse of her drove from him every other thought, every consideration of his prospects or his profession. His one desire was to make this woman his own, entirely. He knew from the beginning that in the heart of the fire that she lit in him was something ill-omened. It was as if he knew that the fire would consume him but cared nothing for it. *Only let it burn.*

He ran to the old mill in the evenings, desperate that she might not come. He abandoned his book, missed his classes and was blackballed by the staff.

When he left Sherborne, he took the train to Tisbury and stayed with Julius at Gifford.

Isadora was not far away, living with Françoise in Salisbury and giving French lessons to young ladies. Letters travelled between Gifford House and Isadora's rented rooms. His were full of passionate promises. Her replies were brief. 'I was glad to have your letter,' one of them ran. Another: 'It is long since we kissed.'

Shortly after that letter he met her at the railway station in Tisbury. They had not seen each other for a month. She was dressed in her black peasant's smock buttoned to the chin and over it her astrakhan coat. She wore black gloves and black leather boots. Everything in black. Jet-black hair loose on her shoulders, so that the paleness of her face seemed lit from within and in her eyes was a hint of wild laughter that was delightful to him beyond all the illuminations to be found in books. They laughed as they met and as they kissed their eyes laughed. The old porter who stared in astonishment and the passengers pretending not to look were nothing to them, left on some other shore.

He had walked in to meet her. 'We can hire a carriage to get to Gifford or we can go on foot.'

'On foot,' she decided.

By the railway station stood the church and they turned into the churchyard to be alone, and into the church itself to be hidden, and as he pulled shut the great iron-studded door, he clasped her to him and she shrugged off her coat which fell in a bundle to the stone floor.

'Not here,' he whispered. He bent to retrieve her coat and took her by the hand up the aisle to the altar.

'Do you?'

'I do.'

'Will you?'

'I will.'

He went back and bolted the door. Before the altar he unbuttoned the fifteen buttons of her peasant smock and she was naked underneath. He took her to the vestry where the cassocks and gowns and headgear hung and pulled everything from the hooks, making a pile on the floor. There among the clerical raiment they lay together, amused by their make-shift bed. 'This must be a chasuble,' he guessed, 'and *this*, I take it, is a capuche, and *that* is certainly a maniple.' She lay laughing in her beauty among the capuches and maniples while he explored what was holy and unholy and in their holy unholiness in the vestry of St. Mary's they were as happy as they ever were, or ever would be.

Later they walked uphill through the town and along Gifford Lane where tall beeches rose from the double hedges, two of them so close together that they had twined about each other as they went up, two slender smooth green bodies wrapped in a lifetime embrace.

'Is that possible for us?' he asked her. 'Is that our future?'

'Oh, do not ask that. This present is all we may ask for.'

He was the male. But in this matter of love, she was always stronger, for she was clear-eyed and she knew better than him the courses love takes. She wanted everything of it, but expected nothing. She wanted him to be everything to her, as he was in this very now, but she knew he would not be. He would be the one to betray her, if betrayal there was, but it was not important until the moment it should happen.

Man-like, he wanted her bound to him, like the beech.

'We are married, are we not Isadora?'

'Today we are. It was all he could get from her.

He introduced her to his grandfather as his betrothed. The old man took little notice of that, or of their arrival on foot, of her having travelled alone from Salisbury or her unusual manner of dress. He took notice of the dazzle of her eyes and the lustre of her hair.

'Come, my dear, I will show you my telescope,' he said after their meal, an excursion to which Kelynack was uninvited. Julius made her sit on the swivel chair and put her eye to the lens, although nothing could be seen but a limitless transparency of sky. He put his arm round her shoulders and swivelled her slowly round, the closest the old man would get to dancing her round a room.

'But what are you going to do with her, Austin?' he asked later, when Kelynack returned after taking her to the train.

'She is not a woman to be *done with*, Julius.'

'She is expensive. All women are expensive and she more than most. She is living in rooms in Salisbury, you say, and paying the rent with French lessons. How long will she be satisfied with that?

You cannot afford her, my boy. You may live here as long as you please, but there's no cash. The rents are down again and what there is gets frittered away on the staff and the horses. I won't do away with the carriage because I can't go places without it, and you know me, I do need to go places.'

'I haven't come expecting your charity, Julius.'

'What *are* you expecting? You've thrown up your job for the sake of this woman. Do you intend marrying her?'

'Yes.'

'On what, my boy? Besides, she's married already.'

'She'll obtain a divorce.'

'What sort of person is this Runciman?'

'Insignificant.'

'Austin, don't be juvenile. Headmasters of large schools are not insignificant. Especially when married to your mistress.'

'He is no longer headmaster. He has gone north, I believe.'

'He has lost his position and his wife. You think he will hand you the keys. He won't. What do you offer in return?'

'She will persuade him.'

'Unlikely, I should have thought. But supposing she can, what next? You will marry her and live in her little apartment while she teaches French. What of your own life Austin, my boy? What about your career? What about Cambridge?'

'Damn Cambridge. I'm in love with her.'

'Evidently. For a month or a year, you can live off that. Then you'll begin to wonder if you did the right thing, and the cosiness will be gone and the chilliness will start. I have twice been married, Austin, and both times I fancied myself in love. I was in love with myself.'

'What do you mean, Julius?'

'I mean that a woman's beauty and devotion are flattering to a man. A man's sense of himself is made glorious when a beautiful woman looks lovingly in his eyes. I'm thinking of your own grandmother, Austin. She was a pretty young thing, with eyes that brought the stars to earth. She moved like a cat, settled herself like a cat. Like a cat she watched the world. But she was spiteful and I knew it within a week of marrying her. Well, I lost her as I lost the first and then I was alone. But nobody felt sorry for me, and nobody needed to. Do you know why, Austin?'

'Why?'

'Because I had all this.' He waved a hand airily, to denote the house, the grounds, stables, farms. 'I had Gifford. A man can live comfortably on his own if he has somewhere to hang his hat. Gifford will come to you eventually, of course, but Lord knows if it'll be worth much by then. Anyway it'll be too late to do you any good.'

'I'm writing a book.'

'You won't write a book while you're dandling that woman, Austin. I'll put my shirt on that.'

Over the winter months, he met her twice a week, sometimes more. For her visits, he borrowed a trap from Julius.

'There's no spring in the springs, and there's only little Molly to pull it,' Julius said. 'You'll have to walk up the hills. But she's a spirited pony, too spirited you may find. She doesn't like dogs, or men with pitchforks, and once she gets excited it's the devil's own job to quiet her. So go smooth and easy.'

The weather turned icy. After the ice came the mud. Anything more than a gentle slope was too much for Molly when they were aboard, so they walked a good deal, uphill. They were invigorated by the exercise in the chill air. If it rained they sheltered in a barn or in the lea of a high hedge. To be together was a joy to them, whatever the weather. In the cold or wet, they pressed close to each other, wrapped in an old tarpaulin. They journeyed randomly, exploring the Donheads and Birdbush, going by Teffont and Chilmark into the Wylye valley, where a string of small villages lay like rough gems along the riverside. Sometimes they went no further than the lake at Fonthill, where an eccentric lord of the manor had once created underground grottoes that stayed dry and warm. But Isadora decided she did not care for them.

'There is something unnatural here, Austin. Whoever made these caves had a feeling for the past, but it was a distorted feeling.'

'They suit us, don't they?'

'We must find somewhere else.'

They found a Dutch hay-barn with a cavernous roof where it was warmer still up among the bales and where they were never disturbed.

He became accustomed to her instincts and moods. She reacted to weather, place and coincidence, to days of the week, numbers on the calendar, phases of the moon. He shared in none of these fancies yet he enjoyed them in her.

'You are partly human, Isadora. The rest is nymph or hamadryad.'

She happily agreed.

'I was born in the forest and I do not know who my father was. A forester, my mother told me. Perhaps after all it was a tree. A handsome young sapling who took her as she slept beneath him.'

'Tell me of your childhood.'

She talked in Russian of her life as a child. In winter they had lived on milk and potatoes and mushrooms. Their existence had revolved around the feeding of the cow. 'If the cow had died, we would have died too. You have no idea how much a cow eats. For six months, we grazed the cow and her calf in the clearings and meadows at the forest's edge. With the money from the calf we bought in grain and hay to keep the cow for the winter. If the winter was long, we boiled potatoes for it and went hungry ourselves. With the spring, the grasses and herbs came back and we were full again.'

He liked to imagine her as a beautiful young peasant girl.

'When I was fourteen, a man came for me,' she continued. But she would not say who he was or where he took her. She would not tell of the long road from the forests of Lukh to the capital and what befell her there, even though he urged her to do so.

'There is no need for you to hear that,' she said. 'What is it that you English say? Ask me no questions and I'll tell you no lies.'

Of the forest and the meadows and the cow she was glad to speak. Their walks in the woods delighted her, as the childhood memories awakened.

'You can eat this mushroom,' she said, stopping at a giant flesh-coloured fungus clinging to an ancient stump.

He laughed. 'That's no mushroom.'

'It's made of mushroom and tastes of mushroom and in Russian it is mushroom. Here perhaps you call it something else, because you don't know what it's good for. You live in a southern country and you are fat and spoiled. Your men are not men and your women … Hah! You have no women.'

'Am I not a man?'

She looked up at him. 'You are a kind of man, Austin. But you are spoiled too. You are living off your grandfather when you should be working.'

'I am working on my book. I will send it to Seeley and he will have it published.'

'He will publish nothing if it is not written.'

'It is progressing.'

'You are lying.'

He was indignant. 'How can you be so sure?'

'I always know when you are lying. But it doesn't matter that you lie to me. It matters that you lie to yourself.'

On one of their excursions they came on a large round barrow near Birdbush. It occurred to him that the amber bead he had been examining when first she had come to his classroom had been found in such a burial mound, which were numerous among the Dorset hills. He recalled the hoard of amber excavated by Schliemann at Mycenae that the archaeologist deduced had formerly been covered by a huge earthen mound. There was a quickening of his historian's curiosity, a connection made between poles.

He was suddenly impatient to look again at Schliemann's book. Isadora took an earlier train back to Salisbury and Kelynack arrived in Julius's library still in his walking boots. He quickly found it and leafed through the pages, studying the sketches of pots and necklaces, affected by the unusual ambience radiated by the dark illustrations of owl-eyed goddesses and great black cauldrons caught at the moment they emerged from the earth, with accretions of rust and soil still adhering to them. The book *smelled* of the Bronze Age, he thought with surprise. It carried an authenticity which went beyond scholarship.

He turned to the description of the excavation itself. The detail was meticulous but enlivened always by a sense of quest, culminating in the finding of the famous gold death-mask, which Schliemann had pulled from the grave with his own hands. 'Today I looked on the face of Agamemnon,' went his telegram to the Kaiser.

Kelynack spent the rest of the day with *Mycenae*, hardly rising from his chair. His supper was served to him in the library. He found the passage describing the finding of the fourteen-hundred amber beads. The graves were in a circular precinct. An examination of soils and levels convinced Schliemann that there had been a forty-foot earthen tumulus covering multiple warrior burials. Swords, spears, goblets. Delicate jewellery. Bones of animal sacrifices, including horses and dogs.

A hoard of Baltic amber in a grave in southern Greece. Emblems of the King's power surely. But why amber? Amber was 'electron' in Greek and Electra the name of Agamemnon's daughter.

Kelynack found himself drawn into the strands of a legendary web, to which the amber was the clue. A charm, she had called it.

He closed the book, got up, shook himself. He went outside into the cold night before going to bed. But neither the night air nor the frosty morning banished his feeling of discovery. He went to Oxford, spent two days in the Bodleian library and talked to Professor Max Müller whom he had heard lecture in Cambridge. He filled a notebook with jottings. After a fortnight, he had a title for his book: The Aryan Dream.

Kelynack had no care for scholarship the major motive of which was invulnerability to attack. Not for him the book fortified with such an arsenal of indisputable fact that the critic was subdued by sheer bulk. Kelynack's conception of his book was more lance than fortress. He expected to be attacked. He wished for it. The tide was with him. The demise of the Church would leave a yawning hole in the fabric of British history. The Church had legitimised the monarchy, blessed industry and thrift, defined a just war. Now the Church was dying and God too, in time. It was a cause for celebration, a release from superstition. But what happened to the soul of a nation when its grand national myths were shown to be empty?

A fresh lineage was required. The Christians could not supply it, nor the classicists. It would be a brief recapitulation of English history, and at its core an idea so strong and simple that even the simplest could grasp it. The survival of the fittest, yes. But who were the fittest? Where were they, since in all generations they must be there?

The word Aryan means noble, he wrote in his notebook. It had been to confirm this that he had sought a meeting with Müller.

'The Aryans were the nobility of the Indo-European race which swept aside the decadent remnants of the old Mediterranean cultures. The Aryans conquered Greece and built Mycenae. It was an Aryan genius that founded the classical age in Greece and, afterwards, Rome. An Aryan kingship lay at the root of European civilisation. In early times, their characteristic monument was the circular barrow and their emblem was amber.' He believed that these Aryan peoples had also brought with them the secret of metal-working, changing the face of the land and the life of its inhabitants.

Chapter One, 'The Amber Routes', would trace the finds of amber in barrow burials – in the Russian steppes, the Caucasus, Anatolia and the Balkans, culminating in Schliemann's great hoard at Mycenae. Then the British finds, indicating the coming of the Aryans to the British Isles. From this, the rest would follow. But the first chapter was crucial and required credentials. He needed himself to excavate. He would unearth warrior graves, amber beads, bronze weapons and season his book with the same kind of darkly detailed illustrations which gave *Mycenae* its authenticity.

There was no Mycenae in England, and even if there were he lacked the means for a major excavation. Schliemann had a hundred wheelbarrows at Mycenae, but Schliemann was a rich man. What did England have, apart from Stonehenge and Avebury, where there was nothing to dig and too many antiquarians sniffing among the old stones?

England had the round barrows. He got out the Ordnance Survey map and looked for the tiny broken circles with their miniature labels in gothic script. Tumulus. Odd word. Tumid, swollen. *Tumulare*, to bury. A sepulchral bump, or tump. He scanned the map, counting dozens between Blandford and Dorchester in an area the size of his hand laid flat on the map.

He must see Biffen. Biffen if anyone would know where the likely barrows were and how best to get into them. Two or three men with picks and shovels could breach these little hillocks in a day or two, surely. In a month he'd have the amber and the swords. In six months the book.

Being with Isadora made him feel lucky. He felt more than lucky, he felt, as he had felt as a child, pointed out by the hand of fate. Fate? He was tempted to dismiss this unreasonable notion. But he had been polishing the amber bead when she had first come to his classroom. 'It is beyond your skill to decipher,' she had said. If she had not challenged him, would he have pursued her?

At last, he shared his great scheme with her.

'There must be no robbery from tombs,' she insisted.

He laughed. 'It would not be robbery, Isadora. Certain artefacts would be shifted from below the ground to behind glass in museums. That's all.'

'It is not all,' she flashed. 'It is all you know, which is nothing. If I bury my grandfather under the ground, with a priest and a service and mourners, and some of his things are cast with him into the grave, are you not obliged to respect that ceremony?'

'We are not talking of your grandfather, my dear.'

'The dead have no clocks. Five years or five thousand, it is the same.'

'The science of archaeology is founded on the contents of tombs.'

'Then it is a corrupted science.'

'Science knows no gods.'

'That is what I mean,' she replied.

'It's true that I could use published records of what has already been found. But they would not have the... force of what we find ourselves. Besides, it'd be the devil's own job to round them up.'

'It is digging up graves that is the devil's own job.'

He went on as if he hadn't heard. 'We'll choose five or six of the biggest barrows and go straight in. Diagonally. If you start from the top, the hole has to be large. From the side, you can tunnel.'

'You'll crawl into a Bronze Age grave on your hands and knees?'

'That's the idea.'

'It's a good idea. It might be mistaken for respect.'

Despite her objections, she came with him on his expeditions, which began to take them further afield, to the heart of Dorset where the barrows were sown among the green uplands as if by ancient giants.

They were together on Bulbarrow Hill, searching for the great barrow that gave the hill its name. From the village of Hedbredinton they were directed one way, but a shepherd on the hill pointed in another and a farmer sorting through the last of a damp hayrick told them the barrow had long since disappeared under the plough. They sat on the high ridge looking out over the tapestry of the vale with its maze of hedges and its clumps and tufts of trees and its measureless history of farm and field disturbed by nothing worse than stormy winds and the inescapable mortality of beasts and men.

'Listen,' Isadora said, taking his hand. 'Let us say that I have a ring, given to me by my grandmother on her deathbed. Let us say that this ring has been on her finger, waking and sleeping, through marriage, childbirth, illness and loss. After it comes to me, I too wear it. I handle it, talk to it even, for it reminds me of the old woman I loved as a child. When I die in my turn, my daughter has the ring put in my coffin, with a favourite necklace and a bundle of letters.'

'I can see where this is leading,' he interrupted.

'The body decomposes. There are only bones, without flesh. The ring falls to the floor of the coffin. When you dig it up, you give it to your own daughter. Will that ring be lucky for her?'

'I see no reason why not.'

'How dense you are, Austin, when you wish! You always deny what you cannot see or touch or weigh in your hand. Let there be two rings then, identical, worn by sisters and their grandchildren after them. Are these two rings still identical, after three generations?'

'Obviously not. They have different signs of wear.'

'That is all?'

'Yes.'

'One of these rings was worn by unhappy people, with tragic lives. The other was worn in happiness and content. No trace of these histories remains in the rings themselves?'

'Only in the mind of the wearer.'

'What is mind? A kind of box kept in the head?'

'I do not think of mind as a box. But I deny that anything in the mind can be transmitted to an object.'

'*Voilà*! You have stated the case to your satisfaction. Here, take this primrose that I have picked and smelled and whispered to of my love. Take it and trample it.'

He did not take it. She threw it on the ground between them and trampled it herself.

Chapter Eight

THE KEEP

Now there was... a castle, called Doubting Castle, the owner whereof was Giant Despair...

John Bunyan

JAMES BIFFEN taught the English language and its literature but his hobby was parish churches, medieval headstones, ancient fords and footpaths, standing stones, the lintels and beams of very old barns, village crosses and field names. Sketches of buttresses and gargoyles were pinned around the walls of his classroom and he was said to be writing a book on country graveyards which had little chance of being finished. 'Too much to know,' he muttered, even though the compass of his studies extended only as far as he could walk in a day or two. He disliked trains and carriages. 'I have two doctors,' he said, 'my right leg and my left leg. Not counting Mrs Biffen of course.'

Most of the downstairs rooms of their large house were almost inaccessible on account of collections of books, bones, stones and pianos. Mrs Biffen liked to play the piano but Biffen never found one to stay in tune. He bought or was given one, it duly went out of tune and was pushed aside to make room for the next. So their kitchen acted as dining-room, sitting-room, study and parlour, as well as accommodating the stove, the pots and pans, the preserves and jams, the bottles of Mrs Biffen's strong wine made from elderberries and rose hips. Two pairs of wellington boots and two pairs of walking boots stood by the stove.

The back door of the kitchen opened on to the yard and it was at this door that Austin Kelynack arrived late one afternoon.

'Ah, Kelynack,' Biffen exclaimed, opening the door. 'They told me you were in Wiltshire.'

'You heard why I left the school, I expect, Biffen.'

'There was some gossip, but the details escaped me. Are you back, or just visiting?'

Kelynack told him the purpose of his visit.

'You want to dig up a *barrow*? Are you sure?' Biffen's voice, always raspy, shot up the scale, as if there were a fault in the vocal chords. He cleared his throat. 'Dorchester way, then. Or The Sleepers over at Shepton. They're very fine. But Wardle don't like people walking over his patch, let alone digging it up. Why barrows suddenly?'

'I'm looking for bronze swords and amber beads, Biffen. I need them for a book.'

'You're better off looking for them in the British museum or talking to Pitt Rivers, who's dug 'em all up over his way. Listen. A burial mound's a big heap of dirt. Dig by all means, but you might burrow for a week and come up with nothing but a horseshoe.'

'There are more than horseshoes in warrior graves, Biffen.'

'Yes, if it *were* a warrior, and if nobody's had the stuff before you and if the rain holds off for a month... there're too many ifs. And you're wanting something for a book that's already written in your head. You've put the cart before the horse, Kelynack.'

'The amber is the clue to the movements of Indo-European tribes.'

'What? Maybe. No. Why? It's a Baltic thing. Scandinavian. Indo-European, what on earth do you mean by that?'

'Aryan.'

'Persian? What would the Persians be doing bringing amber to Dorsetshire?'

'Not Persian. Look, Biffen. We're on different tracks, you and I. What interests you is the locality.'

'The vernacular, I call it.'

'What I'm after is the broad canvas, the migrations of tribes, the diffusion of cultures – where they originated, what they brought.'

'There's tin in Cornwall. Go to Cornwall and find out whether the tin miners sailed off and came back with copper, or whether the copper folk came looking for tin, and where the first bronze was forged.'

Kelynack began describing what Schliemann had found at Mycenae, but Mycenae was a distant horizon for James Biffen. Even Cornwall was far off.

He interrupted. 'A thought has come to my mind, Kelynack. It's a long shot, but it might be interesting to both of us. Sherborne Old Castle.'

'There's no barrow at the castle.'

'There was, I believe.'

'Where?'

'I'll put on my boots and show you.'

'I'm persona non grata in this town, Biffen. Kenelm wouldn't want me within a mile of the castle.'

'Because you left suddenly? Nonsense. Kenelm's a decent fellow. He allows me to sniff around wherever I want. Encourages me.'

'I didn't leave the school of my own accord, Biffen.'

'You resigned. There was a good reason, I'm sure.' Biffen began putting on his boots. 'Come on. There's time for a stroll to the castle before the light fades.'

It was no stroll. Biffen walked with a long rapid stride, defying the conditions, which were partly ice and partly slush, with stretches of double Dorset mud. Kelynack stumbled and slid in his wake. On the bridge over the Yeo, Biffen stopped and gestured at the castle precinct.

'It's higher than the land around. But it's not a natural feature, and you can't only explain it by what was dug out for the moat. I've poked around here a few times and the soil has a remarkable uniformity. It's a loam rather than the mix of stone, gravel and clay you'd normally find in a river basin. It was transported from elsewhere, Kelynack. I wouldn't have thought much of it but for the stories that refer to a mound here once upon a time. Mrs Biffen brought them to my attention.'

He led the way along Castleton Lane. 'There's also a tale among the locals that the gatehouse and the keep are connected by an underground passage,' he said. 'It's not unlikely in a fortified residence. Picture it. The enemy's at the gate, with larger numbers or better weapons. You must evacuate the gate and take refuge in the tower. Arrows and rocks are pelting in from outside and the safest way is underground.'

They walked beneath the arch of the southwestern gatehouse and tramped through drifts of snow to the keep. It was roofed by fronds of ivy winding among the branches of trees and within the high walls dusk had already come. Biffen took up a stick and scratched around in one of the corners of the tower while Kelynack watched him, flapping his arms to keep warm.

'Here we are. Take a look,' Biffen said.

There wasn't much to see, nor light to see it by. The ground appeared to have crumbled away into a shallow pit, littered with old stone.

'If I were looking for the passage, I'd start here,' Biffen went on. 'Clear these stones away, dig out some earth and prod around with a sharp pole.'

'Forgive me, Biffen, but I'm not looking for a medieval passage.'

'My point, Kelynack, is that if this were once a burial mound, we're standing just about in the middle of it.'

Kelynack imagined a great barrow around and above him.

'Alright,' he said. 'And so?'

'If there's an underground passage below our feet, you'd expect it to run along the original ground level, giving the passage a solid basis. Find the passage and you could get at your barrow burial, if there is one, by digging a few feet deeper.'

'Your idea has as many ifs as mine, Biffen.'

'The site's here on the doorstep and not at the top of a windy hill outside Dorchester. You need no vehicle, no camp, no provisions. And while you're looking for your swords and beads, I can investigate the foundations of the keep and the underground passage, if there is one.'

'Even if there is a grave, how do we know the passage leads to it?'

'This place was originally Roger de Caen's palace. My idea is that the Norman builders flattened the ancient barrow to create a raised platform and put their keep exactly over the old burial. Hid it from sight and sealed it up. It's what the Christians did with the pagan stuff. It's only a guess you'll say, but no more of a guess than when you settle on which bump in the hills to dig up.'

'And Kenelm?'

'The excavation will be part of my researches. If you're here to help or observe, Kenelm won't bother with that, whatever the issue between you. Anyway, Kenelm's in Westminster on Parliament duty. He takes it seriously. Speechifies, votes, sits on committees. He won't be back for a month apart from the odd weekend.'

Biffen dismissed the problem with a wave of his stick. He was standing on the edge of the slight depression in the ground they had come to see, the stick – without him noticing it – had been essential to his balance, he stumbled on one of the rocks littering the ground and went over. Scrambling to his feet, he felt a stab of pain in his ankle and sunk again to the ground.

'Help me up will you Kelynack? I've done myself a mischief.'

He shrugged it off, saying it would pass in a minute, but he was unable to stand without Kelynack's support and when they set off towards the town, he hobbled along on one leg with an arm round Kelynack's shoulders. All that was left of the daylight was a deep grey gloom with the ghost-white flashes of snow on the ground.

'Damn it, I've sprained my ankle. I spend much of my life striding over rough ground at all times of day and night and I've never fallen. Not once. Damn it to hell, this doesn't feel like something that'll go away in a day.'

When they got back to the large house in Abbey Road, Mrs Biffen met them at the kitchen door.

'What's this, Kelynack? Biffen leaves in good working order and you bring him back broken.' She settled her wounded husband on a chair by the stove and removed his boot. He yelled out as she pulled his sock off.

'The ankle's broke,' she said.

'Are you sure, madam? You haven't touched it. Felt it, I mean. It was a slight trip, that's all.'

'Good night, Kelynack.'

'I say, Mrs Biffen, don't throw the man out. Stay for a cup of tea, dear fellow.'

'I've no time for making tea, Biffen,' Mrs Biffen grumbled. 'The bone's broken, as I can see with my own eyes without prodding it. The sooner I get it splinted and bound the sooner it will mend.'

'I'm sorry for you, Biffen,' said Kelynack.

'I'm in good hands. None better. She'll have me skipping like a spring lamb in a few days, won't you my dear?'

'A few weeks, more like. Next time Kelynack wants to drag you off for a walk in the snow, remember something else you have to do, Biffen.'

'I beg your pardon, madam, the walk was his idea,' Kelynack said.

'But the purpose was yours, I take it.'

'Ours, I think we might say, may we not, Biffen?'

'Am I really to be chair-bound for weeks, Mrs Biffen? I shall asphyxiate ... I shall petrify.'

'You can finish your book at last.'

'I am minded to go ahead with this excavation at the Old Castle, Biffen,' Kelynack said, with his hand on the door handle. 'Do you think I can do it in your absence?'

'I see no reason why not. I shall ask you to note certain things that interest me about the foundations. If you find a passage, I shall explore it when I'm up and about.'

'And Kenelm?'

'I shall send him a note to await his return. You may be finished before he reads it.'

'I shall start without delay, then.'

'Get Corporal Timmins to help you. He'll have little to do until the new term starts. He can find shovels and a couple of labourers. If you need a place to stay while you're working, there's plenty of room ...'

'Kelynack is familiar with the town. I am sure he can arrange his own accommodation,' Mrs Biffen cut in. 'Good night, sir.'

'Good night. Cheerio, Biffen. I hope your injury mends swiftly.'

It did not. Despite Mrs Biffen's most careful attention, the ankle had to remain bound and immobile for longer than usual.

Biffen's injury suited Kelynack. He would hardly have been tempted by the Old Castle site if it had meant having Biffen directing things in his meticulous fashion. Kelynack had seen him in a trench by the abbey, surrounded by a network of pegs and cords, cleaning a fragment of something with a toothbrush.

He did not know whether to believe in the existence of a burial mound under the keep. Certainly he set no store by Mrs Biffen's folk-tales. But Biffen's words about windy Dorchester hilltops had struck a sour note, and standing in the keep at dusk picturing a great barrow above him had produced a *frisson* whose origin he couldn't explain. Besides, the simplicity of the operation appealed to him. He knew people here, he could find equipment, a cart, men to dig, he would work for a week in what was, for a historian, the most evocative spot in the town. All he needed was to persuade Isadora to keep him company.

She had missed him. Their stolen days together were too few and too brief and she'd had enough of barns and grottoes.

'But *Sherborne?*' she wondered.

He promised he would find a house out of town, somewhere spacious and private, where nobody would bother them.

'With a garden, please.'

'With a garden.'

'Then I will come. For the sake of your book.'

'For the book then.'

She had one more condition, insisting that before a pick was lifted or a shovelful of soil removed, a cockerel should be killed at the site, its blood scattered and the bird cooked and eaten there. It was the custom among her people before an important undertaking, she explained.

'Anything you please, my Hamadryad.'

He drove to Sherborne to look for a house. He drove in sunshine through Corton Denham and Sandford Orcas, Poyntington and Oborne, Goathill and Haydon, lovely villages each of them. He had forgotten or perhaps never noticed how lovely. Seeing them through her eyes, he admired how the dwellings half-hid among the hedges and trees and how the land sprung one surprise after another round a turn in the lane or over the brow of a hill. But the houses he especially liked were occupied and those that were pointed out as being empty had something against them—too dark or too gaunt or their gardens wild and unkempt. From Haydon he followed the track through Sherborne Park back towards Sherborne.

He fed and watered the pony at the *Castleton Arms* and had a meal by a window commanding a fine view of the Old Castle, whose ruined battlements and tortured towers were woven among the innumerable greens of spring. He experienced a moment's envy of Biffen and Grindlay, for whom these horizons were sufficient, and sufficiently beautiful. Did Grindlay ever go away on holiday? No. The notion was superfluous to his life.

While eating, he eyed the houses of Castleton, ranged between the inn and the Old Castle. He thought of the advantages of being so close to the work. He had promised that it should be 'out of town', but Castleton had its own name and character and seemed a long way from Cheap Street and the Abbey Close. He finished his lunch quickly, left the pony in the stables of the inn, walked into Castleton and put his question to the first person he met, an elderly lady whose face was cast in such sharply sculpted forms that they seemed to echo the ancient moods of the land and the patterns of the lives that were lived there.

'Why yes, Mr...'

'Kelynack.'

'Yes, Mr Kelynack,' said this erect, immaculate person. 'The Slape is empty and recently so. The verger has the key. Good afternoon.'

She went on without a trace of the polite or the impolite, poised and prepared. To arrange the flowers in the church? To swim naked in the lake? She would do either, Kelynack felt, in the same uncompromisingly perfect fashion.

The verger explained that the owner, after the death of his wife, God rest her soul, had gone to live with his son in Guildford and had asked him to let the house to a suitable party and settle terms. When Kelynack saw the garden over the hedge, with the japonica in bud and the forsythia blown in a gentle breeze, Kelynack decided not to look inside the house but to pay what was asked and see it for the first time *with her*. He took it for a month, although needing it for a couple of weeks perhaps. The windows would be cleaned, the verger said, and the larder provisioned with the bill for provisions to be paid when convenient. He was disappointed at the shortness of the let but Kelynack said it would be for a month initially.

'What is your reason for coming to stay in Castleton, Mr Kelynack, if I may ask?'

'I am writing a book.'

'How interesting. What, pray, is the subject of your book?'

Kelynack wondered how to answer in a few words. 'It is about the history of England.'

'It has all been written, surely.'

Kelynack laughed. 'Each generation must write new histories.'

'Is that so?' the verger replied, raising his eyebrows. 'It is a curious idea.'

Isadora was surprised to find herself residing so close to the scene of her disgrace but when she saw the garden she made no protest. 'We shall have no cause to show ourselves in Sherborne,' Kelynack assured her.

The house was built in the local honey-coloured stone but from the outside it was a lump of a house, wide and squat, and inside it was built around a curious central hallway extending to the roof. This rather grand feature dwarfed the other rooms and seemed to have squeezed them out of shape. There was a smell of damp in the ground-floor rooms On the first day, they lit a fire in the kitchen and one in the sitting-room and another in their bedroom but the stains on the lower walls showed that this house was damp and always would be, and because of the small windows it would always be dark.

When the verger told Isadora not to worry herself with the stories about the death of the owner's wife, of course she worried and in the end he had to tell her, which he was obviously eager to do. Twenty years younger than her rather severe husband, the lady had suffered from what the verger called a melancholy nature and when her body was found in the lake, it was suspected, 'without evidence, mind you', that she had taken her own life. 'Some of the parishioners even objected to her being buried in the church graveyard,' he added sadly. 'You know that suicides were not to be buried in consecrated ground until fairly recently. One really cannot imagine why. It is the last resort of the desperate. Should we penalise the unquiet dead?'

Isadora made no mention of this to Kelynack and he heard no whisper of it, or of any other Castleton gossip.

But it made her uncomfortable wondering which had been her bed, what had been her relations with her stern husband. A house registers these things, she knew, and stores the memories in its light and shade and moods, and even in the apparently random choice of wallpapers and paints.

A few of the rooms of The Slape were bare of furniture. The others were cluttered with settees, armchairs, reading tables and cabinets with souvenirs that recalled nothing much, photos of unsmiling people who would never smile now, cups that nobody drank from and plates from which nobody ate. Isadora kept mostly to the kitchen.

'You should ask Louis Yeoman to do the sketches of your excavation,' she told Kelynack as they sat together after breakfast on their first morning in the house.

'The boy's not capable of it.'

'Have you seen his drawings?'

'I saw the Ape debate poster. But this is a different matter.'

'We owe him something.'

'What he did for us made no difference as it turned out.'

'That's not the point, Austin, and you know it. He was blamed for the fire because he kept our secret.'

'He is to be allowed back this coming term. He missed some months. So what?'

'Cuff told me he's got a pile of sketchbooks in his study. He's talented, Austin.'

'I don't want the boy at the excavation.'

'You don't want him because of your feeling of guilt, which ought to make you generous.'

'Generous? You expect me to pay him?'

'Certainly you will pay him, if you use his drawings. We shall put him up here and show him our gratitude for what he did. It is common decency, Austin.'

'He is just a boy.'

'Like just a slave?'

'The rumour in the school was that he was in love with you. There were poems found in his pocket.'

'Is it surprising that boys of eighteen in a school with no women and no girls should look at the masters' wives, or at the kitchen maids? You are jealous of him, perhaps?'

'Don't be ridiculous.'

'I shall invite him myself. You have said that you need illustrations for your book. Biffen can't do them and you certainly can't.'

He agreed to get Yeoman's address from the custos when he was in town that day. She wouldn't write, he thought, and if she did

Yeoman wouldn't come. But when he brought the address that evening, she took it at once to one of the innumerable tables in the drawing-room and addressed an envelope. Mr Louis Yeoman, Turnworth Park, Petherton, near Bridgewater, Somerset. Isadora had written the letter already.

The Slape, Castleton, Dorset

Dear Louis Yeoman,

I have been seeking a way to repay our debt to you and to repair, if it is possible, the resentment you must feel in connection with Mr Kelynack and myself. Mr Kelynack will carry out an excavation at the Old Castle in connection with a book he is writing. We would like you to make sketches of the site and the finds, which I know you would do very skilfully. Some of them would be included in his book. There will be others in the party, including Corporal Timmins. He could meet you at the railway station and bring you to join us in Castleton, where we have a large house in which you can have a room to yourself. Timmins will also stay with us during the excavation so that he can see to the horse and take care of the equipment.

Please let me know whether you will be able to join us. I would be so happy if you allow us to make some amends for the injustice done to you.

Sincerely,
Isadora Magdalensky

The verger, once he found that Isadora did not turn him away, came daily for a cup of tea. He was not an old man but he was elderly in his manner. The duties of verger of Castleton were not onerous, and educating a foreigner in the history of that corner of England seemed to him a pleasant and useful addition to those duties. Most of what he knew had been learned from visitors to the castle and listening to local tales. There was therefore no order to his telling and he was ignorant of the quilt of which his stories were patches. But he lived close to the two Sherborne castles, the old and the new, and he was more proud of them than of his small church, which was managed by priests who outranked and occasionally cowed him. As unofficial guide to the Old Castle, he was safe from competition. Biffen knew more, but Biffen was not there, whereas the verger's life, with rare exceptions, was lived within a few hundred yards of it.

With relish, he told Isadora the story of St Osment's curse.

'Osment? There is a *Saint Osment*?'

'A legendary figure perhaps, my dear, but legend or not, the curse has struck repeatedly throughout the ages.

'The founder of the Old Castle, Roger de Caen, died an embittered man accused of treason. Walter Raleigh, who built the New Castle, fell painfully from his horse on his first visit to the spot. He too encountered royal disfavour by eloping with a royal chambermaid and was later imprisoned and executed, and his castle confiscated. A later Baron of Sherborne also ended in the Tower and one of his sons was directly responsible for the outbreak of the Civil War, during which the town was bombarded and looted and the Old Castle destroyed by Cromwell's troops.

'A superstitious person might be tempted to see even the recent drownings in the lake as connected with the old curse.'

'Drownings?'

'There have been several during my own time.'

'Are there no cheerful stories, Sir Verger?' Isadora exclaimed.

There were, he answered, but made bashful by the Arthurian title that the beautiful Russian woman had found for him, he failed to recall any.

When the weather was fine, Isadora walked through the castle grounds to the lake, but the verger had spoilt the place for her. To make matters worse she was accosted by a gamekeeper and told she was trespassing, and in the village she felt that people had recognised her as the headmaster's faithless wife.

She should not have agreed to the excavation, she thought, not for the sake of Austin's book or even for the sake of their love. Compromise was foreign to her nature and made her feel oddly vulnerable, and that was why the deaths in the lake and the fate of the builders of the castles affected her.

Kelynack suggested they omit the cockerel ceremony, but she reminded him that it had been a condition for her coming. She also observed the Lenten fast rigorously, avoiding milk and meat, and on Good Friday she drank only water and ate nothing.

He bought a cockerel from a farmer, bringing it to The Slape in a sack. It spent its last night lying on the floor of an outhouse, with its feet tied together. When he came for it in the morning and went to pick it up, it attacked him, hobbled though it was.

They walked up to the castle keep, Kelynack with the sack over his shoulder and a hatchet in his hand. She chose the eastern wall of the tower for their picnic, where they were hidden from the village and the morning sunshine lingered. He stepped to a tree stump a little way off with his sack and hatchet.

He had killed a chicken once as a boy at Gifford, but this time there was no adult at his shoulder to hold the bird still over the chopping block and to grip it during its death struggle. He closed his eyes as he struck and found that his first blow had not properly done the job. He struck again, desperately. The bird's head was completely severed from its neck, from which came a jet of bright blood. Horrified, he released his hold on the body and the bird flew headless towards the ruins of the tower, its wings beating a dozen times before it hit the wall and collapsed at its foot.

'You told me you knew how to kill a chicken, Austin.'

'I do, I did. I thought I did.'

'Fortunately you do not believe in omens.'

He came close to it at that moment, as the bird flew with no head and spouted hot blood over the wall.

She plucked it while he built a fire. The wood was green and wouldn't catch and it was only when she put down the bird and brought dry kindling that the flames grew strong.

She spitted the bird and set forked sticks on either side of the fire. She kept the bird turning rapidly above the fire, pressing the forked sticks further into the ground as the flames dwindled and the wood turned black and the heart of the fire grew red. She let it take all the time it needed to cook, determined that this part of the ritual, at least, should be right. Long after he thought it ready, she was twisting the spit slowly and more slowly over the embers of the fire, and only when the flesh seemed ready to fall from the bone did she remove the spit. She pulled the bird into pieces with her fingers, steaming hot though it was, and with their fingers they ate.

'It's magnificent, Isadora.'

She nodded. 'It was a young bird and fat for the time of year.'

'When did you last do... do this?' he asked.

'As a child, Austin. There are things you don't forget.'

He thought he would never forget that meal with her under the wall of the keep, and the glitter of the lake beyond the cedars, the spring-scented breeze, the sweet, succulent flesh of the bird.

'The art of the cooking exorcised the clumsiness of the killing,' he said when they had finished.

'Perhaps not, but we ate well, did we not?'

A black-and-white sheepdog arrived from nowhere and lay down at a distance sniffing the air and she threw him the bones one by one and watched him swallow them and heard the cracking of the bones between his teeth.

That afternoon, a reply came from Louis Yeoman saying that he would arrive at Sherborne station the next day. Timmins was there with Kelynack's pony and trap.

Timmins had taught Louis to box. When Louis had first come to Sherborne School at the age of thirteen, he soon learned (as they all did) that sporting prowess served as the only gauge of pluck and manliness, and any boy with none of it was considered 'wet'. Louis disliked rugby football and cricket bored him, but in his first term, driven by a sort of desperate fury, he had won the New Boys' boxing competition, compulsory for all but the lamest ducks. Timmins took him in hand and taught him the craft of the ring and the craftiness that went with it. Year by year, Louis won boxing cups, and although he could never be one of the real sporting heroes, the 'bloods', he was immune from the charge of wetness.

'You're a good boxer because you don't get hit,' Timmins once remarked. Louis claimed he was just lucky, but Timmins said that if it were a matter of luck, his granny would have been world champion instead of darning his grandpa's socks.

A kind of friendship grew between Louis and the big ex-boxer and after sessions in the gym they would sometimes have buns and cocoa in Tuffins tea-shop by the abbey where Timmins would tell tales of ring and camp.

'I'll dig the hole and you draw it,' Timmins said as they drove to the Old Castle. 'They're all there. Mr Kelynack, Mrs Runciman, the pretty maid Frances, two local fellers with shovels and Rugg's lad for the wheelbarrer. Everybody's stood round looking at a place where the ground's given way and wondering how to begin. Kelynack wants what he calls a shaft. I told 'im it needs a big square pit to start, so as it can get narrower as it goes down without cramping us. Too much shovelling, 'e says. He pegged out the ground to mark the entrance to 'is burrow but his idea of pegs is something you put in to show where yer lettuce seeds are. I went and cut 'im some proper pegs and while I was there I cut a few poles and then I fixed up a few things we'll be glad of, like a tent for when it rains and trestles for the water barrel. While I'm away at the station, I said, 'ave a think about what it'll be like working inside a rabbit hole. I'll bet you sixpence, Louis, it'll be a pit in the end.'

'Why Rugg's boy?'

'E turned up and offered. I would've sent 'im packing but Kelynack thought he'd be handy to shift the soil. But Rugg sent 'im along, for sure, which is reason enough to look out.'

When they arrived, Kelynack was at the entrance to the keep, lordly in a snuff-coloured cape. Two farm labourers stood nearby, leaning on long-handled shovels. Rugg's boy squatted a little way off. There was no sign of the women.

'We're ready to start, Timmins,' said Kelynack. 'If you won't work in a shaft, it'll have to be a pit.'

'Yes sir.'

'I've put in some pegs.'

'Then I'll arm myself with a pick and we're off.'

Kelynack turned to Louis.

'So, Louis Yeoman, my ally at the Ape debate. Or were you? I couldn't be quite sure.'

'We won didn't we?'

'Indeed. Perhaps after all it was your poster that won it for us. But can you draw a pot, a bone, a rusted sword?'

'I'll do my best.'

'Will your best be good enough, I wonder. However, there's not much for you to do for now. A sketch of the initial scene, perhaps, before anything is dug. When you find yourself idle, you can help Rugg's lad with the earth.'

'I shan't be idle.'

He sat in one corner of the keep and began sketches of the walls, the array of tools and buckets, the overhanging trees, searching for an idiom for this time and place. A mood, a character, something his pencil could catch and express.

Isadora and Françoise arrived and walked over to where Louis was sitting.

'I am very happy you came, Louis,' Isadora said.

Louis glanced up at her and went back to his sketch. 'Mr Kelynack doubts my ability.'

'And you?'

Louis shrugged. 'It's new to me. Today perhaps I shall finish nothing. Tomorrow may be different.'

'Françoise and I shall sit by you as you draw, if we may.'

'I'd rather you didn't, Mrs Runciman. I can show you the sketches later.'

'But I can stay, Louis Yeoman, can't I?' Françoise asked.

He looked up to see her red lips and saucy smile.

'You will distract me.'

'You don't mind that.'

'Today I do.'

She made a face and went off.

'Françoise is mischievous, Louis.'

'I like her mischief.'

'I do too. I shall send her with tea and sandwiches. You have been travelling. You must be hungry.'

He worked first on caricatures that could be made with a few strokes. Kelynack tall, cloaked, stiffly upright. Timmins, broad-shouldered, a military stripe running down the outside of his trousers – in reality there was no such stripe, always bent over something – the fire, the trestles, the pick. Rugg's boy, short and stick-thin. The labourers, flat capped, shovels as tall as themselves. They were brothers, the younger wiry and cheerful, the older heavy and solemn.

The women were harder work. He didn't want them to appear foolish, or plain. Françoise tended to come out plump and pouting, and Isadora aloof and queenly. In the end he settled for two good-looking women, one shorter than the other, and when they saw themselves later they neither laughed nor protested. Finally he drew a figure to represent himself, with long face, untidy scrub of hair and eyebrows raised in surprise, like one of Cruikshank's eccentric youths. A line of pencils protruded from his top pocket.

The figures were to give an appearance of activity, and to provide a scale. What mattered were the walls of the keep, the crumbling mortar and ruined heights, the branches of the overlooking trees, the complexion of the ground, with its grasses and nettles and its rabble of stones. The forms of rocks seemed random to the casual eye, but they were specific and needed practice.

His first efforts were abandoned at once, but at last he had walls that seemed like walls, grass you could walk on, shovels that would dig, a tent that wouldn't be blown away by the wind.

There was the water-barrel mounted on improvised trestles. By the barrel, a woodpile. Beyond that a circle of rocks and inside it a camp-fire, a tripod and a pot. There was even the roughly built ladder, for when the hole would be too deep to leap in and out.

Louis appreciated these signs of Timmins's ingenuity, which transformed a scene of intrusive busyness into something more appealing. A shelter, a camp-fire, a cooking pot! As there might have been when the medieval walls were raised.

From his corner, Louis heard stray comments from the workers. The soil was loose and full of rubble, the pick could be driven in quite easily here and there. The mood was cheerful because the going was not as hard as it might have been.

The first full drawing Louis attempted depicted the drama of the burnt layer, Kelynack's name for a patch of blackened soil that Timmins and the lads came on in mid-afternoon, about six feet down. It might have been nothing more than the remains of a bonfire of long ago, but they went through it carefully with trowels and then Timmins found a tooth.

Until that moment, there had been a picnic atmosphere, with a camp where tea was brewed, men digging a hole in the spring sunshine, a young artist absorbed with his sketchpad, and two women propped comfortably on cushions against the wall, but now there was a tooth from the mouth of a human being who had burned in a fire. The past, comfortably remote and obscure, suddenly raised its head, like a corpse come alive.

For months the story of Peggy Forgetmenot had been blotted out of Louis' mind by the events of the fire and the abrupt change in his life that was its result. The mention in Isadora's letter of an excavation of the Old Castle had brought vague images of buried cannonballs and rusted pikes but most of all he had thought of seeing Isadora again. When he arrived at the tower, there were other things to occupy his mind: could he make sketches that wouldn't be dismissed or ridiculed, how would he behave towards Kelynack, would Bright appear suddenly to haul him off? Even the burnt layer failed to reawaken the memory of Peggy Forgetmenot. But when the tooth was unearthed, the bleak story came back to him.

He watched the men scoop the blackened earth into wooden buckets and sifted every grain of soil through a garden sieve into the wheelbarrow and as the bones started appearing he thought of the bound body in the wagon, the fire at the stake, the curse of the burned woman.

By the end there were thirty-two teeth, and bones enough for a skeleton. The bones were black and scarred. The teeth, remarkably, were intact. At Kelynack's instruction, the soil was sifted a second time, for a ring, a bracelet, a fragment of pottery or metal, but nothing was found. Françoise had left her seat by the wall to watch the activity at the pit but Isadora stayed where she was.

Louis compressed the events into a single scene viewed from above. Figures were gathered round a pit, looking down, and Timmins was standing at the bottom of the pit with a bone held up in his hand. Louise chose the largest of the surviving bones as a model, a thigh bone—he supposed—which he drew very black, splintering and eroding one end so that it didn't look like something flung to a dog.

The body was a woman's, Mick, the younger labourer, observed. The teeth weren't big enough for a man. She was young, Timmins thought, because all her teeth were with her and seemed little worn.

'This was a castle, a fortress, not a cemetery,' Kelynack remarked. 'She ought not to be here.'

As he spoke he picked up the skull and turned it in his hands.

'You didn't ought to be doing that, sir,' George said.

'Why the devil not, man?' Kelynack exclaimed irritably, but when he looked up, he saw that Isadora was frowning and Françoise had turned her head away.

'Sketch me with the skull,' he called out to Louis, and Louis drew the first three lines of a picture; the bent arm holding the skull, the curve of the cranium and the defiant line of Kelynack's neck and jaw.

'Why was the body burned here, and when?' Kelynack wondered as he stood with the skull in hand. 'It would not have been done while the castle was still in use. The place was abandoned at the time of the Civil War, so this burial took place after that. A woman was burned in the corner of a ruined keep. Who was the woman and why was she not buried in consecrated ground?'

'We've gone and dug up a witch.'

'You keep yer mouth shut, Mickey,' George warned. 'We're along to dig, that's what. What's dug up bain't no business of ours.'

Louis listened to these exchanges, his head bent over his sketch. He added two bold circles for the eye sockets, the outline of Kelynack's cloak, the heap of bones and the flames of the fire in the foreground.

'Why here?' Kelynack continued. 'That's the puzzle. Unless... unless dim memories of a more ancient history survived.'

'More ancient than what?' Timmins asked.

'More ancient than the castle.'

Kelynack put the skull back on the ground with the other bones and squatted there to measure some of the larger bones with the span of his hand, examined what had once been arms and fingers, took out a small black notebook and jotted notes.

'Go on with the digging, Timmins,' he ordered without looking up.

When he had finished, Isadora got up and came forward and began to gather the bones, and Louis put down his sketchbook and helped her. Timmins fetched a handful of old cloths from his tent.

They wrapped the teeth in a small cloth and put them with the bones in a larger one. A kind of solemnity came over all of them and it was done in silence.

'Why such ceremony?' asked Kelynack. 'What's the matter with you, Yeoman? Do the teeth still bite?'

Louis and Isadora tied up the cloth by its corners and put it at the back of the tent.

'Come on, Timmins,' exhorted Kelynack. 'Let's go deeper. I'll take a hand with the pick myself.'

Timmins had made it look easy but the pick was heavy and Kelynack's long cloak got in the way. He cast off the cloak and soon after flung down the pick. Louis saw an irritability in him uncharacteristic of the man who strode in leisurely style across the courts or who took out a book and read when bored by his class.

Kelynack measured the depth of the pit and noted it. He paced out the length and breadth of the keep and noted that too. He went outside beyond the walls and could be seen apparently taking sightings of hills and woodlands. He came back to check on the progress of the pit and grumbled because it seemed no deeper than before.

'The work is best done slow and steady, Mr Kelynack,' Timmins said. 'There's no point in rushing it.'

'Good Lord, man, the soil's loose enough. We can do better than scratch at it like chickens.'

'We can, sir, and we will. If you just go off and sit quietly for an hour or so and come back when the dusk comes on, you'll see what me and the lads have done in that time. If anything turns up in the meantime, we'll give you a call.'

Kelynack stumped off saying he would survey the precinct. Isadora watched him go, knowing that he had surveyed it twice already and wondering at the source of his ill humour. A little later she left with Françoise to prepare a meal for the evening.

Kelynack was soon back to inspect the depth of the hole. He sat down by the fire and made notes. Timmins handed the pick to Mick and built up the fire because the wind had turned chilly. When he had a blaze going, he pulled the pot and its tripod to the edge and brewed more tea. The flames appeared to distract Kelynack, or excite him, because he put away his notebook and stared at them with his eyes wide.

Louis Yeoman worked on the wall of the keep as background to his sketch of Kelynack and the skull, adding the overhanging trees and the wild fronds of ivy as the wind blew cold and dusk drew on. Above the trees, he drew a flight of rooks. He had never drawn a bird in flight and the form eluded him. The rooks became a swarm of outsize bats or winged creatures of indeterminate shape. He gave them open mouths to squawk and screech and he left their eyes in the stark white of the page.

At last he worked on the cloaked figure at the centre of his sketch, the skull in his hand and his eyes staring into the flames of the fire like a sorcerer making a spell. He left the eyes of the figure blank and white like those of the weird creatures wheeling and screaming in the sky.

Chapter Nine

THE SLAPE

… it is most absurdly said… of any man that he is disguised in liquor; for, on the contrary, most men are disguised by sobriety.
                                        Thomas de Quincey

'WE'LL ROAST the joint of beef,' Isadora told Françoise when they got back to the Slape. 'I'll put it in the oven while you get washed, then we can peel the potatoes and clean the vegetables.'

She stoked up the big range, basted the joint, put it in the oven and went upstairs. When she came down later, she had changed into a dress of dark green and brushed out her long black hair.

'You look beautiful, Isadora.'

'It is not how I feel inside, Françoise my dear. You, on the other hand, are pretty within and pretty without. May it ever be so.'

They sat together with potatoes, parsnips, carrots and onions on the table between them. Isadora picked up a knife and began peeling the onions.

'Am I really pretty?' Françoise asked.

'You are very pretty today, and I know the reason why.'

'Tell me.'

'I saw you watching him and with what attention. You cannot hide such things.'

'He is only a schoolboy.'

'I do not refer to Louis Yeoman, and you know it.'

'Then who can you be thinking of?'

'Be careful, Françoise. He may be a good man, but he is not for you.'

'Why not?'

'Because he is an army corporal without money or education.'

'You never had either and when you got close to them you ran away.'

Isadora laughed. 'Don't take me for your example, my dear. I am born for tragedy and you are not.'

'What am I born for then?'

'A large family and good fortune.'

'Maybe I can find them with Timmin,' she said, cutting off what seemed to her a unwanted plural.

The older woman looked at her affectionately. 'Maybe you can. I'm not as sure of things as I used to be. But be careful, Françoise. There is a brute in every man.'

'There was no brute in Dr Runciman.'

'There was a coward in him, which is worse.'

'Isadora, you are crying!'

'It's the onions, Françoise.'

Later they heard the trap arriving and saw Timmins and Louis as they drove past the kitchen window.

'Kelynack must have stayed on at the keep,' Isadora commented.

They heard the pony led across the cobbles of the yard and the sound of a bucket filled and a harness carried to the tack room

'Timmin will need hot water, towel and soap,' Françoise said, springing up from the table.'

She filled a jug with water from the stove and went out quickly before she could be called back. She found him in the boot room at the back, taking off his boots. The room smelled of mud and leather and Timmins brought with him the whiff of the pony and a day's hard work with the pick.

'I never saw you in Sherborne,' he said.

'Perhaps you passed me without noticing.'

'If I had passed within a hundred yards of you, I would remember it.'

'I lived there for three months.'

'You were in hiding.'

'I was not.'

'You have a sweetheart who doesn't allow you to go out.'

'I have no sweetheart, and if I did, he would not be able to keep me in.'

'In any case, he would want to take you out as often as possible.'

'Why?'

'To show you off.'

'I am not a horse or a pig, to be shown.'

He laughed as he followed her to the washroom. 'Be off with you, lassie. I'm going to take my shirt off and I don't want to cause any shock to your nerves.'

'I'm sure there is nothing under your shirt to make me surprised.'

'I wouldn't count on that.' He ducked his head and tugged off his shirt, turning away from her as he did so. On his back was a two-foot cobra, tattooed in yellows and purples, with green eyes. Its head stared out from between his shoulder-blades, the flare of its flattened neck lay about his backbone and the elegant curve of its body narrowed towards a tail that disappeared at his belt.

'You can't see the tail, but who cares to see a cobra's tail when you can see its head?'

'Yes,' she murmured.

'Since you haven't gone as I told you, you may as well stay here and hand me that towel when I've finished.'

She watched his back as he washed vigorously. The snake twitched as his muscles flexed and his sinews stretched.

'Moves about, don't it?' he said over his shoulder. 'I got it in China. They suggested a tiger or a peacock but I wanted something with a simple line, see. Less chance of them making a nonsense of it. Not much luck in a snake, I was told, but I ain't so sure. Seems to me that one bone, plenty of skins and venom enough to kill an elephant isn't a bad design for an animal. What do you think?'

'It's wonderful,' she answered, watching its undulations.

He turned for the towel, water dripping from his hair. 'Don't worry, there's no decorations on the front.'

She stepped closer and passed him the towel, turning her eyes away. But when he busily rubbed his hair, she looked at his chest, his shoulders, his forearms.

'I was a boxer. Perhaps you knew that.'

No, she didn't.

'Boxers have to watch what they eat after they stop boxin'. There'll be no Russian bread for me tonight, lassie.'

'But you must try my bread.'

'Your bread? That's different. I wouldn't miss having a taste of your bread now, would I?'

She returned to the kitchen to find Louis with Isadora.

'We fend for ourselves here,' Isadora was saying. 'We could have had a cook, but Françoise and I preferred to have the kitchen to ourselves. We are roasting a joint of beef. We do not care for English bread or English cheese, but we like the English roast! We roast everything: the potatoes, the onions, the parsnips and the Yorkshire puddings.'

'They are not Yorkshire puddings, they are Minsk pies,' Françoise interrupted. 'Have you ever eaten Russian pie, Louis Yeoman?'

'Never.'

'While you are here you shall have Russian pie and home-baked Russian buns and Russian hotpot. Do you think our Russian hotpot would be too hot for Louis Yeoman, Isadora?'

'I think it might.'

'Here, hot things are necessary. At night, it is cold and dark and there are noises in the walls and the roof. Do you hear them, Isadora?'

'It is only the wind,' Isadora answered.

'They do not come from outside. There is something inside the walls. An old ghost trying to escape.' She turned to Louis. 'It is an old English woman. Made of twigs, like a basket. When it speaks, it does not open its mouth. It just moves its lips. Like so.' She pursed her lips and moved them against each other. 'I'm not sure that it has any lips after all.'

'Stop your chatter and see to the beef, Françoise.'

'She has always been here,' Françoise went on, opening the oven and prodding the meat. 'Since the beginning of things. She does not grow older or younger. She is spiteful because we have come to stay here and comes snooping outside my door at night.'

They heard Kelynack return to the house but he didn't come to the kitchen. Some time afterwards there was the sound of the door to the cellar opening and his step on the cellar stairs. Later they heard him coming up, accompanied by the chink of bottles.

The dining-room table would have seated a dozen. Isadora suggested they use only half of it, but Kelynack said that they should spread out and talk loudly. He sat at one end and Isadora at the other with Timmins on her right, next to Françoise. Louis had his side of the table to himself.

'The wine cellar has produced two handsome bottles of claret,' Kelynack announced. 'Tonight we will drink to the excavation of the keep and the treasures we will find there.'

His face was flushed and his mood expansive. He had sampled the wine in advance, it seemed.

Isadora let him fill her glass but the drink was still untasted at the end of the evening. Louis drank water and Timmins said that he drank only beer.

'Regrettably I found no beer in the cellar, Corporal. Françoise, you shall drink with me.'

Kelynack soon grew merry, with a brittle, self-centred merriment. Each time he filled his glass, he filled up Françoise's glass too. She was a very pretty girl, he thought. She was an extraordinarily pretty girl.

'You are an extraordinarily pretty girl,' he murmured to her.

The table was getting longer, but it was not as long as he thought and his murmur not as soft. It was heard by the company.

'Isadora does not approve of my excavation, Françoise. You shall be our mascot.'

'You are free with your favours this evening, Austin,' Isadora remarked.

'Why not? I am celebrating our excavation, which is beginning, and my book which is nearly finished. A new road opens before me. Fresh horizons beckon. If you will not celebrate with me'—he gestured to her untouched glass—'then I invite Françoise to do so.'

The first bottle of claret was soon empty and the second was broached at once. The table, in Kelynack's view, was not only becoming longer but unsteady too, as if at sea. It was a longboat. There were two longboats, with himself and Françoise in one, and the others drifting slowly out of sight in the other.

'You are extraordinarily pretty,' he told Françoise again, but she was swimming like a mermaid and when he put out a hand to catch her, she eluded him. He picked at the roast meat on his plate, but eating seemed unnecessary. He caught sight of the bottle. A moment ago it had been full but it now appeared to have little left in it.

'Who, pray, has spilled the wine?' he called out. The words were eddied aloft as if he were addressing the gallery. I have made a prayer, he thought, and it has gone upward as it should.

Abruptly he rose from the table, pushing back his chair. It fell on the floor behind him, but it was of no matter. He had no further use for it, and the others... had chairs of their own. He toppled and straightened and went upstairs carefully, uprightly, gravely, as befitted the lord of the manor.

The staircase was broad and easy, with a wall for support, but he bowled twice round the gallery before locating a room he took for his, circumambulating with an air of mischief, as if invisible. From below, they glimpsed his passage behind the balustrade.

'It's a pity he didn't tell us about his book,' Isadora said. 'We might have heard an interesting version of it.'

When the meal was finished, she suggested tea in the kitchen.

'It's warmer and the ceiling isn't quite so far away.'

'I'll see to the fires in the bedrooms, m'am,' Timmins said. 'Then I'm off to Bedfordshire, if you'll excuse me.'

'By all means, Corporal.'

'I must also go up,' Françoise said. She was a little unsteady on her feet.

'I can light you the way, Miss Frances.'

They went upstairs together.

Isadora and Louis drank tea at the kitchen table. There were no curtains in the window, and the moonlight shimmered coldly on the garden lawn. 'We would have eaten more comfortably here, but Kelynack wanted to lord it in the hall. And so he did. Will you show me your drawings, Louis?'

He took a lamp and fetched the sketchbook from his room.

She turned the pages, smiling at Kelynack about to eat a hard-boiled egg, at Rugg's boy eyeing the picnic, at Timmins assembling a trestle.

'You observe us closely,' she commented.

He shrugged. 'People glance at things mostly, just long enough to see that they were what they thought they were. It's different with young children, because the world is still new to them. Once I watched a little girl, in our sitting-room on a visit. She examined everything with her eyes – people's faces, their expressions, their wrinkles, their hands, their shoes, the designs on the carpet and on the cushions.'

'When you draw, you see like a child?'

'I try to.'

She turned to the last drawing.

'This is dramatic.'

'It seemed dramatic. The dark coming. The rooks crying. The ivy slowly dragging down the walls.'

'You are the witness of his excavation, Louis. Later the pit will be filled in and the grass will grow over the place. But your drawings will survive.' She looked again at the drawing in front of her. 'Why have you given him no eyes?'

He had wondered it himself. He had done so unconsciously, it seemed, wrapped in a scene older and deeper than what he saw before him. Perhaps the skull was Peggy Forgetmenot's. The empty eyes stood for the blind ignorance of people who removed from the earth what they did not understand and had no right to disturb, or for the blind cruelty of a man such as Smirk, in the tale. He thought for a moment of sharing with Isadora what he had read in 'The Book of Shadowborne', but decided against it. She would tell Kelynack, the manuscript would be sought in the library and Grindlay consulted. He preferred that Kelynack should dig on with unseeing eyes.

'By the time I made the face, it was no longer him,' he said. 'There was a fire, a cloaked figure beside it. Like a thing of the night.'

She got up from the table. 'Come, you shall see me upstairs, in the manner of the gallant Corporal.'

Outside her room, she turned and kissed him on the cheek.

'Thank you for coming to help us, Louis Yeoman,' she whispered, going in.

He went down for his sketchbook, forgotten on the kitchen table. The old house had grown larger in the dark and the rooms taller. The past of this house was a mournful one, he thought. There had been more sorrow than joy here in these rooms, on these stairs.

Later, in bed, he wondered why the stairway should seem like the focus of the house's sorrow. Because people had borne their sadness upstairs with them in the dark? Or because the stairway stood for a ladder, an ascent? Upstairs to bed. Nearer heaven, the things of heaven. We carry our sorrow toward heaven, and not our joy. Was it true? Why should it be true? There was a line in Ecclesiastes that puzzled him: 'The heart of the wise is in the house of mourning, but the heart of fools is in the house of mirth.' He had wanted to ask Biffen about it. Perhaps sorrow is deeper than joy, he thought, and lasts longer.

In Isadora's room were two beds close together. Both were empty. She set her lamp down on the bedside table and became aware of a figure seated in front of her mirror on the far side of the room.

'What are you doing there, Austin?' She could see only the back of the head above the back of the chair, and only indistinctly. It was not his but the head of a woman. The woman sat quietly, as if staring at herself in the mirror.

'Speak to me!' Isadora commanded.

The figure did not speak, did not turn its head.

Isadora grabbed a pillow from the bed and threw it at the figure in the chair. The pillow passed through the woman's head and landed by the wall.

How very still the room was, as if time had gone away, leaving a hole. All her life, since she was a child, she was prepared for an apparition of this kind. It was in her fate, that the world-between-worlds should make its presence felt in her life. Now it had come with a strange heavy stillness which left her unable to move.

She could not walk up to the figure, touch it, see its face. She could not run to the door and get away. It was as if the woman in the chair had caught her in a web of immobility. She waited.

The light of her lamp was dim beyond the area of the beds. What she had taken for the outline of the woman's hair was a bonnet, she saw, tied tightly to her head. It was what they called a Welsh bonnet, of the kind she had seen still worn in small villages. Beyond the figure was the faint gleam of the lamp on the surface of the mirror but the woman's reflection that should have been there was absent.

The woman was standing up, facing her. There had been no

discernible movement. She had been sitting on the chair and now she was standing on this side of it. There was a lurch in Isadora's stomach, as if the motion that was missing must somewhere be registered. The woman's arm was held out in front of her, pointing towards the door. Her lips were pursed together. No, not pursed but stitched. The seams stood out against the pale skin, crossing and recrossing her mouth. There was no expression on her face, but there was life in the eyes, an intensity. She was looking towards the door. Isadora followed her look but there was nothing there. When she turned back, the figure was gone.

Isadora did not then or later try to convince herself that she had imagined it. And even at the first moment of seeing the figure she had known who it was, or who it represented. The woman whose teeth and bones she had gathered from the ground that afternoon.

Why had they sewn up the woman's mouth? Had they stitched her mouth shut so that she could not scream out when they cast her alive on the flames, there in the corner of the keep? Or perhaps her sewn-up mouth was a symbol for the dumbness of the dead.

The hand had pointed at the door. Indicating what? That she should leave the room, or the house? The woman's gesture had not seemed like an instruction, or dismissal. Isadora went to the door and looked. The door was closed. Nothing in the corner. On the hook behind the door, her own cloak and scarf.

She felt in the pocket of the cloak and drew out two small clods of dry earth she had found among the bones. Something about them had caught her attention and something had prevented her from examining them openly. Later she had forgotten them.

She moved the lamp to the dresser, turned up the wick and held the objects to the light on the palm of her hand. With her other hand she crumbled the soil, which came off in flakes. There were two cubes that she recognised as dice.

She put the dice on the table and sat down. She took a handkerchief from the drawer and wet a corner from a bottle of scent. Using her nails and the damp cloth, she cleaned the earth from the faces of the dice.

One was a white gaming die, marked one to six in the usual manner. The other was red, marked with symbols at first indecipherable. She sprinkled scent on another corner of the handkerchief and rubbed vigorously at the symbols, holding the die to the lamp from time to time to see what was revealed.

A simple cross made by shallow intersecting grooves of white. A pillar made with a single line, rounded at the top. A tower with rudely crenellated summit. A sword or dagger. A circle made of six irregular dots. The last of the symbols was obscure. She took it at first for an owl. But when she held it close to the light, she saw that it was a human skull.

She took up the two dice and on impulse threw them. She glanced at what was on the upturned faces, opened the drawer of the dressing-table, swept them inside and shut the drawer. She wished her ghostly visitor had taken them from her cloak and made off with them. But if a pillow can pass through a head, can the fingers grasp something, can the hand hold it?

She sat on at her dressing-table, unwilling to go to bed. She stared at her lamplit image in the mirror, wondering how she had come to be there, in a cold, uncurtained bedroom at The Slape, under the Old Sherborne Castle. Outside the window, the sky had cleared and the stars were out. The Twins were there, her own sign.

For much of her life she had refused to believe that she had been born under the sign of the Twins. When she had visited Tewari, the Nepali astrologer, in St. Petersburg, she had said that her mother must have been mistaken about the day of her birth. 'I feel no sympathy with the Twins,' she had told him.

'Mothers do not misremember the day of their child's birth,' he had replied. 'You think because you are forthright and impulsive that your sign should be Capricorn or Aries. But Gemini need not indicate indecision. In you, the Twins complement and strengthen each other; they do not fight, or prevaricate. Your outer life and your inner life are one.'

He asked to see the palm of her right hand. 'Here is the signature of the Twins in the course of the life line,' he said pointing to the strong line making its way from her wrist to the base of her fingers. 'In many people this line is unbroken. In you, look, it divides, rejoins, again separates. Just here is a break so distinct that it looks as if a second line begins, separate but geminate.'

Did it mean that her life would change at that point, she had asked.

'The lines of the hand are a palimpsest, not a history,' he replied.

Her life was like a river that was made of two streams joining and dividing, he told her, but their direction was one. In her there was feminine and masculine, strength and tenderness, constancy and impulse, but there was no conflict between them. 'Often in the worlds of Gemini, there is a tension which results in indecision or anxiety,' he added, 'but if the Twins act together, which is their natural function, they make each other stronger.'

She had believed him. From that time, she started to accept in herself what she had thought was a weakness, the way her peculiar sensitivity warred with her impulsiveness.

Now here I am in the world of the Twins again, she thought, as she gazed at the two bright stars. A rightful husband and a wrongful lover, freedom and exile, and on the dice she had swept into the drawer, Skull Two.

Chapter Ten

BEGONE!

At a funeral in China... when the coffin is about to be lowered into the grave, most of the spectators recoil to a little distance lest their shadows should fall into the grave and harm should thus be done to their persons.

James Frazer

KELYNACK WOKE in the morning and remembered which house he was in and, with a shock, which room. Some of the girl's clothes were thrown over a chair. There was a faint scent in the room, as of peppermint.

He remembered admiring her the night before. He remembered filling her glass. But he could not account for how he came to be in her room. He rose from the bed and felt a weight shift in his head, as on a ship when something heavy gets loose in a storm. He was at sea still, but he gathered his things and marched along the gallery without looking right or left. Entering his own room, he said good morning as Isadora woke and continued into the dressing-room.

When he reappeared he was neatly dressed, with hair brushed and shoes polished. His face was a pale grey and something was apt to slide around in his skull, but he gave no sign of it.

'I trust you slept well, Isadora,' he said on his way out.

On the gallery he came on Françoise. Her dress was awry and he glimpsed the bare flesh of her neck and shoulder and was held by this sight against his will. Their eyes met, in a way unmistakable. They both looked quickly away and he murmured good morning as he turned to the stairs, but she did not reply.

At breakfast he could not eat. The tea tasted metallic and after drinking it he felt sick. Nothing in him or around him would stay still in its place, as if the world had been rocked during the night and lost its balance. He avoided the eye of his wife sitting opposite him at the other end of the kitchen table. His wife? Not yet. Not ever, perhaps. Did he want it? Had he ever wanted it?

She seemed set on ignoring the events of the previous evening. She asked him why he didn't eat and offered to make soup for him.

Françoise did not come down, nor did she join the rest of them in the yard. Kelynack walked with Isadora to the Old Castle and Timmins took the trap with Louis and the shovels.

The sight of his excavation failed to restore Kelynack's humour. Timmins, muscular and competent. Drat his competence! Yeoman, hunched over his sketchbook. Drat his eyes! The Rugg boy, who needed to blow his nose. Drat him too.

For a while he laboured with the pick, thinking the exercise might revive him. Overhead, heavy clouds had built a grey dome. The green of the trees was very bright, giving him a headache. How much wine had he drunk? Two empty bottles were on the kitchen dresser as well as the bottle half drunk in the cellar. The world wobbled, loose from its moorings.

'It seems I am unwell,' he said to Isadora. 'I shall go to the house and rest.'

On his way back he remembered that Françoise was at the house and the thought of her was delightful, like rain in a parched land.

'There is something I must do,' Isadora confided to Louis, when Kelynack was gone. 'You can help me if you like.'

'With pleasure.'

'I want to give the woman a proper burial. Away from this place,. Bring a pickaxe and a shovel, Louis.'

She carried the cloth containing the bones and teeth and he carried the tools and they walked over the castle precinct to a door in the southeast wall almost hidden in the ivy. It opened on to the ridge above the lake at a place where three large Lebanon cedars had made their own harbour, their textures and tints exotic and spacious beside the native trees.

'We should find a beech or oak,' said Isadora.

'A beech.'

They came to a beech standing alone on a grand carpet of coppery leaves. Chosing a place away from the trunk they cleared away the years of leaf-mould until they came to a fine soft soil which they scooped out with their hands. When the soil grew firm, Louis loosened it with the pick and Isadora shovelled it aside.

'No foxes or badgers must disturb her, Louis. We will dig until we are tired.'

At last she decided it was enough. They made straight the sides and floor of the pit, placed in it the blackened remains of the woman, covering them with beech leaves and a layer of rocks against animals. Then they replaced the soil and Isadora made a cross of two twigs bound with woodbine.

They stood together by the grave and Isadora recited some words in Russian that sounded beautiful to Louis' ears, like an old poem spoken over a death-ship pushed out into the northern ocean. For an instant, the breeze blowing over the lake brought to him a sense of the centuries of quiet between the water and the wall and when they returned to the tower with its piles of soil and rubble and the grass flattened and bruised, he thought how little they understood or would ever understand of that place, no matter how deep they dug or what they found there.

Isadora decided to go back to the house to see if Kelynack had recovered and find him food. 'He ate no breakfast.'

Timmins nodded, remembering occasions in his own life when breakfast was unwelcome.

'Principals gone off and nothing showing in the pit,' Timmins said when she'd left. 'We could nip down to the *Castleton Arms* and drink a beer, spin the job out for a few days ... or we could knuckle down and get to the bottom of this damned hole.'

'Let's take 'er easy,' Mick proposed.

'Aye, it's a thought,' sighed Timmins. 'But look 'ere, Mick, that sky says rain later and not a shower either. The heaps of dirt will turn to mud and we'll be squelchin' about like pigs in shit and if it rains enough we'll have more pond than pit on our hands. If we sweated a bit we could finish 'er off before the rain comes on.'

'And then go down to the *Castleton Arms*,' said Mick.

'Exactly right, old son.'

It was a very different scene to the day before. No sunshine, no picnic with the women, no Kelynack in his fine cloak. Today there were only paid labourers around a hole, Timmins smiting the ground with a full swing of the pick, Mick, wiry and agile, filling the buckets, George at the top hauling them up and returning them empty. Louis put down his sketchbook and went to the older brother's side gesturing that he would do the emptying and George nodded.

'What do the Corporal mean, finish 'er off?' George asked in a low voice as they worked.

'Get to the bottom of it, I suppose.'

'Who says there's a bottom?'

'If there's no tomb or chest, there'll be rock sooner or later.'

'Don't Mr Kelynack know what 'e's lookin' for?'

'I'm sure he must have some idea, but he hasn't bothered to share it.'

'Here's my idea then. You're a King's School boy and may know better, but the way I see it, there were meant to be an underground passage, which there ain't. Instead we dug up the bits of a dead girl. End of story accordin' to me. Pack up and go 'ome sharpish. Wrong address.'

They got busy with the buckets but later George took up where he left off.

'If the girl were buried in this corner by chance, there baint nothin' underneath, 'cept by another chance that ain't worth the reckonin'. But if she were buried 'ere deliberate, witch or sorceress that she were, what's underneath don't want diggin' up. It wants leavin' be. But you can't expect university gents from out o' town to know about them things, can yer.'

'What things?'

George looked up towards the entrance to the keep. 'Look, 'ere's Ma Biffen. You can ask 'er. She do know, if anyone.'

Mrs Biffen strode into the keep and came up to the mouth of the pit.

'You'll disturb the footings and have the wall down,' she chided.

Timmins looked up from below and passed the pick to Mick. 'Keep at it, Mick lad. I'll be back in a jiffy,' he said, climbing out. 'We ain't bothering the footings, Missus.'

'Then you're bothering something else.'

'What's there to bother?'

'If you don't know what's there, how can you tell whether you're bothering it?'

'Whatever it may be, it's dead.'

'Or inert, Timmins. Don't confuse the two. A thing may be inert for an age and be prodded into life by the point of a shovel.'

'Like what?'

'You're a military man. Think of a feud, fought and forgotten.

Years later a trivial incident revives the memory of the feud and soon it's as fierce as before.'

'Mrs Biffen, you are talking of war between peoples and this is a hole in the ground.'

'We are in a tower, which is a thing of war, inside a castle, a thing of war, and before this castle was, other battles were fought on this spot.'

'How can you know that?'

'It is the nature of the tower to be built where there was a tower before.'

Timmins considered. 'You may be right, Missus,' he said. 'But dead and inert seems about the same to me when it comes to thousand-year-old soldiers and what they fought about.'

'You're an honest soul, Timmins, and you believe the evidence of your own eyes, which is a sound enough rule. But those old warlords knew things subtle and dangerous and if they buried something long ago, it was because they wanted it left alone, which is always the motive for burying something.'

'The hole's empty,' he said, pointing.

'Let us hope so. If you find something, leave it be. Kelynack can prod it and measure it and take it home to put under his pillow. Where is Kelynack?' she asked, looking around.

'Indisposed, Missus.'

'Down tools, then, until he is disposed.'

She spotted the sketchbook lying on Louis' jacket and picked it up.

'I'd prefer you to see the sketches when they're finished, Mrs Biffen.'

She turned the pages nevertheless and stopped at the picture of the figure by the fire under the circling birds. 'This is not archaeology, it is imagination, Louis Yeoman,' she commented.

'Must it be one or the other?'

'Mr Biffen has the answer to that.'

'How is Mr Biffen?'

'Restless and irritable. He has been asking after Kelynack's excavation and I told him I would come and see for myself. I shall tell him that there is no underground passage.' She returned the sketchbook to where she had found it. 'Have you heard, Louis, that in former times people told the future by observing the flight of birds?'

'Mr Grindlay told us the Romans believed in auguries.'

'Did he tell you what had become of that ancient skill?'

'He referred to it as a superstition, not a skill.'

'No doubt he did. But a person who makes a picture of a fire sorcerer with birds screaming over his head might think carefully about the meaning of superstition.' She went close to the boy and spoke her last words quietly. 'Men like Timmins, and good Mr Biffen, are protected by their innocence. Dreamers like yourself do not have the same protection. Be careful, Louis.'

Soon after she was gone, thunder rumbled in the distance. They could smell the rain in the air and they were tiring. The earth was full of stones and the clay came out in clods. Gesturing at the sky, Mick suggested calling a halt.

'We'll crack on until the rain comes, Mick.'

Timmins lifted the pick high above his head and drove it fiercely into the recalcitrant earth.

'Jesus Christ!' he shouted out loud.

'Pick hit summat,' Mick muttered.

Timmins aimed the pick to a point close by and there was the same hollow clunk.

Louis climbed down into the pit and the three of them got down on their knees to see what they had found.

When they'd scraped the soil from its surface, they found that it was a stone slab about three feet wide and long enough for their pit to need enlarging before the slab lay uncovered. At one end was an upright monolith as tall as Timmins, the outer face of which they also cleared. Then they dug out a channel a few inches deep around the slab, which they saw was the lid of a large stone-built tomb.

'Fling us the crowbar, George,' Timmins called out.

'I will not,' said George, crossing his arms.

'Shin up for it, Louis, will you?' asked Timmins.

'You 'eard what the lady said, didn' yer, Corp?' Mick said.

'I 'eard and I un'eard. Go on, Louis lad, bring it down. And the lump 'ammer.'

Louis fetched the tools and Timmins got to his knees, pushed the point of the crowbar under the edge of the lid and gave it a blow with the lump hammer which they thought might split the slab. At his second blow, the great flat stone shifted a fraction.

'No mortar, just the weight of the thing and a crust of old dirt.'

He moved further down the slab and repeated the dose, and once more in a third spot, and the lid was loose.

'Let's 'ave a gander, shall we lads?' Timmins said.

He put Mick on one corner to lever with the pick while he did the same with the crowbar and Louis stood between them and pushed with his hands. The slab moved, with the faint screech of stone on stone.

'Bring a lamp, George,' Timmins called up but George stayed where he was, unmoving. 'Come on, yer great baby, bring that lamp down.' Mick went up for the lamp and the matches and the three of them stood by the open side of the tomb and peered inside as the flame of the lamp lit the interior.

Mick dropped the lamp and went up the ladder. Timmins knelt down, picked up the brass body of the lamp and with his foot swept the broken glass to the side of the chamber.

'Come on, Louis,' he said, putting one hand on the ladder. 'The rain's 'ere.'

Louis climbed slowly up. Inside the tomb he had seen a skeleton with its legs drawn up to one side. The skull had all its teeth and its mouth was wide open.

The rain came in a downpour that drenched them at once. They ran about with tarpaulins and rocks to cover the mouth of the pit. Timmins took two of his poles and thrust them under the tarp so the water would run off. His foot hit against a tool and tipped it into the pit. He took it for a shovel and left it where it was.

The heaps and clods and dribbles of soil around the hole turned to mud in minutes and they took shelter in the tent, wet, muddied, gasping.

''E weren't eight foot tall,' was Timmins's comment, 'but 'e weren't no minnow neither.'

'If you straightened 'im out, he'd be seven foot, I reckon,' said Mick. 'There were a sword next to him, did yer see?'

Nobody had seen it but him.

'That were six foot long, I bet, and 'e were as long with 'is legs bent.'

'What's the point of an eight-foot coffin and a corpse with its legs bent?' wondered Timmins. 'Why not stretch the feller out comfortable? Room for his slippers at one end and his crown at the other.'

Louis didn't mention what else he'd seen. Why didn't he speak out then in the tent, with the raindrops clattering on the canvas above their heads and the men stretched out with mud stuck to their boots and the tools getting in the way if they moved and their shirts sodden beneath their jackets? Why did he keep quiet about the ring of beads that lay at the remnant of neck?

'His mouth was wide open as if he were screaming,' he said.

'Or hooting with laughter,' Timmins said.

'That weren't a laugh, nor a scream. It were a shout.'

'What were it shoutin', Mickey brother, d'you know that?'

'I dunno, George. You tell me.'

'Begone, Mick. That's what. Begone!'

When the rain let up enough for them to leave the tent, Timmins announced it was time for a mug of ale in the *Castleton Arms*. George said he never drank beer and nor did Mick. Mick opened his mouth to object and closed it again because there wasn't much future in arguing with George.

A log fire burned in the hearth at the inn and there was a barrel of beer from the brewery at Myddleton. It had come on a cart a week before and been left to settle and the landlord had tapped it that morning. Timmins said that he'd heard of Myddleton ale but never had the chance to make its acquaintance. The only way to get to know a beer, he went on, was to give it several chances one after the other.

He and Louis grew easy in front of the fire. Timmins told comic tales, with the raindrops streaming down the windows. Louis made a sketch of the soldier by the fire with his mug in hand, adding lines to his forehead and around his eyes, extracting a couple of teeth and creating a disorderly beard for the chin. 'This is how you'll look in twenty years.' Timmins saw it, laughed immoderately and ordered another beer.

When Isadora had arrived at The Slape, Kelynack was asleep upstairs and Françoise was in the kitchen, baking bread.

'I wanted to eat proper Russian bread.'

The loaves were in the oven.

Isadora knew at once what had taken place at The Slape that morning. She knew it because Françoise wouldn't look at her, and she saw it in the unusual paleness of the girl's face and the way her hand shook when she went to open the oven door and inspect the bread.

'The smell of baking bread is not sweet enough to hide what you have done, Françoise.'

'What have I done?' Still the girl wouldn't catch her eye.

'Trespass should I call it?'

It didn't matter what it was called. It was not denied.

'Did you think I wouldn't know?'

Françoise looked at her at last. 'I did not think that you would find out so quickly or that I would be unable to deny it.'

'Then you don't know either of us.'

'I did not invite his attentions.'

'You are weak."

'He... pressed me.'

'You have only yourself to blame. Yesterday morning you flirted with Louis, after lunch it was Corporal Timmins and in the evening Kelynack.'

'I did not flirt with Kelynack. I do not like him.'

'You drank with him.'

'I seemed to have no choice.'

'As you had no choice in the other thing, I suppose. You must pack your bag and leave at once.'

'It's going to rain.'

'It cannot be helped. Shall the three of us sit down to dinner together this evening and discuss the weather?'

'Am I dismissed, Isadora?'

'You are banished. Go to our rooms in Salisbury. I will find you there and perhaps we will discover a way to mend what is broken. Perhaps not. I cannot tell. The train station is not far. Go. I will give you money.'

'I have enough,' the girl said, crying.

Soon she was gone away in the rain, while Kelynack slept on.

He was still sleeping when Isadora took the leather-backed

notebook containing the two hundred closely-written pages of 'The Aryan Dream' and pulled out the pages and tore them into shreds. She read a passage at random.

> The lineage of kings and aristocrats is always fictive. A bastard is legitimised, brute conquest masquerades as just gain, a queen is condemned and replaced, an archbishop installed for the consecration of a usurper. Bloodlines are invigorated by the success at arms of adventurers and captains. Yet the aristocratic principle is maintained and strengthened. It is not in the blood that continuity exists, despite the claims of noble dynasties with their illustrious family trees. Were not the Tudors previously the Tydders, a family of Welsh chamberlains? What were the Stewarts, originally, if not Stewards? We should not confuse principle with pedigree.
>
> Nobility is not an inheritance even if its forms are inherited. But the forms of nobility are not the forms of religion. The English monarchy was founded on the pagan kingships. As for race, who is to say whether any great family, the Cecils or Howards or Bolingbrokes, is free of the blood of Celts, Picts, Jutes, Normans, Saxons or, to employ another terminology, of Danes, Frenchman, Germans and Scots?
>
> What survives is the principle of nobility. As with any principle, it is founded on an intellectual idea – the product of man's intellect, and not of his passions or his appetites. This idea is the subject of this book.

Isadora read this with an admiration that lent poignancy to her careful destruction of Austin Kelynack's work. When she had finished, she took an armful of the shredded pages upstairs and woke him, flinging the stuff over him like confetti.

'Here's your book.'

He couldn't take it in at first, until he picked up some of the fragments and saw the words in his own handwriting.

'Have you gone mad, woman?'

She stood calmly by the bed.

'You tore up our love and I have torn up your book.'

'What the devil do you mean?'

'You crept back here to seduce my maid, and here is the cost of it.'

He denied it flatly. 'Call her up here. Ask her yourself.'

'She has already told me and she is no longer in the house. His attentions were *pressing*, she said. Perhaps you want to chase after her. Take the trap and you may find her on the lane, like a wet rat.'

'You are mad.'

'If I had been mad, I would have killed you as you slept. I considered using the carving knife, the one you used to carve the beef.'

'Your maid has been making up stories.'

'If she had, don't you think I would have realised it at once? You know me so little, despite everything. You're a fool, Austin, which I always suspected, you being an ordinary sort of man. Now I see that you are a coward too, lacking even the courage to say, "I did it and be damned to you".'

'But... my book, Isadora.'

'Words on paper, which you can write down again if there's any value in them.'

'The episode with Françoise was a mistake.'

'A mistake? You took her into your arms by mistake? You undressed her by mistake? Or did she undress herself? Pressing, was her word. Will I go to her room and find her torn undergarments?'

'She seemed to want it.'

'What can you know of that? The husband of her only friend attacks her in her room... Where did it happen? I want to know where. Here, in my own bed?'

'Her room. It was her room.'

'You attacked a girl of eighteen with no one else in the house. By every law, you are her lord and master. You pressed her and because she did not hit you with a lamp, you say that she wanted it? What could she want with you, anyway, a dried-up stick of a man, a failed schoolteacher, a grave-robber, a man who dreams of being lauded at Oxford because he has thrust one more knife into the heart of the Church?'

He had drawn his knees up and held them with his arms.

'Yes, kiss your knees. Hold yourself. Because no one else will. In St. Petersburg, there were captains of dragoons begging for her hand. She could have had the pick of them. What could she want with a desiccated fossil who doesn't know how to make love to a woman? Yes, you heard me. I have had real men make love to me. Men with passion in their hearts and salt in their blood and strength in their shoulders. Men who would have cracked you like the shell of a nut and spat you out.'

'There is no need to boast of your conquests, Isadora.'

'Did you think that Runciman was the only man I ever had?'

'No. That is ... I didn't think ...'

'You had no idea about me, ever. Your little world crumbled when I came into it. And when I go, I shall leave you on your hands and knees, picking up the crumbs.'

'You will go then? You will leave me, because of a ... moment of weakness?'

'I shall leave when it suits me. Put your clothes on. You look pathetic.'

She left him there, clasping his knees.

The rain persisted. She wrapped herself in her cloak and oilskin to look for Françoise. She was not at the railway station but Isadora found her eventually sheltering under an oak. She was still crying.

'Get up, Françoise, your sentence is lifted.'

They walked back to The Slape.

'If he touches you again and I cannot see the scratch marks on his face, everything is over between us.'

'Truthfully, there was nothing I could do, Isadora.'

'Mark my words. They were not idly said.'

When they got back, Isadora cared for her as for a wounded animal, filling a hot tub for her, drying her afterwards, looking among her own clothes for what might make the girl feel pretty.

'You shall move into my room with me.'

Together they threw into a suitcase Kelynack's clothes, towels, hairbrush, his books – everything there was of him in the bedroom and dressing-room. The suitcase was deposited in Françoise's room, from which they removed her few possessions.

'We will leave him in here with his memories. Tell me, did you consent to him?'

'I did not.'

'Then you need not be ashamed.'

'I thought I would live a life without shame.'

'I too thought that. It is easy to think so when you are young. Then the people crowd in around you and the incidents come that bring with them the opportunity for shame, and these leave scars. But like the scars on a child's knee, they do no harm.'

'What if I become pregnant?'

'You will not.'

'How can you be sure?'

'Kelynack will never father a child.'

Chapter Eleven

PITCHFORK

With wicked genii there is also a fluent speech, but harsh and grating. There is also among them a speech which is not fluent, wherein the dissent of the thoughts is perceived as something secretly creeping along within it.

Emanuel Swedenborg

KELYNACK WAS getting the trap ready when Timmins and Louis arrived back at The Slape, fortified, from the *Castleton Arms*. He ignored Louis and spoke peremptorily to Timmins.

'Harness the pony, Corporal. Look sharp.'

It wasn't the way to talk to Timmins, who preferred civility to a sovereign.

'You're in a hurry, sir.'

'Evidently.'

'Too much of a hurry to hear our news p'raps.'

'What news?'

'Why, news of a skull and a sword, Mr Kelynack.'

'You've been drinking, man. I can smell it on your breath.'

'Better beer on the breath than in the barrel is what I say, sir. There's some are proud of the beer in their barrels but I prefer it in the gut, so to speak, where it can do a bit o' good.'

'This accounts for the talk of skulls and swords I take it.'

'Not on your life, sir. Louis and I and the lads put in a spurt and got to the bottom of the pit. Inside the tomb...'

'You opened it?'

'Levered off the lid and fished for treasure in the ancient dirt.'

'A skull and sword you said. Where are they?'

'We settled on leaving things as they were. Considering you'd want to see 'em as they was found. To feel 'em and measure 'em and write 'em down.'

'You should have brought the sword for me to see.'

'Maybe you should have been there with us, sir. Then we'd of known what to do, wouldn't we?'

'I can go there now,' Kelynack murmured.

'Morning would be better, sir. The rain's stopped for the moment, but it'll be muddy underfoot and dark enough to need a lantern, so you'll go down with one hand on the ladder and come up with no hands if you want to fetch the sword. It's not a clever plan, Mr Kelynack. In the morning we can do it together without any fuss.'

'I shall be away for a while. I want to see the stuff before I leave.'

'That's up to you, then,' said Timmins, turning to go inside. 'Mind how you go on the ladder.'

'What about the trap, Corporal?'

'Carry on, sir.'

He went, followed by a dark look from Kelynack.

'You were sharp with him, Timmins.'

'The man doesn't show up for the diggin', orders me about and makes a fuss about a couple of beers. Let 'im fix 'is own 'orse. I'm off to see whether young Frances 'as put together a bite of supper.'

They had to forage for themselves in the cold kitchen. Timmins made a Welsh rarebit with cheese and onions and Russian bread. Neither of the women appeared.

'There's been a tiff, Louis. His lordship off with the trap and the ladies keepin' quiet in their rooms. He drank more 'n was good for 'im last night and made a fool of 'imself, but there must be more to it than that because 'er ladyship's not one to get 'er 'ackles up over one drink too many.'

A while later they heard Isadora's tread on the stairs, and the side-door of the house opened and closed. Timmins nodded his head and raised an eyebrow toward the sound.

Louis sat on at the kitchen table after Timmins had gone to bed. Where had she gone, alone in the dark? Why hadn't she put her head round the door as she passed or left a word about where she was going?

Beyond the window, wisps of cloud scuttled across a heavy grey sky. He put on his boots and donkey jacket and went out. The wind had got up and there was a false dusk, oddly bright without moon or sun, and everything on the move, trees, hedges, grasses. He took the path by the lake shore because his anxiety seemed obscurely connected with the lake, hurrying on with his jacket pulled around him against the wind.

The waters of the lake were picked up and driven by the wind in plumes of spray that spattered his face. He crossed the wooden bridge over the smaller of the Yeo streams and came under the castle wall among the booming cedars, with the fingers of ivy thrown wildly above the ruinous coping. Somewhere here was the door, but he missed it and was turning again when it opened a few yards away and Isadora came hurrying through it, not closing it behind her. She did not see him and he was unable to call out and afraid to run after her and frighten her. He knew at once that it was her, something in her profile or her movement, something intimate to which he was alert. During a lull in the wind he heard her on the wooden bridge where the planks rubbed and squeezed under her tread and he thought of her wild like the ivy and driven like the spray.

Should he go after her? But he was already through the doorway and the wind slammed the door behind him. The path wound muddily upwards towards the keep and as he followed it he heard the whinny of a horse by the gatehouse where it was too dark to see. Kelynack must still be here, and she had seen him... and they had argued or... Be quiet, mind. Stop it and be still.

There was no lantern lit by the shaft. The horse whinnied again and he walked over to the gatehouse and there was the black filly, standing in its traces and tied by the rein to a ring in the wall. 'Steady on girl,' he murmured, patting her neck. 'He'll be back before long.' But it was puzzling where Kelynack could have got to after Isadora's visit. Had she been crying? It seemed to him that he had seen the glisten of tears on her face.

He returned to the pit. There was no sign of Kelynack but even in the gloom he could see that the mouth of the pit lay open. The strangeness of where he was struck him and he crouched with his back to the wall of the tower, wanting something solid behind him. One of the lanterns lay by his feet, on its side. Timmins had driven three six-inch nails into the porous mortar of the wall, one for each lantern. '*This* is where they belong,' he had said, hanging them up, 'and not anywhere else.' He had a place for the matches as well, a niche in the wall. Louis felt for it at head height and there it was, with the matches tucked to the back, still dry. He lit the lantern and swung it over the hole, seeing the tarp and the poles pushed aside, one other lantern unlit, and none on the hooks, which meant that Kelynack had taken the third one with him, wherever he had gone.

Kelynack must be off somewhere and would come back because his pony was there waiting for him. He didn't like to confront the other explanation, but he couldn't avoid it either and it meant climbing down the ladder, just in case. It was an unappealing prospect. Not just because of the one-handed descent, but because of the sense of a thronging dark issuing from the pit.

Not to descend into the pit seemed like a failure of courage. He went down, step by step, and it was further than it should have been, as if the ladder was elongating below him. This peculiar thought took hold of him. Anything seemed possible in that black hole, with the light of the lantern dancing from one side of the shaft to the other, blinding him when it swung too close to his eyes. As he stepped on firm ground at last, he held the lantern above his head. The light lit the great stone slab but he had to reach out further to make it penetrate into the tomb itself. At first he thought his eyes were creating shapes where there were none. But the shapes persisted and steadied as his eyes accustomed to the flickering gloom and he was staring at a twisted body in the stone coffin and when he saw the eyes staring at him he knew that it was Kelynack, dead.

He started for the ladder. But could he be sure the man was really dead? Knocked out maybe. Slipped, fell and hit his head. Were the eyes open when you were knocked out? No. Dead then. As a doornail. Why should a doornail be deader than... than a door? Kelynack was dead as a door... and it was here in his distracted rambling that he was forced to think about what he had not wanted to think about, that Isadora had killed him.

She'd left the house without a word, she'd been here at the castle and run away and now here was his body, dead as a door. The door joke insisted on interfering with any more serious thought, protecting him, in its peculiar way. She might have done it. Could it have been an accident? He must examine the body to see how it had died.

He crouched over the edge of the tomb and held up the lantern, ignoring the open eyes and mouth, in pain or shock at the encounter with Death, looking instead at the body, splayed over the edge of the coffin.

He thought Kelynack might have fallen into the tomb breaking his neck on the edge of the lid, which would explain the contorted position of the body, with one leg twisted this way and the other that, and an arm bent outside-in. Moving his lantern, the light fell on the man's torso and from the abdomen protruded the prongs of a fork, curved and glinting in the light of the lantern. The blood that had oozed from the wounds formed a dark patch spreading over the trousers and shirt.

She had killed him with George's pitchfork. The thin curved tines had been driven right through his body.

Was she capable of such fury? He wanted to deny it, but always in Isadora he had been aware of the quality of extreme – her extreme beauty and extreme grace and extreme... detachment from the ordinary. She might, he thought, if wronged or humiliated, be subject to a moment of violence.

George's pitchfork was preferred by him to rake or digging fork. His brother Mick used to tease him – 'as if th'art married to the darned thing'. George kept it clean and sharp. ''Er's no use if 'er's blunt'. Perhaps the strength of a woman might be enough to drive the needle-sharp prongs through a man's stomach.

She had grabbed up the pitchfork and – surely she cannot have meant to kill him – stabbed him. Nothing else could explain her manner as she fled from the castle. She had attacked him as they stood at the top of the shaft and pushed the body into the hole. Perhaps it had been the fall onto the lid of the tomb that had killed him – but there would be no talk of an accident with the body run through by the prongs of a pitchfork.

I could turn it over and pull out the fork, he thought. I could pull out the fork, but the wounds would be there still, and if I take away the fork and destroy it, George will miss it, there's nothing surer than that.

The deed could not be concealed so the body must be. The fork withdrawn and cleaned, the body disposed. Up the ladder carrying the body to ... to the lake? Impossible. But wait, the body can go into the coffin and the lid be put back. He said he was going away for a while. Release the pony, destroy the trap and then Kelynack has left as he said he would, nobody knows where. With him gone, the excavation is over. We come back here, fill in the hole, leave everything neat and tidy...

Put the lid back. Destroy the trap. For that I'll need Timmins. How to tell Timmins that she killed him? Even Timmins, who thinks the world of her, wouldn't understand *that*. Nobody would except me. Françoise perhaps, but I can't get Françoise out here in the dark with the body, and what would either of us do with the trap? Timmins can pull it apart with his bare hands and fling the bits into the lake. But first: get the fork out.

Get the fork out is four words. Turning a corpse in a coffin and making it lie still when you start tugging at what's stuck into it means getting in there and shifting the limbs about and putting your foot on the torso so that the body stays where it is while you extract the darned fork, whose tines seemed to have grabbed hold of whatever's inside. The innards. The tines were twisted up with the innards.

Then his foot slipped when he was pulling and the body reared up at him from the floor of the tomb. God.

The fork came out at last, bringing nothing much with it except more blood, mercifully. But there was more blood now around the holes, the upper part of the trousers were saturated. If Timmins saw that, he'd know. He wouldn't miss two holes in the belly and a bucketful of blood and take it for a man breaking his neck in a fall.

So he had to get the lid on by himself. It was half-way on and half-way off. He remembered what a job three of them had had with the lid, solid stone two or three inches thick.

He used the handle of the pitchfork as a lever and it broke. He thought that being shorter it might be stronger but it snapped again. He managed to wedge a flattish rock under the coffin lid thinking if he could tilt it he might shift it but it wouldn't budge. The light of the lantern flickered, gave off a curl of black smoke and went out.

He had no fear of the body, no feeling for the death. But the dark swallowed everything. The sense of something thronging returned and he thought he could hear a low humming noise. Climb the ladder in this black nothingness, fetch the other lantern? It might also be low on oil or empty.

He thought the slab might have caught on something, some small obstacle and if he pulled instead of pushing, he might move it. There was still nothing before his eyes but a blanket of black, his foot missed the slab and he pitched helplessly forward striking the top of his head against the other side of the tomb. As he landed on top of Kelynack's corpse, he was aware of nothing, not where or who he was or anything at all.

Later when he had forgotten the pain and the blood on his clothes and the cold stickiness of the body underneath him after he woke, he remembered that moment of lying senseless on Kelynack's corpse in a tomb older than the abbey – older than any existence that could be comprehended – and it seemed to him as if Somebody, Somewhere had assembled a uniquely peculiar set of circumstances

in a uniquely peculiar place in order to conduct an experiment...
With himself, with his life.

The thronging shaft and half-open tomb, the murderous prongs of the fork, the thick blackness when the light went out, the Sisyphean struggle with the slab and a crack on the head that might have brained him – when he put all this together in his mind, he knew that he might have been found in the morning dead in Kelynack's arms or have been fetched up gibbering ready for an asylum, or he might have recovered his balance on the coffin top and pulled the slab neatly home. The difference between these outcomes, he thought, was no more than the throw of a dice that skittered and tumbled across the floor to show *this* sign or *that*, and not *that*. The large question was – Who cast the dice?

This unanswerable question was no doubt connected with the dream that followed. He decided to call it a dream and then thought trance was a better word, or concussion if you were telling a doctor, or vision if you didn't baulk at the idea, but none of these conveyed the vivid sense of reality as he climbed out of the tomb and groped for the ladder in the impenetrable dark with his arms out in front to tell him where the wall was, and found himself in a hollow space that was not there before.

The reddish light that dimly lit this space suggested an unseen maze of tunnels and somewhere a distant source of light or fire or whatever else may exist when you go below the surface of things. He saw the rock walls of a passage as if lit by a lantern of red-tinted glass, with their seams and knuckles of rock. The passage opened out into a wider chamber and the wall of rock opposite him was alive with soft trickles and plashes of water making their way down its face. The light was stronger or his eyes more accustomed and this face of rock was intricately beautiful, worn smooth in places by the water and elsewhere carved into shapes and traceries, as of figures and limbs, some of great grace and delicacy while others were awkward, blunt and somehow threatening.

He was gazing at a figure whose lower limbs were distinctly smooth and feminine, when something, not water, began to move in the lowest part of the rock face where bulbous shapes crouched among the mosses and waterweeds. In a metamorphosis altogether miraculous, a wraithlike figure emerged, detaching itself limb by limb from the flanks and lirks of wet rock. It slipped from the shadows and protuberances that had contained it and slid towards him across the floor, sending forth a shaft or root from its base and attaching itself to Louis' feet.

A faint jolt attended this conjunction and he shivered, as if a charge of something had leapt upwards through his body. The cascading wall was gone like a piece of scenery from a stage, and he and whatever-it-was were sitting together in an alcove by the side of the passage, himself on one rock and the other on a second rock, still joined at the feet.

'You were fortunate,' said the other in a voice low and fluent like the place he had come from. 'If one of the others had got to you first, you would have found yourself upside down hanging from your ankles or in some other most discomfortable situation.'

'Why are we joined at the feet?' Louis asked.

'It is the unalterable arrangement between a person and his

shadow. It is rarely noticed, being unremarkable to the person and to the shadow a fundamental condition of existence.'

The word 'fundamental' was stressed, perhaps because it was so utterly opposed to the being that said it. As they spoke, the shadow's personality became stronger. At first it was like water or wind, assuming its shape and temper from the surroundings, but as time passed it became more robust and more disposed to be argumentative.

'You are not my shadow,' Louis said.

'You arrived without one, a most dangerous undertaking, and I reacted more swiftly than the others. It may have looked simple, the business of emerging from the rock, but it isn't. I have done it before and most of the others have not. There is one, however, who has done it many times and you were fortunate that he was concealed somewhere very deep or gone off on one of his errands, because in *his* company you would not have lasted one second.' The shadow clicked his fingers to denote this tiny portion of time. The gesture was expressive but no sound resulted. 'You see? Our footfall makes no sound, nor our hands or our bones. The voice is borrowed from inside your head, of course.'

'What are you made of?' A series of important questions was beginning to queue up in Louis' mind. I must remember, he told himself, to listen to the answers and not to lose myself in getting ready the next question.

'I am made of you,' the shadow answered smoothly. 'How could it be otherwise? I use your lineaments in the light that comes not from the sun.'

'Who is the one you spoke of, with whom I wouldn't last one

second?' Louis also clicked his thumb and finger, to see whether there would be the usual sound. There was.

'There is no useful answer to that question. I mentioned him because I want you to be alert to the extreme dangers of this place.'

'Dangers of what?'

'Everything. Most people who stumble in here do not stumble out again.'

'They die.'

'Looked at from your point of view, that is correct. They change state is how I should put it but it amounts to the same thing.'

'What do they die of?'

'What people usually die of. Fear is the commonest cause. Greed. Confusion. Stupidity.'

'I thought most people died of old age and accidents.'

'When you are old, you will understand what old age is. You take it to be the decay of the body, but that is only part of it and not the most important part. Old people are more fearful, greedy, confused and stupid than the rest. That's why they die more often.'

'That,' replied Louis, thinking of his grandmother, 'is an uncharitable and spiteful...'

'Don't yield to fear, greed and confusion,' interrupted the shadow. 'The rest is unimportant. I may think of you as callow, disloyal and dishonest, but what does that matter to you? Same for the old folk. How to live with themselves, that's the problem, especially if bound to a chair or a bed in a narrow room.'

'How to feed themselves is a more real worry, I should have thought.'

'More old people die because they stop eating than because they have nothing to eat.'

Louis thought this might be true. 'You can think, then. Or do you borrow your thoughts as well as the rest of you?'

'Thinking is what we do. We are a kind of thought caught in the absence of light.'

Louis argued that as far as he could see a shadow could never have any life of its own. The shadow disagreed, pointing out that sorcerers and magicians of all times knew the importance of shadows, especially in the early morning and late evening when the shadow of a man might reach the foot of a mountain or stretch out across the ocean. At midday, he went on, a man's shadow is weak and almost worthless, doing nothing but lying in a shapeless pool at his feet, but when he walks in the woods at eventide with the sun at his back it runs before him, rippling over roots and climbing trees, moving at speeds and performing actions inaccessible to human beings. At such times, he concluded, a shadow may gather a rare kind of energy which if a man knows how to unlock it he may use to fly, or to dart through the water like a fish.

'Why doesn't a shadow die when its owner dies,' Louis asked.

'Ownership is a false description since a man can not live without a shadow, which is not true of anything else he might own, from a house to a harrow. The relationship is geminate,' the shadow continued, expounding on the relation between light and shadow, how shadow was a child of light – given shape by light, given birth by light – yet a negation of its parent. Shadow in fact was a principle of life on earth, just as light was and he told stories from ancient legend as evidence. Louis found these stories unlike anything he had heard, apparently arbitrary and without meaning yet belonging to the magnitude of stars and planets, death and purgatory, the wisdom of astrologers, things large and very old and entrancing. Afterwards he knew there was much he did not grasp of the shadow's words and much that he did not remember.

'Where are we?' he asked eventually.

'It has many names up above. Land of the Shades, the Underworld, Tartarus.'

'Why here?'

'If you mean below the Old Castle at Sherborne, it is a misapprehension. You came by means of the Old Castle, which being a Caer Sidh in the ancient tongue, is an entrance. There's another at Glastonbury, another at the Giant's Grave, another at Silbury, several in the barrows, or what's left of them. They all lead to the same place, which being beyond Time is also beyond Space. Here is where we are and now is when we are and that's all there is.'

'I arrived by accident then.'

'The old warriors used these entrances to reach the Underworld if they had the courage. You came here because you started the fire and fell in love with the wrong person and climbed into the Forger's Pit at dead of night — a series of follies you might have avoided if you weren't so ... confused.'

The shadow tensed. The sinews or tissue that held him together grew taut and the rest of him drifted away leaving a thin coil of something. 'He's coming. The one I told you about. He's coming *fast*,' the shadow whispered urgently. 'Swap with me.'

Thinking he meant change places Louis jumped up.

'Swap forms, you fool. It's you he's after. Be me.'

Louis stole a glance over his shoulder. There was nothing but the reddish glow of the passageway, but again came the sense of a thronging multitude somewhere beyond.

'Turn your attention to your feet,' the shadow hissed. 'Put yourself in your feet. You will feel a pull. Yield to it. If you do not, you may die.'

This was said with such urgency that he complied, and as soon as he turned his attention to his feet, he was aware of the pull as of a powerful wind.

A sudden resistance arose in him against being dragged out of his body and he fought against it. I am in my head. The head is where I live, he thought. He shut his eyes tight and had the sensation of a third eye between the other two, an inner eye full of space and light. It was a gateway, he realised, to another place, and he stayed there knowing it for a refuge.

No entity came. No masterful spirit, prince of ghouls, ring wraith or thrall. There was nothing but him and the shadow, made of him. When he ordered the connection at his feet to be severed, it was done, with the same jolt as before and when he opened his eyes again, he saw the coil of black shadow retreating and dwindling, with its voice now barely audible, like the last moan of wind at the death of a storm.

'I nearly swallowed you,' the shadow wailed. 'So. Nearly. Swallowed. You. Down.'

When Louis got back to The Slape he went quietly upstairs not to disturb the women and roused Timmins with the whispered words 'I've killed Kelynack'. Timmins caught hold of him like a poacher catches a bird.

'Steady on, Timmins!'

Timmins saw who it was and removed his big hand from his neck.

'Louis, don't ever creep up on me and play games in the middle of the night. Don't ever do that.'

'It's not a game.'

'If you need me, knock at my door and I'll be up in a flash, or as close to a flash as I get these days. Now, say it again.'

'I've killed Kelynack.'

'I thought that's what it was. Go down to the kitchen and stoke up the fire and put the kettle on the hob and when I come down tell me once more and I'll believe you.'

Timmins came down in what he called his boiler suit, a shapeless, baggy thing that had once been blue. He explained it was what the boiler men on trains wore and he used it for painting or fixing up or taking apart, and Louis was glad to see him in it because there was the trap to be dismantled, which was the first task according to him.

'Let's go step-by-step,' Timmins said. 'Mr Kelynack is hurt.'

'He's dead.'

'In our hole at the castle?' Timmins asked, examining the state of Louis' clothes, hands, boots, hair. 'You found 'im?'

'Yes.'

'But you didn't push him.'

Louis hesitated and Timmins gave him no time to go on. 'I know you didn't.' 'How?'

'Because you're a bad liar, one. Because you're not the sort to push people down holes, two. Because you ain't blubbin' or shiverin' or spillin' your tea. Three, four, five. What were you doin' in the hole in the first place?'

'The pony was at the gatehouse, a lantern was missing. I thought I should take a look.'

'You went to the castle looking for Isadora, didn't you?'

'No.'

'You went out because she left without a hello or good-bye and you were worryin' for her. That's because you're carryin' a torch for her, as anyone can see with half an eye. I heard you go out and I knew why you was goin'. Tell me the truth Louis, or I'm off back to bed.'

'I saw her, she was... You know how composed she always is, how whole she is. She was like a wild thing, Timmins, and when I found the body, I knew she must have done it. That's why I had to get the lid on, to stop you from seeing the holes in the body.'

''Ang on, 'ang on. Not so fast.'

He repeated his words, slower.

'Shame you went to the bother of trying to shift that bloody great slab. The first thing I'd 'ave done if I found the lid on would've been to take it off again and see why it was on. I'm a nosey parker, Louis, and I like to know what's what.'

'I set the pony free.'

'Did you now?'

'I led her back here, with the trap. I unhitched her and gave her a slap on her rump and she trotted off.'

'I see.'

'What we've got to do is take the trap apart and throw the bits into the lake.'

'What you've got to do, old son, is go to bed,' said Timmins. 'And what I've got to do is take a walk to the castle and climb down the 'ole and take a look. And there'll be no argument about that, so don't start.'

Still, he put the trap in the barn before he went and shifted a few bales of straw so it couldn't easily be seen. When he came back as it was getting light, he put a few more bales of straw around and over, locked the door of the barn and put the key in his pocket. Then he went in and made himself breakfast and waited for the household to stir. When he heard the women on the move but neither of them came down, he knew it had been more than a tiff and wondered what it had to with Françoise, who would have called in at the kitchen to pass the time of day otherwise. There was an ache in the region of his heart when he realised that she wasn't coming.

'Well, lordy me, Corporal Timmins,' he said to himself, 'who would of thought it at your age.' It wasn't so much his age that bothered him but his penniless condition and lack of any prospects to interest a fine young girl like her. 'Dammit, you old toe-rag, give over thinkin' on that maid when there's a battle to be fought.'

Louis came down later with his eyes sunken and tense. He went off while his tea was brewing to check on the trap. Timmins saw him from the window, heading for the barn. When he came back, they looked at each other and knew they were on the same side.

'What did you do with the pitchfork?' Louis asked.

'It were broke up already. I picked up the pieces and threw 'em in the tomb before I shut the lid.'

'You did shut it then.'

'It only needed a prod to go back to where it was when we found it so I thought that was best.'

'It didn't look like an accident, did it?'

'That's 'ardly the point, Louis. The point is that our lady upset the good citizens of the town by cheatin' on 'er lawfully wedded 'usband, ran off with the history master and, worst of all, came back to these parts, where she should never 'ave shown her face again.'

'She didn't go near the town that I saw.'

'Here's near enough, old son. If this gets out, she'll be found guilty by the populace, even if she can prove she was in bed with pneumonia when it 'appened. She's a foreigner, she's the most beautiful woman they ever saw and she's an adulteress. Forgive my tongue what said the word, Louis,' he added, seeing the look on the boy's face, 'but they'll be callin' 'er worse than that.'

'What do we do?'

'Here's my idea. We pick up the lads. We tell 'em the excavation's done with, that Kelynack's took the stuff and gone off and told us to fill in the pit. Then we all set to and fill it in, and you can make some pictures to show that the job was done in order and official.'

'Kelynack will be missed, sooner or later.'

'It might be much later, old son.'

Chapter Twelve

SMELL OF A RAT

Though the mills of God grind slowly,
Yet they grind exceeding small;
Though with patience He stands waiting
With exactness grinds He all.
  Henry Wadsworth Longfellow

MOLLY THE pony had taken her time returning home. There was spring grass and freedom on the way and they tasted fine. When Julius was told that she had appeared in the courtyard at Gifford, he commented that his grandson wasn't much for looking after horses and would soon be over to fetch her back. A few days passed and a few more and Kelynack didn't come and there was no letter or telegram. Julius thought of something he had to do in Sherborne and when his business was done he talked to the custos and learned that the digging was finished and Austin Kelynack gone a week before. So he went to the police station to have a word with Constable Bright.

When Bright saw the expensive carriage and the pair of chestnuts, each with the same white flash, he got out his obsequious look and wore it throughout the afternoon. He suggested they drive to The Slape, informing the old man it was where Austin Kelynack had been residing during the excavation. The door of The Slape was opened by Isadora, who told them that Kelynack had left at night when the roads were wet and she hoped there had been no accident.

'We would have heard of an accident, Mrs Runciman,' Bright said, 'and somebody would have found the trap.'

Julius put his arm round her and assured her that there must be a simple explanation, but as they returned to Sherborne he was damned if he could think of one.

'I smell a rat, your lordship,' was Bright's comment.

'I am plain Mr Kelynack, Constable. Please make the usual enquiries locally and inform the other local constabularies of Austin's disappearance. Send me a telegram at Gifford if there's anything to report. Or if there is not,' he added, and drove home.

While they were at The Slape, Bright had heard a man's laugh issuing from inside the house followed by a girlish squeal and these noises had irritated him. The soldier and the young Russian filly were up to some game, but what game exactly? What makes a girl squeal?

He considered the situation at The Slape and found it offensive. Two women, a soldier and a schoolboy sharing a house. It occurred to him for the first time that Isadora was the subject of the vulgar verses found in Yeoman's pocket. Perhaps Mrs Runciman was in the habit of granting favours to schoolboys as well as to members of staff. What sort of favours? Bright drew a breath and leashed his imagination for the time being. The fact was that Yeoman was at the house and Kelynack wasn't, which surely suited the boy very well, and the soldier too. Since Mrs Runciman was said to have no money, the rent of the house had no doubt been paid by Kelynack. Very nice. Very nice indeed. Somebody at Castleton would know about the rent. But first things first. Where was the trap?

The next day he started his search at the Old Castle, where there was nothing remaining of the excavation but a patch of dug soil in the keep surrounded by trampled vegetation, a scrap of torn tarpaulin, a holed bucket and a roughly built ladder. He made a circuit of the castle wall, poking among the brambles and nettles, and finding nothing.

He walked back into town, following Long Street. As boys, they had called it Rich Man's Row, or simply Rich Street, to go with Cheap Street. The Conduit they called 'the conker', in accordance with the usual schoolboy disparagement of the old and peculiar. Down Rich Street, right at the conker, up Cheap Street, left down Abbey Road to the cubbyhole of the custos.

'Afternoon, Custos.'

'What are you after, Bright?'

'Where's your boy?'

'Where I put 'im.'

'I want a word with him.'

''Ave your word with me.'

'Kelynack's disappeared.'

'Then what?'

'I want your boy to tell me when he left and why.'

'What's it to you?'

'You'll hear about it sooner or later.'

'Boy says Kelynack 'opped it on account of what they found at the keep. At the bottom of the 'ole were a tomb. Inside the tomb were a skellington with its mouth open, and among the bones were a golden sword and a pile of jewels.'

'Where was Kelynack?'

'I'll get to that. The rain came on and they ran about, and the boy said Timmins brought up the stuff in a sack. It were rainin' cats and dogs by then and they scarpered. Boy went down the ladder in the pissin' rain, but there was nothin' there but the bones. Whatever was in there was took away, 'e said, and that were the night Kelynack drove off. Boy were over at The Slape later and saw Kelynack gettin' the trap out.'

'It was pouring with rain, you said.'

'Boy came back and 'ad some tea and went off again when the rain let up.'

'In the dark.'

'Stick to the point, Bright. Kelynack's gone off. Wot's 'e gone off with? That's yer first question. And next, who do it belong to?'

'To Lord Kenelm surely.'

'You'd 've thought so, but you'd be wrong. Hulme says there's a law called Treasure Trove making anythin' dug up the property of the Queen. If she finds out about it, nat'rally. My bet is that they dug up somethin' worth 'avin' and Kelynack made off with it.'

'Where's the trap then?'

The custos shrugged. 'A pony don't get free of a harness without someone unbucklin' it. The pony 'ad no bit and no bridle when it arrived at Gifford. I know that because I asked old Kelynack about it. You never thought of askin' that, Bright, did yer?'

'If the horse were set loose, the trap must be around somewhere.'

'Somewhere between 'ere 'n Bristol.'

Bright took his leave and from the window of his den, the custos observed his progress across the courts as far as the Head's lodge.

The School Governors had given Hulme the use of the headmaster's big study overlooking the courts, and Hulme had brought in some grandiose furniture of his own. These articles had belonged to Hulme's grandfather, who had spent his life in a Somersetshire parsonage with the proper complement of heavy oak desks and large oak tables and pew-like benches that over long years had acquired the dark solemnity Hulme thought appropriate to a Reverend Headmaster's study. Kenelm had noted the new furniture and bluntly warned Hulme against 'moving in'.

Bright found Hulme installed in what was more throne than chair behind a desk which had required the door to be taken off its hinges to get it inside.

'Ah, Constable,' said Hulme. 'I have a bill for eight hundred pounds for the repairs to Science Five, reminding me that we have not yet got to the bottom of that matter.'

'The fire was started by the boy Yeoman, Headmaster. A case might be made, but we lack solid evidence.'

'Yeoman did not act on his own, Constable. It was a conspiracy. I could point out to you the boys likely to have been involved.'

'My enquiries have led in a rather different direction, sir. I believe the fire may be connected with the... indiscretions of the headmaster's wife.'

'Indiscretions? There was more than one?'

'It is a delicate matter to discuss before a churchman, sir.'

'At this desk, I am headmaster of the King's School first and Our Lord's humble servant second. You may speak frankly.'

'You may recall that the boy was in possession of some verses. The subject was a woman, in a state of... undress. Unfortunately Dr Runciman permitted the boy to destroy the verses, but they indicated an improper feeling for an older woman. It seems that she had called out to the boy. *Summoned* was the word used.'

'Extraordinary!' The implications were beyond Hulme's imagining.

'Indeed, sir. I had put the verses to the back of my mind, but in the light of recent events, they have come to the fore.'

'What events?'

The constable informed Hulme of Kelynack's disappearance, ending with the revelation – made with an appearance of embarrassment – that Yeoman was now living with the Russian women in Castleton.

'Good Lord! Is his father aware of this?'

'That is more your province than my own, Headmaster.'

'Quite right, Constable. I shall write to the boy's father at once.'

'I wonder, Dr Hulme, if that might be postponed for a few days.

There is a connection, I am convinced, between the fire, Kelynack's disappearance and the goings-on in Castleton. It would be helpful not to disturb things until I have discovered what that connection may be.'

'Very well, Bright. I wish to be kept informed on a daily basis. The good name of the school is at stake.'

Bright had no sooner gone than Rugg arrived. He didn't trouble with a pretext for his visit, assuming rightly that Hulme would at once repeat whatever had just been said.

'Bright is taking up the matter of the fire once more, Custos. Yeoman did it, he says.'

'My own testimony suggested it, Headmaster.'

'What do you know about the family, Custos?'

'Old Yeoman don't come often. Dressed like a gen'leman when 'e does. Nice pair of 'orses and decent carriage. But 'e pays late and always takes off a few items. The Chief – Mr HH, I mean – took 'im to task for it once but it didn't make no difference. Yeoman calls 'imself a farmer but doesn't get 'is hands dirty. I 'ad that from the boy Louis when 'e were still a nipper and didn't give 'imself airs. Good little chap 'e were then but 'e were took under Mr Grindlay's wing and Mr Biffen's, won a handful of prizes and got like they get when they do too much readin' and not enough runnin' about.'

'I'll be blunt, Custos. I want to know if Mr Yeoman could afford the bill for the fire if it were proved that it was started by his son.'

''E's got two hundred acres near Bridgewater. There's money, but it ain't readily spent. 'E'd fight a court case is my bet and the lawyers would make off with most of the cash.'

'The bill for Science Five is eight hundred pounds, Custos!'

'It were me what passed you the bill, sir.'

'It would pay for a new cricket pavilion.'

Rugg made a swift calculation. Actual cost of pavilion 500, plus builder 200, Rugg 100. 'You'd get a good pavilion for eight 'undred, Headmaster.' Or, preferably, builder one, Rugg two. 'But you'd best stay away from the Law. Old Yeoman might pay up if 'e knew that 'is one and only son won't get to Oxford if 'e don't. That and the shame of it if the story got about.'

'Threat of expulsion and humiliation.'

'That's the ticket, sir.'

'It must be done this term, while I am… before any permanent decision is made on…' Hulme cleared his throat. 'The new pavilion will be called the Hulme Pavilion, with a brass plaque to say so.'

'Very good, Headmaster.'

'At the top, the School Crest. Then the name.'

Returning to his den, the custos sent word for his boy, who was keeping an eye on the wrapping-up of the works at Science Five. He was found and came.

'What did yer lay yer 'ands on, twerp?'

The boy shrugged. 'Bit o' dressed stone. Odds and ends of timber. Builder's man took the rest.'

'Did 'er? I'll 'ave a word. You can wheel it 'ome and stack it proper later. For now, you'll stick close to Bright.'

'Till when?'

'Till I say so. Don't let 'im out of yer sight. 'E knows something I don't. Find out what. See what 'appened to the stuff dug up at the keep. Gold and jewels or a heap o' bones, I want to know where they are. Get up to The Slape this evening when they're at their supper. 'Ave a look round the yard and keep an eye open for Kelynack's trap.'

'Kelynack went off. I told yer.'

'Maybe 'e did and maybe 'e didn't. Don't tell Bright that yer goin' for a snoop up Castleton way.'

'I weren't born yesterday.'

The custos reached out swiftly, caught hold of the boy's ear and gave it a good twist.

'I know when you were born, twerp. I were the one what made yer. I'm still makin' yer. When yer made, go off and get a 'undred pound and bring me fifty. Then we'll 'ave a new account. Until then, it's thre'pence a day, and nothin' if there's no result.'

'Ought to be a tanner,' said the boy, still twisted up.

The custos increased the pressure, like winding a clock. 'I've known ears come right off.'

The boy was doubled up, but made not a sound. The father released him.

''Ere's thre'pence for today's business. And 'ere's another thre'pence because you may 'ave to be out and about with Bright and if 'e doesn't stand you to a hunk and a wet for dinner—which knowin' 'im 'e won't—yer'll 'ave to buy it yerself. Tell 'im I sent you. Tell 'im that particular. If 'e squawks, send 'im 'ere.'

''E wont squawk,' said the boy, pocketing the coins with a grin. That grin represented a triumph of Rugg family life. A day's work was worth three pennies, the strap was ever ready on its hook and ears could come right off, but Rugg's boy felt a glimmer of pride that the constable should defer to the custos.

Bright didn't squawk and Rugg's boy found nothing at The Slape because it was too dark. But the next day he was there with Bright and they shifted the bales in the barn while Timmins stood at the door with a thunderous look. Right at the back, behind the last bale, was a bit of broken panel with four yellow letters on it. The letters were UBBA and Rugg's lad knew them at once for the middle part of the name of Hubbard the coachmaker, and Bright caught on later and pretended he'd known all along.

Not a scrap of iron was found, not a fragment of padded seat or wooden spoke. Just that one piece of board with the four yellow letters.

'What's that, Bright?' Timmins asked.

'Piece of Kelynack's trap, that's what.'

Bright disliked soldiers. He disliked their flash uniforms and the way they went about in groups and the sense they conveyed of having something large and powerful at their back. Timmins had no uniform and went about on his own, but he smelled of the army and ran after little Russian maids.

'Kelynack left with the pony and the trap,' Bright went on. 'Pony turns up thirty miles away and what's left of the trap turns up in your barn.'

'That bit of panel don't mean nothing. It's what's on all of Hubbard's wagons. The geyser who owns The Slape had one, I s'pect, and broke it up for firewood when it got old.'

He picked up a hay bale and started to put the barn to rights.

'Hold on, Timmins. We're not finished here yet.'

He strolled about, studying the stalls and inspecting the shelves. On one shelf, a ball of twine with cobwebs, hoof oil, and a curry comb. On the ground, clods of dry soil that had come in clinging to hooves and wheels. Two large wall hooks, bearing a flat cap with a hole and an old bridle with torn reins. Jetsam of hay stalks and hay seeds. Inch of dust throughout.

Bright's mind was of the smug sort, building castles before it had the bricks to make them. So, the Russian woman had killed her lover with the help of the schoolboy and the soldier, and the soldier was after the maid, and the boy was an arsonist, and all of them were sinful at The Slape.

'Hop out and find where they make their bonfires,' he told Rugg's lad. He watched Timmins stacking the hay, tossing the bales as if disappointed with them for not weighing more. He made a mental note that when it came to arresting the soldier the handcuffs should be well oiled and swiftly applied because you wouldn't want any mistakes with this feller.

The boy came back and said the fire site was round the back and Bright went to look. There'd been timber burned there he thought and not long ago, but when he spotted what he thought was a curl of blackened paintwork, it fell to pieces in his fingers and might have been something else. He didn't need it anyway. What he needed was the body.

They might have thrown it in the lake, but he didn't think so. They might have taken it somewhere and dug a hole and buried him, but they'd need to have done it at night after a day's rain.

Then the thought came to him – they had a hole already, didn't they?

'We'll 'ave a look round at the Old Castle tomorrow, Timmins. Dig up that pit of yours.'

'Do what you like. There's nothing in the pit but an old skeleton with 'is mouth open.' He eyed the constable quizzically. 'Looks a bit like you'll look later on, come to think of it. All mouth and no brain.'

'I'll want you there tomorrow, Timmins. Bring the Yeoman boy. Or I'll lock up the two of you, on suspicion.'

He gave Rugg's boy sixpence and told him to fetch a blanket and sleep out at the keep that night. Nobody could dig up the pit and remove something from it in a night, but if the case came to court, he'd have the chance to show off what he'd done and he wanted nothing missing in front of the chief constable, the coroner and the judge.

Rugg's boy took the coin and fetched his blanket to the keep, but the blanket had the place to itself until dawn next day, because he didn't fancy a night there on his own and preferred to earn his sixpence in the outhouse at home where there was a door to shut and an old mattress to do as a bed. He was back at the tower at first light and rolled up in the blanket and slept for a couple of hours in the spring sunshine. Bright found him there when he came with two of Rugg's sweepers. The custos arrived later, in a rare excursion outside the town, having been alerted by Bright, who wanted a better witness than sweepers. There was no sign of Timmins or Louis Yeoman.

The soil was loose, the men hardly needed the picks. Bright and the boy unloaded the buckets while Rugg watched from a tree stump. The abbey clock was chiming the long twelve when they came to the lid of the tomb.

Bright went down with a crowbar and Rugg's boy followed him after being told not to. The slab shifted at once, releasing a stench that had the custos reaching for his handkerchief at the mouth of the pit.

Only Rugg's boy got a good look at the corpse. Bright was content with a brief glance. There would be a coroner for the dirty work, he thought. The labourers were shocked by the stench and turned away. But Rugg's lad was peering into the tomb as the lid came off and saw with a terrible distinctness the staring face and the twisted body.

He was first up the ladder. Bright and the others followed. They withdrew a little distance from the pit to avoid the smell.

'I'll wire Chief Constable Jukes to come over from Dorchester with the coroner,' Bright said. 'They'll hardly get over before late in the afternoon and someone has to stand guard over the body until then.'

'Me and the boy'll can do it,' Rugg said.

'I don't want anything touched, Custos,' Bright warned.

In the end nothing was, because the custos was the wrong shape to climb down and his boy, despite bribes and threats, flatly refused to.

Bright went to The Slape before returning to town to send the telegram to Dorchester. Her first reaction was what counted. She was an actress, of course. She was a *courtesan*. He knew it from his favourite periodical *Alley Sloper*. In *Alley Sloper* bejewelled Indian temptresses were courtesans and the pretty bedmates of dukes and princes, their flimsy gowns hinting at a marvellous voluptuousness. It seemed to Bright that his long acquaintance with those seductive pages were a preparation for this moment when he would arrest two of these foreign harlots. Yes, two. For surely the little plump one with the big lips could be had too.

It was a policeman's prerogative to come to a person's house by whatever route he chose, and Bright exercised it when there was reason and when there was none. He circled the front of the house at a discreet distance and entered by the garden. He came to a place where a tall yew hedge ran between him and the house and from here he could hear voices. When the hedge ran out, he stepped out onto a small terrace. It was a sheltered spot that caught the afternoon sun, paved with mottled granite flags, ringed with stone pots planted with primroses and violas and partly roofed by an ancient wisteria coming into bud. Bright was oblivious to these qualities yet there was a quiet intimacy among the four people round the table that discomfited him. They all looked up but nobody stood.

'Mr Kelynack's body has been found in the tomb under the keep,' he announced.

He watched Isadora as he spoke. She dropped her fork, her face paled, her hand went to her mouth. It was perfectly done, he thought.

Timmins's expression was impassive. The maid gave a kind of yelp, like a lapdog. The boy kept quiet, his face turned away.

'The body was put inside the tomb and the slab pulled over him,' he continued. 'He was murdered. One of you did it, or all of you.'

He had the rest of it ready – the trap broken up and burned in the yard, the hasty filling of the pit – but he wasn't given the chance to produce it. Isadora stood up, steadying herself with her hand on the edge of the table.

'Your behaviour is outrageous,' she said. 'Corporal Timmins, please show this person out.'

Timmins rose from his chair.

'Mrs Runciman, you are not in a position...' began Bright.

'I am in my own house, where you have intruded in such unmannerly fashion. If he does not leave at once, Corporal, eject him without ceremony.'

Françoise was at her side and took her arm. They turned and went through the french windows into the drawing-room.

'I have some questions for you, madam,' Bright called out, but she didn't look round.

Timmins stood up. 'You heard Mrs Runciman's instructions, Bright.'

'I have things to ask you too, Timmins.'

'Not 'ere and not now, you 'aven't.'

Chapter Thirteen

SKIAPHAGOS

'I'm asking you this'—and No-man struck the stones of the road with his great oak cudgel—'because I must know! Are you just playing with these supernatural influences, with these Powers as you call them, or do you take them as actually real, real as this stick, real as the cap in your pocket?'

John Cowper Powys

THAT DAY and the following morning Isadora kept to her room wishing to be left alone. Timmins told Louis they ought to warn her of the danger she was in before Bright came back, but Louis worried that it meant admitting to thinking she had killed Kelynack. He didn't know what to make of the fact that she hadn't asked to see the body, but on balance he wished she had.

Louis had not been well during the fortnight since his ordeal in the shadow pit. He had moments of confusion and sometimes had difficulty in concentrating on what he was doing. It was as if, he thought, he was not quite all there. There was an ache in his neck and left shoulder, like a weight pulling him down on one side. Once or twice his left hand seemed reluctant to do what was asked of it. At other times there was a sharp, stabbing pain over his left eye.

'It's that crack on the head,' Timmins said. 'A man in the Crimea got a crack on the head like that and couldn't remember who he was. You need something to cheer you up. Let's catch a pike in the lake and bake it for supper.'

'We can't go fishing today, Timmins.' It seemed frivolous, irreverent.

'On the contrary, old son. This is exactly the right time for fishing. What'll we do if we stay 'ere? Mope about and worry for what we can't do nothin' about? We'll leave Frances to look after Isadora and we'll 'ave a natter while we wait for the fish to bite and come up with a plan.'

He walked into Sherborne and came back with rods and lines, some hooks and two handsome floats.

'Borrowed from Thorneycroft,' he explained. ''E makes the floats 'imself.'

'What shall we use for bait?'

'Bread.'

'We won't catch pike with bread.'

'Are we that fussed, Louis? Bream, chub, tench – whatever's in there. The hooks are big'uns and if we stick a fat ball of bread on 'em, we won't be bothered by tiddlers. I ain't one for tiddlers. I like to see a fish bend the rod and splash about a bit or there's no fun in it.'

Françoise refused to be left behind, having had enough of the house.

'It's haunted, Timmin.'

'Better sleep in my room, Frances.'

'Your room is very small and there's only one bed in it, Timmin.'

'You can use the bed and I'll stand guard against the boggarts.'

'You are the boggart.'

He laughed and said he was too big for a boggart.

Not much fishing was done on their rod. The line went one way, the bread the other. She cast into the reeds and Thorneycroft's precious float bobbed away in the current. They had more fun retrieving it than fishing and when she suggested a walk round the lake, he agreed.

'You'll be glad to be rid of us, Louis.'

Louis watched their erratic progress round the lake. As the two figures grew smaller, a chill breeze sprang up, shivering the surface of the water and the pain in his shoulder came back.

When he looked for his float it had gone under. He seized the rod and struck. The rod tip bent and the line hummed.

He couldn't get the fish close enough to the surface to make out what he had hooked. A tench, holding to the bottom as they do? But this was bigger than any tench he'd heard of. A carp maybe, but he knew nothing of them. 'Stately and subtle', Isaak Walton wrote, but where had he read – not in Walton surely – that the carp was the soul-fish, growing to a great size in the still depths? He'd read it, or dreamt it.

The fish didn't run for the reed bank, just stayed immovably on the bottom, too big to reel in on the fine gut line. He looked up to see if Timmins was within shouting distance and thought he might be, but the two bright figures on the bank were gaming among the buttercups and he didn't shout out.

He heaved on the rod, quickly lowered the rod tip, tried to reel in and couldn't. How large was this fish? Larger than the twelve pound pike he'd caught on the Parrett. The line went slack and he thought he'd lost it, but the fish was swimming up towards him and he made out a black shape oddly like sea skate or sting ray, which he'd seen on fishmongers' slabs. He reeled in the slack line peering into the depths of the lake and saw the shape looming towards him through the water. He had an impression of arms or wings and just then the pain in his shoulder hit him sharply and made him catch his breath. He reached for the knife which Timmins had left with the rest of his fishing-gear and cut the line.

Afterwards he cursed. The size of the fish had been a trick of the light in the murky water, the pain in his shoulder was brought on by the strain of the rod, the wings were an illusion of his precarious mind. When Timmins came back he told him his line had caught in weed and said nothing about the fish.

After tea at The Slape, the ache in his shoulder and side was worse, and he remembered what the thing in the pit had told him about the shadows of sorcerers which darted through the waters. He left the house and walked into Sherborne to find Grindlay. How he could tell Grindlay his trouble he didn't know, but Grindlay had made the translation of 'The Book of Shadowborne', and would hardly have done so if he thought it nonsense.

Perhaps it was nonsense. Better that it should be. But the tale of Peggy Forgetmenot was no invention. The woman's bones were now buried by the lake.

As he walked into Sherborne, the pain above his eye was like a knife twisting in his brow, making him wince.

Grindlay was not in the library, which was locked. Tuffins tea-shop was also closed but Tuffin came to the door, sticking his red head out and pointing out grumpily that Mr Grindlay's quarters had a separate entrance. There was a narrow unlit staircase, an uneven landing no bigger than a bath-towel and a door with a card pinned to it saying G. Grindlay in spindly letters that looked as if it had been there as long as the door. Louis knocked, there was the sound of a chair being pushed back across bare floorboards and the door opened to reveal Grindlay's pale full-moon face, lower in the doorway than it should have been, as if Grindlay grew more gnome-like when at home.

'Good Lord, Two-and-a-Half, boys don't come here. Nobody comes here.' But the door continued to open and Mr Grindlay's withdrawal to where he had been sitting seemed an invitation to enter so Louis went in. There was space enough for a bed, a chair, a table, one narrow wardrobe and one trunk. A frayed carpet lay by the bed, thin cotton curtains bordered the single window but were not drawn. His 'quarters', Tuffin had said grandly. This was a cell and struck Louis in his precarious state of mind as somewhat dismal.

The one luxury was an abundance of lighting. Half-a-dozen lamps were lit in the room, some of them with white globes fitted over the funnel glass. There was a lamp on the top of the wardrobe, one on the trunk, two on the desk and another sharing the floorspace with neatly-stacked piles of books.

'Two-and-a-Half, your visit embarrasses me. I have only one chair, so you will have to perch on the bed. The pot of tea that Tuffin's girl brings me is left with half a cup at the most. I would suggest a move to the library but I cannot face additional bouts with those miserable stairs. It is not the stairs that are miserable, you understand, but the old person forced to negotiate them.'

He poured the remnants of the tea into the only cup and the boy took it and sat on the bed.

'I trust you do not object to drinking from my cup. People have become sticklers for what they call etiquette. The word is French, I believe, denoting ticket, like something you might purchase at a fair. The passing of the cup was an agreeable custom among Greek philosophers and medieval churchmen but the etiquettists must derive their rules from elsewhere.'

Louis followed these remarks with difficulty. His attention was caught by the multiple shadows thrown by Grindlay's head on the walls and ceiling and for a moment he wondered which Grindlay he was talking to. There was one very large and clear shadow on the ceiling that seemed particularly imposing and rather threatening.

'Forgive me Two-and-a-Half, I am infernally didactic. You have been in a predicament since we last saw each other. I was disappointed you did not call in to select some books for your exile.'

'I was allowed to come back,' Louis said with an effort.

'I am aware of it. The acting headmaster keeps me informed to an extent. But I detect that your return to this old town has not been an invigorating experience, Two-and-a-Half. You appear dejected.'

Louis tried to concentrate on what had brought him there.

'You have heard about Mr Kelynack's death, I'm sure, Mr Grindlay.'

'Kelynack is dead?' said Grindlay, astonished. 'When did this happen?'

It had not occurred to Louis that the news would have failed to reach his ears. He had imagined it running through the town like fire through stubble.

'He was found yesterday in the tomb under the castle keep. They believe... Constable Bright believes... that Mrs Runciman killed him.'

'It was no accident then?'

'It seems not.'

'This is what you came to tell me?'

'No, sir. I assumed you would have heard of it.'

'I hear little but the chiming of the abbey, Two-and-a-Half. Nobody visits but Tiffin's girl with the tea, and I suppose that she too was ignorant of this dreadful event. Immured in a tomb? What a ghastly thought.'

'It was I who found him.' Perhaps he should not have admitted this, even to Grindlay. But it was done. 'He was lost and I climbed into the pit after dark and the lantern went out. I must have fallen into the tomb with the body, knocked my head...'

'Good lord, boy. This is not some kind of elaborate joke is it?

No. I see well that it is not. You appear to have lost your equilibrium, Two-and-a-Half.'

'That's why I'm here, sir. I fell into the shadow pit and nearly lost my... my life or my soul, I can't tell... I don't feel well, sir. I don't feel whole.'

'Shadow pit?'

'I read your translation of 'The Book of Shadowborne', sir. It fell from the top shelf the day you...'

'The book is legend or folk-tale. Fairy-tale I might say.'

'Then why did you translate it, Mr Grindlay?'

Grindlay gave him a long searching look.

'Excuse me, Two-and-a-Half. This is a lot for me to absorb at once. I believe that if it were any other boy but you I would send him to the sanatorium for a sleeping draught and a week in bed. But I owe it to you to be honest with you. I started the translation of "The Book of Shadowborne" – many years ago – out of mere curiosity and to exercise my grasp of medieval Latin. I found the text obscure in parts and mischievous in others. Were it not for the evident age of the manuscript, I would have dismissed it as a hoax. Yet there were also traces of an unusual insight into certain matters that convinced me to take it seriously. How much did you read?'

'A few pages at the beginning, then the story of a woman called Peggy Forgetmenot.'

'That story appears among other stories of the same ilk, which may be fancy or fact. There is no way of telling. But the shadows themselves, the so-called shadow pit, reminded me faintly of Plato's allegory of the cave. You are familiar with it, I expect.'

'You read it with us in the fifth, sir.'

'Did I? I generally avoid it. It represents a large leap for young heads. And a still larger leap for old ones. We watch a shadow play on the wall of our cave and take it for reality. If Plato was right... Well, it's not the time for that... the point is that I came to think of the story of the stealing of men's shadows, like Plato's cave, as a kind of allegory, referring metaphorically to the stripping of men's illusions. Perhaps you did not read that far.'

'No, sir.'

'In the usual medieval fashion, the story was set about with evil demons, the chief of whom was called Skiaphagos. I recall the name because I was unsure whether to translate it literally as shadow-eater, or shadow-stealer. I chose the second, I believe.'

The conspiracy of lamps and shadows competed for Louis' attention with the drift of Grindlay's words. The old man opposite him was a talking head dimmed and dwarfed. He wished he could draw the curtains to exclude the multiplication of lamps in the window glass. The play of light and shadow, the darkness of night without and the reflections of the scene within, unsettled him. He wanted to say something about metaphor and illusion but he couldn't. He couldn't say anything. He thought if he opened his mouth nothing would emerge but a balloon of air. He pressed the palm of his hand to his forehead, wincing.

'Two-and-a-Half, you are indeed unwell.'

'A headache, sir.'

'This headache is a symptom of your malaise?'

Louis nodded.

'Then you must consult a doctor. There are doctors in town of course, but I am not acquainted with them. The matron at the school sanitorium, perhaps?'

'Not the sanitorium. I'd prefer my own bed.' His bed in an empty dormitory? His bed at The Slape? His bed at Turnworth? Islands in a wild sea.

'We shall pay a visit to Mrs Biffen, Two-and-a-Half,' said Grindlay getting up. 'I'm not sure why I should think of her. An association with the story of Shadowborne, apparently, that I am unable to account for.'

Hands in pockets, Louis followed Grindlay in his slow descent of the stairs into the windy chill of the alleyway, past the Conduit, a humpback on its knees, up a totally deserted Cheap Street below a mournful ribbon of sky, with the shops crouched bad-temperedly on either side. A plague town with no door open, lamps of mustard yellow flailing vainly against the night, the cobbles writhing under his feet, Grindlay cloaked and bent, and in the black shadows under the buildings blacker shadows, flitting between doorways.

They came to a large house with no light showing at its windows.

'Knock,' Grindlay summoned and Louis thought it must be a rule in this dark game that he be the one to knock at this door. It was a well-known entrance to him in truth but he had left the familiar world behind and when Biffen answered the knock, Louis was as surprised to see his English master as Biffen was to see him.

'Yeoman!! We are on our way to bed. Who is this with you?' Bent and hooded like an ancient monk, Grindlay stepped forward and made himself known.

'Forgive me, Biffen, this boy is unwell. I thought Mrs Biffen...'

'Come in, come in my dear sir. Come in both.'

In Mrs Biffen's kitchen, a lamp was soon lit, the range stoked, the kettle pushed on to its hotplate and Louis Yeoman installed in the armchair by the stove.

'You've heard about Kelynack, I suppose, Grindlay,' Biffen said.

'Yeoman has only now informed me.'

'Awful business. He was in this kitchen larger than life a few weeks ago. Was he not, Mrs Biffen?'

'It was the night you broke your ankle, Biffen.'

'So it was.'

'You're lucky it wasn't your neck.'

'I say, that's rather harsh, my dear.'

'I am extremely glad that it was not, Biffen,' she went on. 'Here's another casualty of the keep, I suppose,' pointing to Louis.

Grindlay set off on an explanation but Mrs Biffen cut it short.

'I've got eyes, Mr Grindlay. Sit yourself at the table with Biffen.'

'Once down, Mrs Biffen, it'll take a crane to lift me. If you permit, I shall leave Yeoman in your care and make my way. A headache, he said, but a bad one as you see, and he complains of...'

'He shall tell me himself. Biffen, step out with Mr Grindlay and see him home. Refresh him with a glass of rum at the *Cross Keys* and don't hurry back.'

Margot Biffen saw how the boy held his hand to his face with the palm pressed against the eye. She noted the circle of tension around his visible eye and the way his gaze jumped wildly round the room. She bent down and reached behind the cooking range and pulled out an earthenware roof tile of the kind called Roman which she placed on the hottest part of the stove.

'Be off with you,' she said to the men.

She removed Louis' hand from his face, examined the left eye and brow and took his pulse in three places on the left wrist and the same three places on the right. She selected a few pinches of dried herbs from the clay pots on the mantelpiece, each marked with a hand-painted symbol.

'A pinch from the cow, of course, and one from the goat, and several from the pig. The pig is a strong creature, Louis, and keeps healthy in unpromising conditions. Cleverer than the cow and easier than the goat and more affectionate than either. But you're from a farming family and know all this.'

'We have no goats.' It was Louis' first comment since setting sail from Grindlay's anchorage.

'No? A goat needs a woman, as hens do, and you're a household of men, you told me. A man can do very well with a cow and often has a real affinity with a pig.'

When the pain above his eye eased, he could see well enough. He counted twelve clay pots on the shelf, six of them were marked with a farm animal painted with a few bold strokes – pink pig, white goat, gold cow, beige sheep, chestnut horse and black hen – and the other six with symbols or signs, made with the same Chinese simplicity, two strokes for a sword, a tower with three turrets, a cross, a ring of rosettes or stones and what appeared to be a skull, which even on Mrs Biffen's kitchen shelf bore its usual malevolent look. Louis was glad that no pinches of herbs were drawn from that pot.

'The tea's for afterwards,' she told him. 'First we need heat.'
'It's only a headache, Mrs Biffin.'
'You've had many like it, I suppose.'
'No.'
'Other aches and pains?'
'My shoulder.'
'Arm?'
'That too sometimes.'
'Left leg?'
'No.'
'I warned you to be careful with that nonsense at the Old Castle, Louis.'
'It didn't seem quite like nonsense.'
'What did it seem?'

She turned the tile on the range, checking its heat with the back of her hand.

'It seemed... that there was something to be discovered. A key to a door.'

'That's all very well. There are such keys and they must be sought by those with a mind for it. But why at the bottom of a hole among things buried by strangers long ago? Ancient objects carry traces of the past, Louis, and I don't mean mud. They are better not fiddled with.'

'I haven't fiddled with anything.'

'Is that so?' she muttered, raising her eyebrows.

'The bones of the young woman on the first day. Nothing else.'

'What woman?'

He told her of the burnt level and what was found there.

'How careless of me to miss it,' she said, as if to herself.

'There was nothing to be seen by then, dark smudges on the wall of the pit.'

'There were only bones?'

'And teeth.'

'What became of them?'

'We buried them by the lake. Mrs Runciman and I.'

'It was well done. And after that?'

'There was an old tomb at the bottom of the pit. A skeleton, a sword. They are still where they were, I suppose.' He ought to tell her of the events of that night, he thought, but he hadn't the heart for it.

'How did Grindlay find you?'

'I went to his room.'

'This pain came on at Grindlay's?'

'He told me the story of a demon and it scared me.'

'What demon?'

'Skiaphagos, he called it. The shadow-stealer.'

'You're not a child, to be frightened by goblins. Goblins must be put in their place.'

Again she tested the heat of the tile. Apparently satisfied, she took a cloth from a drawer of the kitchen dresser, wrapped it round the tile and put it firmly over his brow, instructing him to hold it there. It was pleasantly warm at first but as the heat came through the cloth, it got hot and then hotter still until the heat of the tile merged with the pain over his brow and it was hard to tell which was which.

He took away the tile saying it was too hot to bear, but she pressed it back into position. 'That little flush of heat is nothing to what you're going to put up with in a minute.'

She allowed him to put it down at last, unwrapping it and returning it to the stove. She took hold of his head and began working her fingers around the ridge of bone above his left eye – it was not a massage, it was a kneading, a squeezing, a pinching, an assault.

'There's a knot,' she said. He felt her strong fingers grasping something above the bone, flattening it, beating it into submission. When she had so thoroughly kneaded and squeezed that he was on the point of crying out, she picked up the reheated tile, wrapped it once more in its cloth and put it where it was before. A torrent of heat surged around his eye, brow, cheek, head.

'Scarfag don't much like this, I can tell you.' She chuckled.

'Scarfag?' he asked blearily.

'Grindlay's goblin.'

The tile came off again and the hard fingers were back and he felt wrung like a rug after a wash. She gave him the tea and made him drink it to the last drop. When he was led upstairs and put in a bed heaped with blankets, he was only dimly aware of it. When he woke in the morning, his head felt dazed and emptied but the pain was gone. There was no ache in his shoulder and when he flexed his arm and fingers they did as they were asked.

Mrs Biffen cooked him breakfast, which in her house on a good morning was the full English with fried bread, fried tomatoes, a sausage almost long enough for a draught excluder, rashers of streaky bacon cooked crisp and two fried eggs envelope-style. Also on the table was a loaf of bread you could use for a lifebuoy, a head of hard cheddar, golden butter and greengage jam. 'If you don't care for the greengage, there's quince,' but he said greengage was good.

She made him tea with pinches of pig and pillar, explaining that it had a different purpose from the one she had made the night before. He should drink three cups, she ordered. It had a blackish, pungent taste, but everything else on the breakfast table was perfect.

'What's happened to Scarfag, Louis?'

'Gone back to where he came from,' he answered.

'Scarfag indeed. What will the old boy think of next? Have you ever wondered, Louis, at the people who are drawn to this place? Obsessive bookworms like Grindlay, diggers and delvers like Biffen, who admires nothing more than a gargoyle, men for whom a cricket pavilion is a kind of temple, money-getters pretending they're something else. An odd assortment, Louis, called by the odd humours of the place.'

'What about yourself, Mrs Biffen?'

'I'm the oddest of all! But there's work for me here and in this instance I have made a poor fist of it. I didn't think Kelynack's hole would arrive plumb on the Old Smith's grave or that we'd have boys burying bones by the lake. We'll have to go there and see what can be done to put a stop to it.'

She put on her walking boots, which were not very feminine with tall uppers, straps and buckles. 'I had these made by the Hound Street cobbler to my own design. I walk in places where women are not expected to unless they are herders of swine. Who cares to cobble a proper boot for a herder of swine? Come. We'll waste no further time.'

There was a crude hand-painted sign saying keep Out! at the entrance to the keep and the mouth of the hole was covered by two tarpaulins weighted with rocks, on top of which had been piled Timmins's poles and trestles.

'It'll all have to come off, Louis.' They did it together, Mrs Biffen working with brisk agility. The ladder was standing in the pit, and the lid of the tomb was still half-open, but what was inside couldn't be seen from above.

'I'd rather not go down, Mrs Biffen.'

'I'd rather not either, but there's things need seeing to and you may be able to help. Light that lantern, Louis.'

She went down the ladder with a sure step, and he came after with the lantern.

The skeleton was on its own in the tomb, but the skull had been turned on its side, its gaping mouth turned away from them.

'There was a sword, you told me,' said Mrs Biffen peering into the tomb.

'They must have taken it out.'

'It will have to be put back. What else has been taken?'

He didn't mention the necklace of beads, which no one knew of but him.

'The old Smiths, who once ruled in these parts had five signs,' she explained. 'The headstone is the Pillar, the skull is the Skull of course, and above us is the Tower. The Sword is missing as we know, but there's the Circle missing too and they would not have buried him without the Circle. Hold that light up further.'

She got on her knees and leant over the tomb and examined its contents carefully by the light of the lamp.

'Here!' she exclaimed. 'Bring the light closer here.' She pointed to the neck and he lowered the lantern over the area, knowing he should speak up but the longer he left it the harder it was.

'There was a necklace,' she murmured. She ran her finger over a row of small indentations on one shoulder. 'The stones lay here for so long that they left their imprint on the bone. Somebody took them too.'

'Rugg's boy maybe.'

'Either him ... or *you*,' she said. 'Give me the lantern.'

She took the light and put it close to the headstone where there was a series of faint marks about half way up.

'The same five signs,' she said, pointing. 'Pillar, tower, sword, circle, skull. I have finished here. We can go.'

At the top, he snuffed out the lantern and hung it on its hook, avoiding her eye.

'You're like a child hiding behind its hands,' she chided. 'You're an odd bird, Louis Yeoman. I don't mind that for I'm one myself. But where is the necklace?'

'What necklace?' She just looked at him. 'I saw it when we first opened the tomb,' he admitted. 'Then when I came here at night and Kelynack was dead, it was ... in his hand.'

'In his hand? Are you sure?'

He nodded.

'And you took it from him.'

'He dropped it. Well, you can't say he dropped it because he was past doing anything, but it dropped. I picked it up and ... after that I don't know. I didn't see it again.'

'The pocket of your jacket.'

'When I remembered a couple of days later, I looked in the jacket but it wasn't there. I couldn't think where else to look.'

'It must be found and be returned to the tomb. If one sign is missing, the charm is incomplete. I shall put a crucifix with them, naturally, but the five must be there.'

'Perhaps I dropped the necklace somewhere that night.'

'Unlikely.'

They replaced the canvas and other objects.

'Now I shall visit Mrs Runciman,' Mrs Biffen announced.

He asked her if she needed him.

'Certainly not!'

There was something he had to get from town he said and went off at a run. She watched him go, wondering at his sudden haste, but it meant he was well again, which was what mattered at present. She pottered about the castle precinct for a while, eyes on the ground, but if she was looking for something she didn't find it.

Isadora's eyes were rimmed with red and her face was very pale but she did not turn away Margot Biffen. They sat together in the drawing-room of The Slape.

Mrs Biffen's person was unremarkable. People passed her in the street without a second glance. If they noticed her at all, they saw a shortish, commonplace person with heavy walking boots. There was in her eye a sharpness close to brilliance but few saw it.

There was no exchange of pleasantries between the two women and Kelynack's death was not mentioned. Mrs Biffen refused the offer of a cup of tea and they sat in silence. They had met once or twice at functions in the town, but had exchanged no more than a few words. Yet the silence was oddly companionable. Isadora understood Mrs Biffen's visit as a gesture of solidarity, the only one of its kind. Mrs Biffen for her part seemed to be deliberating what it was that she had to say, and when she had said it, she left.

'There is a kind of arrogance in blaming ourselves for what happens to people around us, Isadora Magdalensky. As if they have no destiny of their own.'

It would have seemed a cryptic comment to an onlooker, but Isadora responded with a faint smile. Perhaps it was the rare use of her own name that occasioned the smile, or perhaps not.

Outside, Mrs Biffen found Louis on a garden bench reading from a large, leather-bound manuscript balanced on his knees.

'So that was what you went for!'

He nodded, watching her.

'You know it then,' he asked.

'It was written by one of our people, Louis, and donated to the school library by another, for safe-keeping. Oh yes, I know where Grindlay's goblin came from, just as you did.'

'He felt there was a connection between you and this book that he couldn't account for.'

'He's not called gnome for nothing,' she commented, and he laughed at hearing Grindlay's nickname from her lips.

She sat on the bench next to him and he told her what he had been unable to tell her the night before.

'The death of Austin Kelynack was accidental,' she told him when he had finished. 'Nothing happens for no reason, but the reasons are so many and so various that to call something accidental is the closest we can get. In this case, accident seems the wrong word for something with such a strong element of cause and effect, but the causes lie beyond our ken. Skiaphagos is, as I said, just a goblin, which in turn is just a name for something formless, but maleficent for all that.'

In her oversize boots, Jersey-knit fisherman's jacket and corduroy trousers, she was not womanly, nor maidenly nor old-maidish, neither spinsterish nor teacherly, by no means elegant yet not inelegant. A farmer's wife, some might have thought, but she was not wifely. She belonged, Louis thought, to a different category of women, raised in different climes or in an age when there were more women of this kind, defiant and original. A mate for Puck, a Queen for Oberon.

'Let the goblins and the shadow-stealers alone, Louis,' she concluded. 'We have a more urgent and practical concern. Constable Bright has what he takes to be a murder and he needs a murderer. He will look no further than Isadora Magdalensky. I have warned her that she must defend herself, but I doubt that she will make much effort to do so. Any jury in these parts would convict her so it must not come to a trial. You must go to Bright and tell him what you and Timmins did that night and why. Meanwhile I shall do what I can to sow the seeds of doubt in places where it may make a difference.'

When she had gone, he took the manuscript to the study, put it among the other books and sat down at the desk to think. He and Timmins had made things worse for Isadora because by replacing the slab they had put an accident out of the question. But who would believe in an accident anyway, since it required Kelynack to have fallen on to a pitchfork standing upright in the tomb with its prongs in the air? She would be brought to trial, convicted by a hostile jury and die at the end of a rope in Dorchester.

At every point in the events that led to Kelynack's death, he had been involved, not as a witness but as a catalyst. Without the catalyst there is no reaction, Thorneycroft had told them. He was responsible, so he must be the one to mend things.

As he sat at the desk, he considered the idea of confessing to Kelynack's murder. He had a motive – jealousy, and revenge. He had more than once wished that the man were dead. But he doubted that he had the strength to create this fiction and repeat it over and over, to judges and juries, to Timmins, to his father, to Isadora herself. Besides, she would never allow it.

An unused notebook lay on Kelynack's desk, with pen and blotter ready at its side and it was this that suggested a more subtle plan. He found two bottles of ink in a drawer, one blue and one black, sharpened the quill and wrote in bold letters on the first page: Journal of Louis Yeoman. Castleton, April 1878.

It must not be hurried. It needed care and forethought for there must be no errors. He would change between inks, use the blotter for some parts and leave others to dry in their own time, to make it clear to a reader that the entries were made at different times.

He dated the first entry April 18 and referred to events that had taken place a little over two weeks before. Late that night, the journal reached the present and here Louis stopped. Subsequent entries were made during the following fortnight.

The fictions of the first half of the journal were inserted among the facts so that like partridges in a field their colour blended with what was around them.

Chapter Fourteen

MOON IN GEMINI

There was a time the crow was white
Turning black at dead of night
The robin's breast was yellow-filled
Reddening when blood was spilled
The croak of chough was silver-tongued
The cheeping sparrow many-songed
The thrush caught fishes in the brook
The little wren outflew the rook
                    Louis Yeoman

A*PRIL 18* Today they started digging at the keep and I made sketches. They found bones and teeth which they thought belonged to a young woman. In the evening Kelynack drank too much. Afterwards, Isadora admired my sketch of the fire and the birds. Birds are difficult and these do not resemble any bird I have ever seen. I meant them as crows, then changed them to ravens, which

Biffen said are considered oracular. Odin had one on his left shoulder and one on his right, one called Mind and the other Memory. I don't remember their Norse names. Humming and Mumming or Hoomin and Moomin. I wanted the birds in my sketch to be ravens because of an episode from my childhood which I had forgotten, or buried under a lot of other clutter. Why should I remember being unable to eat some overcooked mushy peas and my father calling me a fussy and ungrateful boy, yet forget the Raven, which fluttered on the margins of my mind and my dreams for years.

It was my twelfth birthday and my father gave me a Four-Ten sporting gun to initiate me into the art of hunting big game in Somerset (rabbits, snipe, partridges). I was unable to shoot like a man. The detonation scared me, the recoil bruised my shoulder. In the trees behind the house I shot what my father called a small scavenging bird (a chaffinch). I held the tiny bloodied body in my hand. How quickly its eye clouded over and lost its light. Window of its little frail sky-loving soul slammed shut.

I persevered in this manly sport, blasting off and missing. I think my eyes were closed as I pulled the trigger. Then I shot a large black bird in the treetops and for an instant it seemed an achievement, to deliver death at a distance. The bird twirled downwards like a sycamore pod and landed. Head still erect, legs sound, eye sharp. Only the maimed wing dragging on the ground. It hopped away from my grasp, took refuge in a thorny thicket, pecked at me when I reached in for it (What did I intend? to wring its neck, beat out its brains?). Its beak was black, therefore not a crow but a rook, or as I came to believe, a raven.

Whatever its lineage, it was unquestionably superior to the young sportsman timidly pursuing it. Its eye was more brilliant, its feathers finer (glint of red, vermilion, peacock green). Hardly bigger than his booted foot, its gift of flight cruelly stolen, but still fearless, vigorously attacking his hand. It would have pecked out his eye had he been close enough. What exemplary courage, what stern dignity, what a fierce glitter-black eye! Like a wounded admiral of the woodland quarterdeck.

I left it where it was, wishing for its wing miraculously to heal. *Corvus non bene relictus.* The next day it was nowhere to be seen. A fox must have got it, or a stoat or buzzard. It was my last shot. I told my father that I feared lasting damage to my shoulder. 'Something peculiar in my bone structure,' I suggested. 'Something lily-livered in your gut,' he said.

I was haunted by the raven. In moments of cowardice, of carelessness, of pretending to be what I was not, I saw its stern eye and glossy cloak. It became a part of me. The dark, winged, night-time shadow, mocking my efforts to make of myself a man.

April 19 Kelynack was unwell. I should call him Mr Kelynack, but I do not want to. This journal is private to myself and there are no rules except the ones I make for myself. So far there are two rules: Do not allow anyone to read it; Do not give up this journal until the last page of the notebook is written. Herein fail not.

If I wish to call him Kelynack, or Sir Knacker, knight of the Long Table, I shall do so. I was glad when the Knacker felt too ill to stay at the keep and the work went faster without him.

Isadora and I buried the remains of the woman under a beech by the lake. She spoke some words in Russian. Her voice in Russian is sweeter and darker and more lovely. Like Russian honey.

Timmins, Mick and George dug on and I helped them. As the soil became almost too heavy and stony to dig, we hit on a tomb. Inside was a skeleton. We expected this, but nobody expected the way his mouth gaped or the empty fury in his missing eyes. (Perhaps the fury was in the open mouth, mirrored in the hollowed eyes.) Mick said there was a sword, but I didn't see it. What I saw was a necklace of beads, but I kept my mouth shut.

We got wet in the rain and afterwards I drank ale with Timmins at the inn. At The Slape the Knacker was about to leave. He would be gone for a while, he said. Good. He told us he would call at the Old Castle to see what was in the tomb. Timmins warned him it was unwise in the dark and the wet.

April 20 We went to the keep in the early morning and found that Kelynack had been there. The slab had been replaced. I suppose he took the sword with him. Would he have taken the skull also? I doubt it. How did he shift that great stone on his own, I wanted to know. Timmins thought that with the slab loosened, it would have been no more difficult than shutting the drawer of the dresser.

When the lads arrived a bit later we filled in the pit. I thought we should leave it as it was, but Timmins said that Kelynack had shifted the slab as a sign to us that the excavation was done with. Why else would he have done so, alone in the dark? If I wanted a record of the tomb I should draw one, he added. For that we needed to remove the slab and look more carefully at the arrangement of the bones, I said.

'Arrangement of the bones?! There was an old bloke six-and-a-half-foot tall with his knees drawn up, smiling or screaming. What else do you want?'

Mick told me where the sword was lying. Neither of them wanted to reopen the tomb, and nor did I.

Back at The Slape, I worked on the sketch using a full page diagram from the encyclopaedia to help me with the bones. I drew it all very carefully and at the end it looked like the skeleton in the encyclopaedia bent at the knees. It had no age, no atmosphere and no originality. The skull's open mouth looked inane. I kept the sketch as a record of the dimensions, thinking Kelynack might want them. But he will not want it for his book.

Besides, the manuscript is no longer.

Timmins thinks there was a tiff. More than a tiff, because when I came into the study to write up my journal, the floor was covered with fragments of his manuscript. I recognised his writing. It is a small and beetling hand for a man so sure of himself.

Isadora says she does not know when he will return. She gives no reason for his sudden departure and does not want to talk about it.

April 22 On one of the torn fragments of the manuscript I found what must have been the title because they were the only words in capital letters. THE ARYAN DREAM. I was surprised by the word dream in the title of a history book and I made nothing of Aryan.

Iranian? On other scraps were 'far-reaching vision', 'profound legacy', 'noble inheritance'. I detect his emphatic tones, his confident style, his alignment with the strong.

Among the shreds I found one complete sentence, a marginal scribble: 'Amber is ἤλέκτρον in Greek. Electrical attraction the source of the amber's emblematic value.' I keep this fragment as a bookmark for my journal.

I am glad that she tore up his book.

April 25 Last night, I sat here in the study with her. The evening was chilly and we lit a fire. She took a cushion and lay by the fire with her head supported on her hand. My journal was on the grate, with Kelynack's bookmark sticking out. She saw his handwriting, pulled out the slip of paper and read it.

She asked me what I thought electricity was. I told her what Thorneycroft taught us about magnetism and poles and a charge of invisible particles. Her question was: why had this invisible power, which could make heat and light without a flame – why had it been discovered now, and never before? She didn't think it was because people were cleverer. She didn't think that people got cleverer just because time passed.

I told her what the ancients said about the first age of gold, the second of silver and the third of bronze. Ages in decline as men got further from the truth.

'Electricity is a power that was not meant to have been found, Louis,' she said after a while. 'It will take us further from the raw materials of God. This new age that is beginning will be the age of electricity, more dangerous than iron, baser than bronze, plunging more quickly towards the abyss.'

'What abyss? The end of the world?'

She shrugged. 'Towards a new beginning, perhaps. I can't see so far. If I see further than some, it is because I am not much entangled in desires and fears. Especially now Kelynack is gone from my life. I am free. I need nobody, and nobody needs me.

April 28 Kelynack's grandfather came looking for him because the horse had arrived home without the trap. Isadora did not seem worried. I hope he has gone to Oxford, or London, or Athens.

April 30 Bright came looking for the trap. Why would he look in the barn of The Slape? Timmins said he found something he thought was a clue. A panel with lettering on it. What lettering, clue to what? I asked. Four letters, clue to nothing, he replied.
He told me Bright planned to dig up the hole at the keep tomorrow and wanted us there to keep him company. Will we go? Not on your life, he exclaimed.

May 1 Kelynack is dead. Bright arrived while we were on the terrace and announced that his body was found in the tomb under the tower. 'One of you did it or all of you,' were his words. Isadora ordered him off the premises and told Timmins to see to it. She went upstairs and kept to her room for the rest of the day. Françoise took her some food in the evening but brought it back untouched.

I feel nothing about his death. I should, I suppose. Perhaps Bright's accusation shocked me more than the news he brought.

He understands Isadora no more than he understands a wren, or a water mill. She is incapable of violence. Timmins, who has known violence, thinks the same. Oddly, Timmins is also incapable of violence. He would have been a champion boxer but for his dislike of hurting people. It was Hulme who told us that, years ago. He is a bear, but a tender-hearted one. Ask Françoise. Ask anyone.

Bright has not forgiven me for eluding him over the Science Five fire. He was sure from the first that I had done it. He knew that I had matches in my pocket, and Hulme and the others would have told him there was a rebellious streak in me. Rebellious against what? Against Hulme and the others. Not Biffen and Grindlay but the dense ones.

What Bright couldn't do was to find a motive. Hulme imagined a conspiratorial protest, as if Sherborne were the Paris Commune. Yes, Science Five was disliked because it was used for detention. None of us approve of the futile copying of lines. Good teachers don't give detentions. Grindlay never does, nor Biffen. Runciman didn't. Only the dense ones. But, burn down a room because it was used for writing lines? The real rebels among us would sooner burn the chapel.

Bright couldn't find a motive because he didn't know what I felt for Isadora. He might have got on to that if I hadn't torn up the poem. Bright is sharp. His instinct told him I'd started the fire, despite the smokescreen about the time on the clock and seeing Kelynack in the Close. I made a mistake about the time and slipped up about the train and he nearly had me. But Runciman probably thought that a Classics scholar and poetry prizewinner must be a decent fellow.

Am I not a decent fellow? It is impossible to say that I am. I am odd, confused, unreliable, independent, selfish, prone to imaginings, slave to superstitions. Somewhere is something weak and timid.

It is hard to say why I let the match drop among the papers. I can think of reasons but none that excuse the deed. The papers were full of lines in Latin, the same thing over and over. There was something wretched in them that deserved to be burned. I thought the paper would burn but not the room. I was shocked later when I saw the roof in flames. But dropping the lighted match was really to do with *them*. I was jealous of him, disappointed in her, angry at an adult world which seemed deceitful and somehow cheap. It made my love for her cheap.

I wanted a bonfire on which to burn my love.

There were noises from below. I was afraid of being found. I ran away, telling myself that only the papers would burn. How did those feeble flames struggling with the reams of paper reach the roof a little later? It's a mystery to me even now.

Afterwards I could not confess. 'Oh what tangled webs we weave, when first we practice to deceive!'

I didn't want to give Bright and Hulme the satisfaction of being right. I didn't want to be banished by my father when he learned the truth. I wanted to go to Oxford, despite pretending not to care. I was afraid of the consequences of what I had done and I saw that I could avoid them by denial.

It was I who brought all this on Isadora. If Bright could have had me, he would have left her alone. But now it is too late for that.

May 2   Fishing. Lost a big carp. Suffered from a headache. Went to town and Mrs Biffen fixed it with a roof tile. A roof tile! She is a remarkable woman. She also is convinced that Isadora could not have done it. It was an accident she says ... but *who closed the tomb?*

The answer is: whoever killed Kelynack.

(i) A vagabond, a thief. He sees the trap outside the Old Castle, goes on the snoop, finds Kelynack in the pit. Rugg's boy has been putting it about that there was treasure in the pit, a rumour that would travel well in certain quarters. The vagabond kills Kelynack because he thinks he's there to bring up the treasure. Discovers that he's done it for a rusty sword, stuffs the body in the tomb and pushes home the slab.

(ii) Somebody settling an old score. A man like Kelynack must have made enemies. There he is on his own, in a hole. An argument. A tussle. Pitchfork handy.

These sound far-fetched, but every murder is far-fetched. Neither of my versions are as far-fetched as Isadora running him through with a pitchfork. Mrs Biffen pointed out that not even a strong woman could have driven the two prongs of a pitchfork through a person's belly. One prong maybe, she says, but not two. I was impressed by this unsentimental observation.

May 4   Bright came officially to put some questions. He saw Isadora in the drawing-room and I expected them to be closeted there a long time, but it was done in ten minutes. Isadora told us that she had said the exact truth and nothing more and when he tried to make her repeat it, she refused. 'Are you hard of hearing, Mr Bright?' When she came from the room her eyes were flashing and blooms of colour flowered on her cheeks. I saw that she was more upset about the whole affair than she admits.

Timmins was longer in the drawing-room. He went in cross and came out crosser. 'The damned pitchfork,' he grumbled. 'I told him I must of kicked it down the 'ole. I kicked something in while we was scurryin' about with the tarp. Which way does a pitchfork fall, 'e says. Downwards like anythin' else, I says. Prongs up or 'andle up, 'e wants to know. Depends how it was when it started off, says I. No it don't, 'e says. 'E'd tried it with another pitchfork. Nine times out of ten it fell with the prongs downwards. That's mechanics, Timmins, he goes.

'But did you try this, I says: The fork's lying along the edge of the pit. A foot hits against the 'andle, at the top. The fork topples in, 'andle first, and slithers down the side, without ever gaining the momentum to cause it to flip in mid-air. When it reaches the bottom, 'andle first, it drops straight into the half-open tomb where it nestles nicely in the corner, prongs up, waiting for someone to slip up and fall on it. It's the exception that proves the rule, I said.'

Then it was my turn. Yes, Kelynack told us he was going away. Yes, he intended calling in at the keep. None of us went out. We went to bed early. No, I did not hear Mrs Runciman go out. In the morning, the lid was closed. I never saw the fork.

Once more, same questions with extra padding, same answers.

On my way out, I said: Mrs Runciman is a very kind and good-hearted person, Constable, and whoever killed Kelynack it was not her. *Who started the fire in Science Five?* he asked fiercely, out of the blue. Vagabond or thief or someone settling a score, I answered.

When Bright had gone, Timmins and I thought we'd managed it alright until Isadora confessed she'd told Bright she was at the castle that night and had an argument with Kelynack and run off in tears.

'Lordy me,' Timmins called out.

May 12   A week since my last entry. Reason: I lost my journal, which I'd inadvertently left on the window-sill of the kitchen. It was a sunny morning, I'd been writing at the kitchen table in the sunshine and drank a cup of tea at the open window, looking out into the garden. I forgot the journal on the windowsill where Rugg's boy picked it up, intending to return it, obviously. But first it went to Rugg and then to Bright and Hulme and to the chief constable of Dorset. It was passed around and read and digested and the upshot is that I am to be charged with starting a fire with malicious intent, but what we hear from the Tuffins and Biffens is that no charges are to be brought against Isadora. The rent of the house has been paid for another week, at the end of which she will leave for Russia.

May 13   Timmins talks to Tuffin who drinks with Rugg who hears what Bright's up to from his boy who knows what we're doing because he's watching us. Thus we receive an account of our own doings at several removes. Rugg's boy can be seen here often, his shock of hair behind a bush, his legs disappearing swiftly round a corner or his nose pressed against a window. Timmins promises to catch him out one day out in the open and bowl him over like a ninepin, with a spud. Mrs Biffen has been to see Bright and the coroner and the under-sheriff, whoever he may be. She thinks that Bright is determined to charge Isadora with the murder but the chief constable wants more evidence, or a confession.

A few days ago Timmins told me that he is going to ask Françoise to be his wife.

Later he came to let me know she had accepted but that Isadora's got to be asked as well. He clears his throat and looks embarrassed. Out with it, I said.

'I thought you might do the askin' on my behalf, being as you're silver-tongued. She always looks like the sun came up when you're around.' I told him it would be better if he did his own asking and that if she refused I'd somersault into the lake. I wanted to do it that moment because of what he'd said about Isadora but I made as if I hadn't heard.

May 14 Today the shadow pit was filled in. Bright wanted it left but Mrs Biffen has been badgering the under-sheriff, claiming that it was a mortal danger to visitors to the castle, in spite of Bright's notice. He yielded finally and it seems that he can overrule the constable, which nobody knew, not even Bright. Timmins thought we'd better fill in the pit ourselves and hurl a few big rocks in to make sure it stayed done. Mick and George came and Timmins paid them out of his own pocket, adding the day and a half they were owed. They wouldn't accept the half-day so Timmins went and bought George a new pitchfork when we were finished.

Rugg's boy could be seen lurking by the curtain wall and once came into the keep but Timmins picked up a stone and tossed it up and down in his hand and Rugg's boy kept his distance after that.

Mrs Biffen was there with a crucifix, a ring and a kitchen knife, with which she climbed down and placed on the tomb before we started. I offered to go for her but she insisted on doing it herself. She was down there a little while, standing over the tomb murmuring, or praying. I asked her later if a kitchen knife was appropriate and she said brusquely that the point of a symbol was what it symbolised not the article itself.

Timmins insisted that the work be thorough. As we got close to the surface, we threw in a lot of large rocks followed by two wheelbarrow loads of smaller ones and when we'd covered them with soil, Timmins had us all tramping up and down over the top of the pit. Mrs Biffen watched these measures with approval.

Isadora and Françoise had stayed at the house and cooked a turkey with roast potatoes and roast carrots and Minsk pies and spring greens. We were seven at the table: Isadora, Françoise, Mrs Biffen, Timmins, George, Mick and me. Biffen's ankle has healed but she hadn't allowed him to come because he'd have held everything up by ferreting around in the pit.

I saw her out when she left. 'Do the right thing with what comes to you from the shadow pit,' she admonished. 'They're not toys to be fribbled with.'

She meant the beads, I suppose, which had gone through a hole in my jacket pocket. How did she know I had found them?

May 15 Timmins and Françoise were married at Castleton church. They went and talked with the vicar, in preparation for their wedding. 'There's no doctrine,' Timmins told us. 'The man's got a pig he's proud of, so we 'ad a chat leaning over the wall of the sty. 'E talked about the pig mostly. What 'e feeds it and how much it'll weigh by next Christmas.'

'Is he going to kill it?' Isadora asked.

'Frances asked 'im that too. It were the closest 'e got to talking religion. 'E said that if you could understand looking after a pig affectionately and enjoying the taste of it roast at Christmas, you might get an idea about why there has to be suffering in the world. 'E 'ad tears in 'is eyes when 'e said it.'

It made me think of the Walrus and the Carpenter, but Timmins reckoned the vicar had a point and Timmins sees things pretty clearly.

How Françoise looked coming up the aisle in a frock of brilliant white, with her rook-black hair and the tears in her eyes of midnight blue cannot be rightly written. When they drove away in a hired brake, she clung to Isadora. Timmins stood up with the reins in his hands, unmanned.

'God dammit, I'm blubbing,' he muttered. 'This business 'as made a watering can of me. A song, Isadora! For God's sake a song!'

Isadora sang something in Russian, of a loveliness indescribable. She told me later it was a farewell sung by a girl to villagers who had taken her in when she arrived as an outcast. 'A stranger such as I', was the refrain.

Timmins and Françoise disappeared down the drive while Isadora sang the song to the end.

May 16   There are only the two of us here. I told Isadora there will be no trial over the fire. I am expelled from the school and will not be allowed to sit the Oxford exam. I said I was happy with that because I have decided I don't want to go to Oxford.

There is an end-of-term mood in the house. Isadora has packed her bag, she told me. There was mischief in the way she said it, as if once the bag is packed the rules no longer apply.

She is leaving the day after tomorrow and I wonder, if I asked her, whether out of friendship or sympathy, she would let me kiss her.

May 17   This is our last day, she said, let us spend it far from here.

We put fresh bread and cold beef and hard-boiled eggs and cherries in a bag and walked all morning, avoiding the lake, the castles, the town and all familiar ways. We walked up the sunken tree-lined lane that Biffen once told me was the old south-bound highway. Our path took us through villages where neither of us had ever ventured. Caundle Marsh, Holywell, Kings Stag. We started in sunshine, but a wind got up and drove in the clouds from the west and the sky grew dark and threatened rain. We'll have our picnic in the wet, she said laughing.

We came to a village whose name I didn't learn. The place was very still under the dark sky. There was a row of small cottages on a slope and above them we could see the spire of the church. There was no sign of life in the cottage gardens, in some of which the spring flowers were almost hidden by wild grasses and waist-high weeds. The rain came on in a sudden downpour. We can go to the church to shelter, I suggested, but she stood unmoving in the middle of the track with her arms held out and her face to the sky. She was wearing a pale yellow cotton frock which I recognised as belonging to Françoise. She was soaked in a moment and the water ran from her face down her neck. Let's run to the church, I repeated, but she shook her head. No churches, she said, we'll go in here.

The front garden of the cottage beside us had gone to weed. The little gate hung half-open with tall grasses growing up it on either side. We went in and found the front door unlocked. The narrow doorway was made for elves and I had to stoop to enter. You could see at a glance that nobody lived here, or had done for a long while. There was an abandoned armchair, and an ottoman couch covered with sheets.

'This is trespass,' I said.

She put her finger to her lips. 'It is a gift.'

Outside the sky grew darker still and thunder rumbled not far off. She took up one of the sheets from the Ottoman and as she went through into the kitchen she pointed at the other sheet. 'That one's for you.'

The storm blew away at last, but our clothes were still not dry and our picnic was still uneaten. We sat on the Ottoman and ate, wrapped in white sheets. She said it was too late to walk back and would I mind if we camped there for the night. Upstairs we found some old blankets and one dry bed and made our camp and in the kitchen we found half an old bottle of cherry brandy. 'That will do instead of a fire, Louis.'

May 19 We walked back in the morning by a different route, coming through small villages with few houses without a whit or whiff of ugliness. Even the mud in the lanes looked fresh and wholesome. 'I waited until my last day here to see the best of your England, Louis,' Isadora remarked.

In the evening, she was sad. The thought that I might have caused it was painful to me.

'You are anxious about tomorrow, Isadora.'

She shrugged. 'A journey once begun has a way of taking care of itself. Before it starts, it can seem difficult, and this one more than most. To be truthful, Louis, there is an aspect of this journey which I have avoided thinking of.'

'It is a long way.'

'That in itself is nothing.'

'You will be on your own, without Françoise.'

'I do not mind solitude.'

'The sea may be rough.'

'It's what the sea is for.'

'You worry about what awaits you in your own country.'

'I anticipate nothing so fear nothing.'

Whatever the source of her anxiety, she didn't want to say it and it was only in the middle of the night that I woke with a start and realised what it must be.

She had arranged for the carter to come for her. I will come with you to the station, I told her.

'Let us walk then, Louis.'

'What about your things?'

'You can carry them,' she said laughing. I imagined going with a trunk on my back, but I would have carried one on my head as well. When she came out of the house, she had two small satchels, one over her shoulder and one in her hand. 'I've left my clothes for Françoise,' she said. 'What she can't make fit she'll give away.' I took both satchels and remembered Françoise carrying my bag to the same station, when I was a schoolboy and she a maid.

We found the carter to tell him he wasn't needed. We walked along the river, over Blackmarsh meadow. Birds chirruped from the banks and heavy bumblebees lurched among buttercups. I wished the way would go on and on. And so, in its cussed way, it was over before it had hardly started.

We sat on a bench on the platform at the station.

I took out the necklace.

'Please take it.'

She turned it in her hands.

'The beads are amber.'

'Yes.'

'And the chain gold.'

'I found it in the tomb.'

'It is very beautiful, Louis.'

With a bodkin and a toothbrush, I had removed every speck of earth, every particle of crusted matter. I had polished the beads and the links of the chain and then polished them again.

'You might think it unlucky, Isadora.'

'Do you think it unlucky?'

'Not for you.'

She rubbed the beads against her dress and drew them over the cloth, whisking up particles of thread and fluff.

'If I needed to sell it, would you mind?'

'It's what I thought. There are places in London, I suppose...'

'It happens that I know of one. When I first arrived in London I was obliged to sell a few things, but none of them was as fine as this.' She looked up at me with eyes whose brightness betrayed the bauble for what it was.

'I wish I could keep it to remind me of you', she said. 'But I need no necklace for that.'

She had something for me as well, in a velveteen jewellery box. It rattled when I shook it but I wasn't to open it yet.

The train was coming, the narrow cone of white smoke visible before the sound of the engine reached us.

'Kiss me good-bye, Louis.' I thought she meant peck on the cheek, as people do. But she took me in her arms and hugged me close and I loved her. 'Come with me to Russia,' she whispered.

What a word is this Russia! A glow of warmth in the northern cold, mother of myths, goddess of gods. To Russia with Isadora without farewells. A cabin with Isadora on the high seas!

I opened my mouth to say 'I will come'.

The bars of my cell lay shattered. In a world of no reason, I was free to go, or to stay. In a vision that came and went quicker than thought, I saw a boy dumb on a quay at the heel of his queen. In the very now, beyond the platform where I stood, were beeches aloft in a breeze, beyond them the shimmer of the Yeo stream, somewhere beyond that an elfin cottage in a village with no name.

'I cannot come,' my voice said.

The stationmaster blew his whistle and the train started to move out and she kissed me leaning from the window and I waved her good-bye with a hurt like a rock caught in the cage of my chest and walked away from the station with hot, salt tears in my eyes, on my cheeks, on my tongue.

ALSO AVAILABLE FROM THE SUNDIAL PRESS

ALBION'S DREAM by Roger Norman

RED DIE by Roger Norman

FLORENCE Mistress of Max Gate by Peter Tait

A PAD IN THE STRAW by Christopher Woodforde

GHOST GLEAMS W. J. Wintle

A CAGE FOR THE NIGHTINGALE by Phyllis Paul

PATTERNS ON THE SAND by Gamel Woolsey

THE SAILOR'S RETURN David Garnett

UNCLAY by T. F. Powys

KINDNESS IN A CORNER by T. F. Powys

DURDLE DOOR TO DARTMOOR Wessex Essays of Llewelyn Powys

STILL BLUE BEAUTY Wessex Essays of Llewelyn Powys

CHRISTMAS LORE AND LEGEND by Llewelyn Powys

THE JOY OF IT by Littleton Powys

THE BLACKTHORN WINTER by Philippa Powys

SORREL BARN & THE TRAGEDY OF BUDVALE by Philippa Powys

HESTER CRADDOCK by Alyse Gregory

KING LOG AND LADY LEA by Alyse Gregory

DEMOPHON by Forrest Reid

LIFE, BE STILL and other stories by H.A. Manhood

ALBION'S DREAM
by ROGER NORMAN

Edward Yeoman and his cousin John Hadley begin to play an ancient, handmade game called Albion's Dream without realizing, at first, that events they set in motion on the board are also transpiring, in parallel, in real life. The first clue comes when Edward notices that faces on the game cards resemble actual people, particularly his tyrannical headmaster, Tyson. Still, both boys feel compelled to play on. When the game falls into the hands of Tyson and the unfortunately named Dr. Fell, the boys are accused of occult practices and threatened with expulsion. In a riveting denouement, Edward is proven innocent and Tyson is replaced—exactly the outcome for which the boys had played. Although the author clearly sets forth the struggle between good and evil, his best storytelling is in the gray areas between such extremes: Edward's capacity for the dark arises from ordinary boyish wishes. Moving handily between board action and school scenes, Norman masterfully manipulates a large number of characters, locations, and ideas.

ALBION'S DREAM | Paperback | The Sundial Press | ISBN: 978-1-908274-19-9

RED DIE
by ROGER NORMAN

In October 1916, Lance-Corporal Jack Yeoman arrives back in England from the trenches of the Western Front. Guided in his movements by a pair of unusual dice he carries with him, he returns to his home in deepest Dorset and arranges a secret rendezvous with his adoptive sister Maggie at a village pub. But his recklessness in word and deed soon land him in trouble and he finds himself a hunted man. His war-wounded brother, an embittered stone-builder, the vindictive local squire, and a sinister priest – all have their reasons for pursuing Jack as he flees deeper into the heart of his native land and deeper into the mystery that envelops him.

Several others are drawn into his sphere through the roll of the dice, some of whom are more than they seem. But there are other forces at work in this haunting tale of reality and illusion, of the living and the dead, a tale of natural potions and supernatural powers in which the threads of human destiny unravel and intertwine. As Jack seeks to come to terms with his conflicting loyalties and beliefs, with the death of his father, with his love for Maggie, events build to their violent climax on All Hallow's Eve on Giant Hill at Cerne Abbas.

RED DIE | Paperback | The Sundial Press | ISBN: 978-1-908274-20-5

RED DIE by Roger Norman

Reviewed for *The Long, Long Trail* by Anthony Head

'Whenever war is spoken of / I find / The war that was called Great invades the mind …' So the late Vernon Scannell, one of Britain's most accessible modern poets, begins his poem *The Great War*, noting how it was this war and not the one he himself fought in that he 'remembers'. It's an irony not lost either on many non-combatants from later generations similarly haunted, for whom the First World War represents a watershed between the imagined innocence of a better day and the cynicism of the modern era.

Among contemporary writers inspired in one way or another by the war is Roger Norman, author of the acclaimed debut novel *Albion's Dream* in the 1990s, whose second novel, RED DIE, is set in October 1916. This intriguing tale of earthly and supernatural forces relates the story of Jack Yeoman, a deserter from the Western Front who returns to his native Dorset, guided by the messages he reads in a strange pair of dice. He soon finds himself a hunted man, though not all his pursuers are what they seem.

RED DIE is not a 'war novel' in the strictest sense, straddling as it does certain other genres, notably the ghost story, and in this it differs from such works as Pat Barker's *Regeneration* trilogy or Sebastian Faulk's *Birdsong*. But the horrors of the trenches serve as both impetus and backdrop to the narrative and provide the moral heart of the book. In its delineation of differing attitudes to the war, it pitches the pacifist against the patriot, provoking unrest in a rural community where the distinctions between truth and propaganda are not always apparent. It's a work that raises questions about ignorance and knowledge and the formation of opinions in times of war (with apparent modern resonances), as well as the individual's dilemma in dealing with conflicting desires.

Among the gallery of engaging characters is the stonemason Bill Bate, rejected for service due to a missing 'trigger finger' and all the more bullish and boorish as a result; Jack's invalided officer brother Capt. Charles Yeoman, a man for whom duty and honour are paramount, but who nonetheless tries to help his brother before the vengeful local squire and his cohorts can reach him; and Cockler, a quick-witted Londoner adept at humorously disguising the fact of his own desertion. Jack's adoptive sister Maggie and the mysterious Mrs. Dooley, owner of a local pub, provide a steadying female influence, the only main characters who do not broadcast their opinions about the war – very much the work of men – and whose actions are not swayed by it. After a dramatic narrative climax atop a famous local landmark, Jack ultimately returns to the Front – but to reveal the circumstances in which he does so and what happens thereafter would be to destroy the particular pleasures of reading this compelling book.